W9-AJS-818

—————————— ★ ——————————

The fog was as thick as if the rain had been crushed into unmoving mist. She held quite still for several minutes. Noise, she reflected, sometimes echoed in fog making distorted, disoriented sounds, but now there was no sound. A chilling shudder swept over her.

Hesitantly she moved forward, veering too close to the edge of the swamp, quickly side-stepping in time to avoid the full force of the blow aimed at the back of her head. It felled her, and she sprawled full length on the soggy ground.

The man grunted, lifted her slight body and heaved her into the swamp, where she slowly disappeared into the slimy green sludge.

The man grunted again, turned and hurried toward the highway.

—————————— ★ ——————————

DOROTHY KLIEWER

MURDER
IN THE SWAMP

WORLDWIDE.

TORONTO • NEW YORK • LONDON
AMSTERDAM • PARIS • SYDNEY • HAMBURG
STOCKHOLM • ATHENS • TOKYO • MILAN
MADRID • WARSAW • BUDAPEST • AUCKLAND

If you purchased this book without a cover you should be aware
that this book is stolen property. It was reported as "unsold and
destroyed" to the publisher, and neither the author nor the
publisher has received any payment for this "stripped book."

*To my son-in-law, Charles Bradish, for his support and
encouragement of my writing endeavors.*

MURDER IN THE SWAMP

A Worldwide Mystery/April 2004

First published as *There...in the Swamp!*
by Hilliard Harris Publishers.

ISBN 0-373-26490-9

Copyright © 2002 by Dorothy Kliewer.
All rights reserved. No part of this book may be reproduced
or transmitted in any form or by any means, electronic or
mechanical, including photocopying, recording or by any
information storage and retrieval system, without permission
in writing from the publisher. For information, contact:
Hilliard Harris Publishers, P.O. Box 3358, Frederick, Maryland
21705-3358, U.S.A.

All characters in this book are fictitious, and any resemblance to
actual persons, living or dead, is purely coincidental.

® and TM are trademarks of Harlequin Enterprises Limited.
Trademarks indicated with ® are registered in the United States
Patent and Trademark Office, the Canadian Trade Marks Office
and in other countries.

Printed in U.S.A.

MURDER
IN THE SWAMP

ONE

DEEDRA MASEFIELD wasn't happy with the assignment Clete Bailey, editor at the Daily Spokesman newspaper, had given her. In the first place, she had been sent to Rufus two years earlier when two women from down state had mysteriously disappeared. At that time a state police car had caused a delivery van to skid on the icy road and crash into Lake Percifal, a tiny elongated lake of uncertain depth. Percifal wasn't where she wanted to be over Thanksgiving.

Now Clete reported that the latest rape victim had been discovered in the swamp at the lower end of Lake Percifal, a virtual swamp. Dead only a few hours, the woman had disappeared the day before while jogging near the tiny lake.

"Clete, you mean you've actually rented that empty rat-infested store-building expecting me to live there in that…that…"

"Calm down, Deedra. There's a murderer running loose in that county. This makes the third body found along that highway in the last four months. The sheriff there thinks the killer might live around Percifal or Rufus. Somewhere close to that highway. You are an investigative reporter, aren't you? Specializing in murders? Or do you want me to assign this story to Bryce Paxton?"

"You wouldn't!" Deedra challenged, but knew that Clete meant what he said. "I assume you want me to leave post haste?"

Clete nodded. "The rent's been paid, a TV installed, you can take your laptop and cell phone. Buy groceries at the supermarket here, we won't honor those sky-highs up in forestland. Just snoop around, get an idea of the country, a composite of the killer's M.O. Background for profiling. You know the kind of thing we want. Now, get going. You'll want to settle in before it gets dark."

Deedra's reputation had been earned by being a tough and clever reporter, and sometimes she regretted it…deeply, but was now forced to live with it. Sometimes she would have preferred the convenience and comfort of her own home after hours. She gave Bryce a flippant, triumphant smile as if she had just landed a choice story, and strode to her cubicle where she grabbed her handbag, camera, a bag of film, and swaggered out of the newsroom unaware that Bryce watched her leave with a frown.

Deedra still drove the Scout, the one that had performed so beautifully while she was investigating the murders up at North Ledge. Now, however, the Scout needed a paint job, and a general over-hauling. It didn't help knowing that they were no longer in production either…almost obsolete. She had the oil changed while she was loading up on groceries using the newspaper's credit card. That, she thought with satisfaction, was something Bryce didn't have. He hadn't proved himself that valuable yet, hadn't had enough front-page stories.

"Looks like you're going out of town again, Deedra. Big story?" the station attendant had known her for several years.

"Murders up around Rufus."

"Weren't you up there a couple of years ago?

"Yep. I'm not looking forward to spending Thanksgiving up there. Somehow I'm always sent out of town whenever it's near the holidays," she grinned trying to convey her frustration in an I-don't-mind manner, had to play the ready-for-anything reporter.

Deedra didn't want anyone to realize how soft and gentle she really was, how deeply she had been hurt by Deke Thomas, by the few women who had walked away with her beaus without a backward glance. She was still looking for Mr. Right…only each time she held out hope…the vision vanished. So she maintained the aura of an independent, resourceful woman of the new millennium, capable of going it alone. Only she didn't want to. She wanted a husband to be there on those sleepless nights that were occasionally haunted by visions of rats. Wanted someone to know how being confined in the cellars of the awful abbey with that mutant boy who had squashed rats to death in his oversized hands, had affected her. Now, on her way to Percifal, she prayed there wouldn't really be rats in the old store building.

The highway leading up to Percifal was scenic, old oaks and scattered pines dotted what had once been mining country. There were rugged-looking houses set back from the highway, and a few pastures where cattle and sheep gleaned an existence on the sparse vegetation. Several gas stations and general stores eked out a living by their very convenience. Two miles from Percifal Deedra drove through the small town of Rufus, California, named, the sign proclaimed, for Otto Rufus, pioneer who had settled a cattle empire there in the late 1800's. There had been grass aplenty then, before the droughts and pollutants. A town of 8,000 people, Rufus boasted the stores of necessity, but Deedra saw no sign of industry, and vaguely wondered why anyone would deliberately choose to live there.

From the police reports, Deedra knew the murdered women had all lived in or around Rufus or Percifal. The latest victim had owned a fabric store in Rufus, was well-known, and had no vices or secret men in her life. Her female friends reported no known enemies or close male friend. Her ex-husband was an officer in the Navy and on board a ship in foreign waters at the time of her death.

When Deedra reached the swamp that was part of tiny Lake Percifal, she saw the yellow crime-scene tape, and noted a sheriff's patrol car parked on the shoulder. She parked the Scout in front of the patrol car and went over to talk to the two men in uniform, flashing her press card.

The taller of the two men was the sheriff, the other a sergeant. "What can I do for you, Miss?"

"Deedra Masefield, Sheriff. Daily Spokesman. I believe Clete Bailey alerted you?"

The not-quite handsome sheriff's blue eyes twinkled. "Yes. I understand he's situated you in that vacant store over there," he nodded toward a building across the small lake. "He said you are to pose as a writer seeking inspiration away from the bustling city," Sheriff Aaron Blaine grinned. His blue eyes had the power of penetrating a person's thoughts, and Deedra was instantly aware that he knew of her dread at the prospect of residing in that old store building.

Deedra nodded.

"This is Sergeant David Keller. And since I know why you're here, the body was found half-out of the swamp right there. Killer was probably interrupted, possibly didn't want the body discovered for a few days and was trying to get it into that swampy water.

Woman's name was Priscilla Dawson, 32 years old, lived in Rufus, and owned a gift and fabric shop there. She was known to run a mile a day, usually south of Rufus, however. Why she changed her route that day, we don't know.''

"Cause of death?" Deedra was getting emotional vibes about this calm and interesting sheriff with his icy blue eyes.

"Raped and strangled with some kind of cord. Forensics suspects it's a baling twine. Buy it anywhere. We've got men checking the local farm and hardware stores to see if we can get a match.''

"The killer using the same M.O.?" Deedra took a photo of the crime scene.

"Yeah. There are a few variations evidently caused by the environment at the scene of the murders.''

"I understand the three women were all found along this highway?''

"Yes, but not murdered here. The bodies were all dumped in this area. Where their deaths took place, we have no idea at the moment. Forensics hasn't found any clues to that…yet." The sheriff's jaw clenched in a frustrated and determined way.

Deedra received the strong impression that this killer would have to be super clever to avoid Aaron Blaine's dedicated determination. Aaron, she mused, was a lawman to admire, tenacity probably part of his persona. Covertly she glanced at his ring finger. No wedding band. Her interest increased. The sergeant sported a new wedding band, and was decidedly better looking than the sheriff whose craggy features presented a person of strength and toughness.

"Let's see," Deedra remarked. "The first murdered woman, Darlene Hernandez, was found just north of Rufus in a ditch alongside the highway. She had been missing for four days."

The sheriff nodded.

"The second victim was Thelma Hansen, 34 years old, lived this side of Rufus at the end of a remote lane. She didn't return home from work in the city. Took a Greyhound bus each day that picked her up and let her off at the end of the lane leading to her home. Driver claims he let her off there as usual?"

"Yes, and witnesses on the bus confirmed that. There were no cars or people around that anyone noticed. As far as we could find out, she didn't plan to meet anyone.

Husband is a salesman and was on an out-of-town trip. We checked him out rather thoroughly, he couldn't be the perp."

"Hm," Deedra murmured. "Guess I'd better settle in before dark." Deedra waved and started walking toward her battered Scout.

"Keep your doors locked and your cell phone handy!" Aaron Blaine shouted after her.

The vacant store's wide front windows faced the tiny lake and looked dismal in the late afternoon, long shadows cast by the tall pines on the knoll above shrouding it. The store sign hung askew, held in place by only one corner, the remaining paint peeling as if the building was afflicted with a strange and ugly disease. Slightly up a knoll was an abandoned gas station that stood in silent testimony to better times. There was sudden movement and a dark-colored cat skittered around a corner of the gas station, saw her car, and raced to a shelter under the empty store building.

Deedra shuddered, "Hope that cat is a rat-catcher!"

Still she hesitated getting out of the car. Why was she so reluctant?

Gritting her teeth, she located the keys to the store and approached it with elevated pulses. The door creaked open, alerting any rats of her arrival.

The place had been swept clean, an old sofa and matching chair were placed in front of a 27-inch television set resting on an old store crate. At least the TV was new, she mused. The furniture items were all that occupied the large room, which obviously had been its place of business. Through a draped doorway a hall led to a bedroom and an antiquated bathroom. She turned on the faucet in the claw-foot tub. Rusty-colored water sputtered out in a series of complaints. After a few minutes the water ran clear, but cold. There was an electric hot-water tank off the kitchen in a makeshift utility porch. She checked to make certain the pilot light was on, and breathed a sigh of thankfulness.

With the lights on in every room, she carried the supplies inside, throwing her sleeping bag down on the bed where an old, but clean mattress had been placed. "No frills here," she muttered.

There were empty plastic crates and old wooden boxes in a screened back porch with which she created a writing center in the living room, clustered around her laptop. Fortunately she had included notebooks, paper and pens, aware of the inconsistencies of electricity in places like Percifal and vacant old buildings with antique wiring.

Deedra had finished carrying in the supplies, had locked the Scout, planning to settle in with a cup of hot coffee, but had paused on the wooden porch to give one last glance around when out of the shadows alongside the gas station, a man appeared.

"Who are you?" he rasped.

"I'm Deedra Masefield. Who are you?"

The middle-aged man surveyed her through a frown. It was too dark for her to see the color of his eyes or the cut of his facial features. She received the impression that he was not friendly, however.

"I'm Claude Hoover. I live over there." He pointed to a small house to the left of the gas station. A dim light filtered across the intervening space. "My wife is…ah…nervous. She gets frightened over strangers. What are you doing here?"

"I'm an author, I need to finish a novel I'm writing." This was literally true—Deedra had three chapters written on a novel that would probably be finished in 2020. "I rented this old store building to spend my vacation away from the city and distractions, you know what I mean."

Claude inspected her for a moment before he nodded. "You're only here for a week or two then?"

Deedra smiled. "Yes. I must get inside and warm this old place up. I'm glad to have met you, Mr. Hoover."

The man nodded and strode off into the shadows. Through a window in the bedroom she saw him climb the rickety porch of the nearest cabin, and disappear inside.

Though she waited a moment there was no further movement.

Deedra got coffee started and ate the sub sandwich she'd bought earlier. The coffee sustained her and by the time she'd devoured the sandwich was ready to commit notes to the laptop, and to send an e-mail to Clete.

Her notes finished—her eyes drooped. Just on the brink of sleep, she caught the sound of cautious footsteps outside the bedroom window. She was suddenly fully awake. Without turning on a light she peered through the torn curtains. A man of medium height with a heavy jacket moved toward the front of the store.

She scurried barefoot to the front, the floor cold and somewhat gritty under her feet. The man was circling her car, testing the doors to see if the car was locked. He turned his flashlight on the license plate, inspected it a moment as if looking to see if there was an insignia of any kind like doctors use, then doused the light. He continued on to the gas station where the flashlight was beamed against its facade. Evidently finding nothing disturbed, the man vanished into the shadows behind the gas station. He did not appear to be the Claude Hoover she had met earlier.

Deedra waited a few minutes, the cold seeping through her, then retreated to the bathroom where she ran a tub of hot water, gratefully slipped into its comforting warmth. The man, she reflected as she lay in the water, was simply curious, was perhaps leery of strangers. Naturally the residents here would wonder at anyone's audacity in renting the vacant old store. However, writers were attributed with quaint and varied characteristics and as long as she wasn't planning on making the store her home, they would probably accept her presence without undue suspicion. It wouldn't be difficult to play the part of an author, her profession after all, was writing. It was the reporter of news that she had to disguise. Tomorrow she would set out the tools of her trade…and the unfinished manuscript. Any snoops would find nothing here to indicate her investigative reporter status. Her laptop had a password should anyone try to access it.

She slipped back into the comfort of her sleeping bag and closed her eyes.

Outside her dingy abode, the man had returned and had listened as water ran into the bathtub, had seen the light in the bathroom filtering through the tattered shade, and knew that the person within had probably seen him examining her car. When quiet settled within the old store building, the man moved away scarcely making a sound, then walked unhurriedly toward a cabin near the end of the road that ran in front of the cabins.

WHEN DEEDRA AWAKENED in the morning, a thick fog hung over the landscape completely shrouding the lake, and only dim lights indicated the location of the cabins.

From studying a map obtained by Clete, she knew there were seven occupied cabins, and a vacant one. That an old road at the swamp end of the lake led to the highway though not usable because the ground beneath was unstable, the swamp had encroached below the surface causing a quicksand affect.

After breakfast she was standing at the front window drinking coffee when she heard car engines warming up, then one by one various cars and trucks drove past onto the paved road leading to the highway, their headlights making only faint illumination in the heavy fog. She noted two pickups, one delivery truck, and two cars though she could not see the drivers. The vehicles were not new, dents here and there showing signs of weathering and constant use. It would, she reckoned, be difficult to keep a car clean and shiny here.

She phoned Clete who sounded grumpy. Probably hadn't had his third cup of coffee yet. She told him of her conversation with the sheriff and of the man who snooped about the store building and her car.

"There's a fog here thick enough to slice this morning. Talk later."

The morning TV news had no further information about the latest murder, and showed a clear picture of the swamp where Priscilla Dawson's body had been discovered. The commentator did state that the swamp was not where Priscilla had been killed, had met her death elsewhere and her body dumped there. All three murder victims had been killed somewhere else, their bodies taken to another place for disposal thus preventing the finding of valuable forensic evidence.

Waiting for the fog to lift, Deedra went over the case facts of the two earlier victims thought to be committed by the same killer. The M.O. in each case was similar. Each victim in her early 30's, each a resident of or around Rufus, perhaps each an acquaintance of the killer, each raped and then strangled. Only in Priscilla's case was the murder weapon, the twine, recovered.

According to the information Clete had received from the sheriff, each victim's list of friends and co-workers had been carefully checked and no common denominator found. There didn't seem to be any connection between the women nor did they share close friends or acquaintances. The second and last victims were obviously accosted on the highway, Thelma at or near her bus stop. Presumably Darlene Hernandez had been in a similar situation though no one knew exactly when she met her killer, only that she had been missing for four days. The M.E. thought her death had taken place three days after her disappearance. Where Darlene had been held captive was still a mystery.

There were few clues for the sheriff's people to follow. It was concluded that the killer either lived or traveled through that part of the country either daily or at least once a month. Traveling salesmen whose routes included Rufus were being checked out. So far none of the known regular salesmen had been in that area at the times of the murders. It was evident, however, that the killer was acquainted with the area.

By 10:30 the fog had lifted and Deedra set out to walk about the cluster of cabins and along the lakeshore. She needed to know who was at home during the day, what they did and who they were. The sheriff had told her that most of the residents had lived there twenty years or more. Only Neil and Marsha Landen were new to Percifal. There was no record of crime there and no record of domestic violence.

Deedra's assignment was to get a story, preferably the first story on the capture of the killer, in lieu of that, to assess the possible suspects. She was not a police officer so was not expected to get results in solving the crimes…just get the story. But she knew, and Clete expected her, to delve into it as if she was an undercover cop. It was the reason for her posing as a writer, and she sighed under the stress of that expectation.

There were lights on in three of the cabins, one in the middle of the group, one with a dark cabin between, and one at the very end.

Deedra walked along the edge of the small lake, noting the cloudy water where no one fished, where the swamp was encroaching with its masses of green glob. This was a dying lake, she'd heard about it when she had been in the area two years earlier. A natural phe-

nomenon, scientists claimed, nature taking back a gift
it had once bestowed. An underground source had been
clogged by an earthquake a few years earlier and gradually the fresh water source closed off, leaving part of
the lake a swamp and the rest gradually being overtaken
by slimy sludge. Here and there she caught sight of
frogs in various sizes, their color a blending in with the
swamp. They had a plentiful food source in the variety
of winged insects that hovered over the sludge.

Deedra was aware that a woman in a wheelchair had
been watching through a window of the last house, but
she made no indication that she saw the woman, continuing to stroll along the lake. Arriving at the end of
the swamp she could see across to the crime scene tape
strung around the area where Priscilla Dawson's body
had been pulled from the swamp's slime, a patrol car
was parked on the highway shoulder and a uniformed
man was measuring the distance between the swamp
and the pavement.

An unexpected shudder shook her.

A vacant cabin with a forlorn mien, its front steps
already broken and wooden shakes missing from the
roof, was situated back from the others. She walked up
the knoll to inspect it, noting recent tire tracks in what
had been the backyard. A glance at the other cabins
showed carports, backyard attempts at gardening, and
large back porches. The residents evidently sat on those
porches on hot summer days when shade from the pine
trees on the knoll above provided a pleasant coolness.

Knowing Clete expected her to drive in to Rufus,
learn what the residents had to say about the murders,
and glean background material, she retraced her steps.

The woman in the wheelchair was still at the window,
watching but not giving any sign of welcome. She

looked somewhat familiar to Deedra, then she realized that the woman was the wife of the man whose delivery truck skidded into the upper part of the lake two years ago. The woman had also been in the truck at the time and had barely escaped with her life. A back injury from that accident now confined her to that wheelchair. Deedra searched her memory for the couple's names. Melvyn and Emma Randolph.

Deedra had stayed in Rufus on that first visit. The story that had sent her there was the disappearance of two women from a large city to the south. They had last been seen at an antique store in Rufus. Nothing was ever heard from them again even though the California authorities had sent out missing person's bulletins on them, finally concluding that the women had gone off together to start a new life having heard a rumor that the women might have had a sexual liaison. Deedra remembered that one of the women's husbands had vehemently denied that assertion and tried to sue the city's police department.

On that visit, Deedra hadn't interviewed anyone living at Percifal.

At the moment, Deedra was trying to figure out why Priscilla's killer would dump her body in the swamp when he had not bothered to hide the other two victims.

Her thoughts were interrupted by a voice from the porch of Claude Hoover's cabin.

"You the writer person that's rented that old store?"

The woman was very thin, had once been beautiful, but the loss of weight had taken the softness from her features. She was neatly dressed, her hair freshly combed.

Deedra strolled toward her cabin. "Yes, I guess your

husband introduced himself last night. I'm Deedra Masefield.''

The woman nodded.

Deedra was close enough now to see that her eyes were very blue, a soft blue like a baby's blanket, and as clear as water.

''I'm Jocelyn Hoover. I guess Claude told you I'm a bit put off by strangers, but you seem harmless enough. Would you care for a cup of tea? I don't get many visitors.''

''Thank you, I'd like that. It's cold out here.''

Deedra followed the woman inside, surprised to find the living room full of comfortable chairs, a sofa, a stone fireplace with interesting objects on the mantel, walls decorated in soft pastels. There were shelves of books, a large screen television, a VCR, and CD player with a ''tower'' of CD's alongside. Soft music sounds emanating from the background told Deedra that Jocelyn Hoover played music often, perhaps to fight against loneliness.

''Your house is charming. The outside doesn't give a hint of such a comfortable home,'' Deedra said as Jocelyn poured a cup of tea into a dainty cup.

Jocelyn smiled. ''We just rent this cottage, and as long as we don't insist on new house paint and things like that, the owner doesn't raise the rent, and we don't have to pay property taxes here. Looks can be deceiving, you know.''

''I notice an easel,'' Deedra pointed to a room just off the living room, ''are you an artist?''

The woman flushed. ''Well, I try to paint. I'm not very good at it, but some things in nature seem worth trying to capture.''

Her answer told Deedra that she was, indeed, an artist no matter how talented. "You paint landscapes then?"

Jocelyn placed her frail cup into the thin saucer. "Mostly, though sometimes I try to paint birds. I keep a feeder in the back yard to attract them." Jocelyn did not offer to show Deedra any of her paintings, however.

"It's terrible about the poor woman they found in the swamp over near the highway. Did anyone around here know her?" Deedra kept her gaze out the window where she could see the patrol car parked along the highway.

"Not that I know of. I heard she lived in Rufus." Jocelyn sighed, a trembley sort of sound. "No telling what a person could find in that old swamp!"

Deedra changed the subject to a mundane topic and after a little chat, thanked her hostess and went back to the old store. She mustn't get too friendly, mustn't seem nosy. People living in such remote areas were leery of strangers, always questioning why anyone would want to live so far away from "convenience."

She busied herself writing a feature story on Percifal, careful to work where she could be seen through the wide store windows. It paid off. About 1:00 Jocelyn Hoover and another middle-aged woman, who Deedra quickly learned was Harriet Stratton, knocked on the front door. Jocelyn handed her a plate of freshly baked muffins when Deedra opened the door with a smile.

"My those smell scrumptious!" Deedra quickly ushered them inside. "Cold out there." She gestured them to the sofa and chair.

The women seated themselves on the sofa, leaving the chair for Deedra. They looked around with the interest shown to new arrivals.

Deedra placed the muffins on a makeshift end table near the women. "Can I get you tea, coffee?"

Both ladies shook their heads. "No. We've just had lunch. Harriet and I lunch together often. She noticed that someone had moved in here, so I thought you might like to meet her."

Harriet Stratton smiled in a hesitant manner. A plain woman, she concentrated on neatness, but her eyes had the alert intelligence of many quiet unassuming people. This was a woman who knew much and kept a strict code of ethics.

"Our husbands work near each other in Brockton. Sometimes they drive to work together. But today Claude has a dental appointment and will be home earlier than usual, so Harriet's husband drove his pickup in."

"My husband's name is Dwight. He manages a grocery store in Brockton." Harriet smoothed her clean and attractive housedress as if any wrinkle met with her disapproval. She glanced out the window obviously thinking of something other than their conversation.

"Harriet used to run this grocery store for Dwight while he worked in Brockton," Jocelyn explained. "It's been closed now for nearly ten years."

"Then you must own this store building?" Deedra asked.

"No. We leased it from the owners. They died a few years back and the property went to their heirs. I don't rightly know who owns it now." Again Harriet smoothed her smooth dress.

"Which house is yours, Harriet?" Deedra needed to keep the conversation going and glean as much as she could from the women.

"It's the one marked 3. Just up that slight knoll behind this old store," she replied.

Just then a patrol car drove past, traveling on to the far end of the roadway.

They rushed outside to watch and saw the sheriff and another deputy get out and walk to the dirt road that led around the swamp to the highway.

"I wonder why they are looking there?" Jocelyn asked.

"For tire tracks," Harriet replied. "I don't think they'll find any. Dwight and I walked over there right after they found that Priscilla person. There weren't any."

"Why would they even think there might be?" Jocelyn asked, a frown forming on her thin features.

"In murder cases they examine everything very carefully," Harriet replied in a solemn voice.

Deedra threw her a curious glance. The woman had evidently given the matter deep thought.

"What about the sheriff? Is he capable of handling a serial murder case like this?"

She quickly learned she had ruffled Harriet's feathers by suggesting the sheriff might not have the qualifications. "Of course he's capable! He's a graduate of U.S.C. Just because we're a remote county, doesn't make Aaron Blaine a non-entity!"

"Sorry! Just wondered if his department had the man-power," Deedra replied.

Harriet calmed. "He relies on the State Police labs if that's what you mean.

County budgets have been cut, of course, but in this case the governor has ordered that all resources be available. I'm sure nothing is going to be overlooked." Harriet decided it was time to retreat. "I must get back.

I've some baking to do." She strode up the slight knoll to her house, her back straight and determined.

Deedra and Jocelyn had followed her outside.

"Let's go inside, it's cold out here!" Deedra suggested. She added another chunk of wood to the fireplace and put pellets into a stove at the back of the room.

"Harriet and her husband, Dwight, have known the sheriff since he was a boy. You wouldn't have known that, of course. Aaron's sort of role model for the young people around here. We don't have many big cities here, Brockton the biggest, but it's in a different county. This old store here was a gathering place for people of the area twenty years ago. Harriet and Dwight got to know nearly everyone who lives in this area. Aaron is perhaps their favorite person."

"Then there are houses close to the highway that can't be seen from the road?"

"Yes. You'll notice locked mailboxes here and there, and where there's mailboxes there's lanes leading to homes. Residents work in Brockton or Calif which is now called Half Town."

"Calif?" Deedra was intrigued.

"Named by an old gold prospector who didn't find any. Said he'd traveled from Vermont to California and didn't find any gold, so when he did, he would finish the name of the town." Jocelyn smiled. "There're about 400 people living there year around now, and no new homes have been built there for years. There's a gas station, a coffee shop, an automotive repair, a dentist and a post office. It's just too far from city conveniences to really make substantial growth. A retirement home was built there twenty years ago, but it didn't have the facilities to attract people rich enough to live there.

Most of those apartments are now rented to people on
Social Security. Once a month a bus takes them to
Brockton to buy groceries and for doctor appoint-
ments.''

"This doesn't sound like a community that would
spawn a serial killer then," Deedra remarked.

"Nooo, though the swamp seems to attract such
things!" Jocelyn stared toward the swamp in an almost
hypnotic way.

"Have other things happened around the swamp?"

"Perhaps there are shades of long ago, the fog plays
tricks on the imagination, you know. You think you see
something and when the fog lifts there's nothing there,
of course. A swamp is an ugly thing!"

Deedra sensed there was more to Jocelyn's remark.
"Did you ever paint the swamp?"

A flash of what Deedra thought was fear darkened
her clear blue eyes. "I've not tried for several years
now. There're only those old snags, and that greenish
slime, of course. The fog hangs over it and sometimes
the mist creates ghostly images. I try not to look at the
swamp when it's foggy."

Deedra wanted to question her further, but just then
Claude drove past and Jocelyn hurried away. Was the
woman afraid of her husband, or had she just wanted
to put an end to that particular conversation?

Deedra made notes of things she had learned, and
was putting on a fresh pot of coffee when Sheriff Aaron
Blaine knocked on the door.

Somewhat surprised, Deedra gestured him to the
chair since she had notebooks spread out on the sofa.

"Coffee will be ready in a minute," Deedra remarked by way of a greeting.

"Need that," Aaron sank into the chair and placed

his hat on the floor. "I saw you chatting with two of the natives?"

"Yes. Jocelyn Hoover and Harriet Stratton. Interesting women. I was trying to get background on the area."

"Do they know you are a reporter?"

"No. I've told them I'm a writer. And they've checked out my writing stuff." Deedra glanced toward the upturned boxes holding her laptop, printer, various papers, and a cup containing pens and pencils. "Harriet even took a quick peek at the title page of my novel."

Aaron grinned. "That ought to satisfy her, and cultivating her is a good idea. She has a vast knowledge of the people that reside in this area. Wouldn't surprise me to learn after we capture him, that she knows this killer. She might unwittingly give you a clue sometime. We are certain now that the killer lives this side of Rufus. Of course, he might live in Brockton, but most of those resident's travel toward Sacramento and not on this highway. It's been many years since water sports or fishing in Lake Percifal attracted anyone. Now the swamp repels visitors and the lake is steadily shrinking."

"What about Half Town?" Deedra suggested.

Aaron smiled. "So you've already heard about Half Town?"

"Yes. Jocelyn filled me in."

"We've checked out the residents there. It's a retirement community, most of the men too old to have committed these crimes, many don't even own cars, don't think our killer is there. We've been doing background checks on Rufus people. Haven't found any with a sheet on rape or assault. A half-dozen were involved in domestic disputes, but all are divorced with the exes in other parts of the country.''

"So you've developed a profile of this murderer?" Deedra was quite aware of this sheriff's muscular body, his aura of virility, his repressed desire to capture the fiend who stalked local women.

Again Aaron smiled, this time it extended to a twinkle in his sharp blue eyes. "Always the investigative thinker, eh? Yes, we have. We believe this killer is between 40 and 50 years old, lives in this part of the county, and simply takes advantage of women who are temporarily alone. That he doesn't stalk any particular woman, just happens to see them walking alone or whatever, and takes advantage of the moment. The victims were all different types. Two blondes, one with dark hair. The only thing they had in common was their ages. All in their early thirties.''

"Any suspects?" Deedra hoped her admiration for this man didn't show.

Aaron Blaine sighed. "Not at this point. We've checked out nearly everyone with a prior in nearby counties. Nothing suspicious there." The sheriff leaned back and savored his coffee. A look of weariness made his features looked pained, but the look vanished almost as soon as it had appeared causing Deedra to wonder if she had only imagined it.

"Any of your suspects living here?" Deedra gestured to the cabins that formed Percifal.

"Right now we don't have any leads to suspect anyone, but serial killers come in all types. Most are ordinary and seemingly unassuming. That's why I requested Clete to send you up here. I need someone to keep an eye on what goes on here in Percifal. We don't have the man-power to watch everyone, and I knew Clete would want a story.''

Deedra felt a start of surprise. "You know Clete Bailey?''

"Known him most of my life. We grew up in Rufus, went to Rufus High. I guess Clete doesn't talk about that?" Aaron grinned.

"No, he doesn't.'' That certainly explained Clete's intense interest in these murders. Had Clete known any of the victims or their families?

Aaron nodded. "Figures. Clete owns property just this side of Rufus, and the house his parent's owned in town. So he still pays taxes here.'' He paused. "That's partly why you're here. His interest and my request. I need someone unknown to the natives and not connected to law enforcement.''

Deedra nodded realizing that Aaron was probably acquainted with Sheriff Gavin Blair, whose county was slightly north in old gold country and the site of two murders in a "ghost town'' called North Ledge. She was here as an unauthorized deputy, not really as a journalist. Clete did have a way of getting the most for the money.

"So I'm to socialize with the residents, but remain aloof,'' Deedra suggested.

"Right. You know the agenda. Don't contact me by e-mail. A couple of these people are computer savvy. Use a pay phone when you can otherwise the cell phone is okay. You might want to write up character sketches on the men here.'' Aaron drained his coffee cup then reached into his jacket and drew folded papers from an inside pocket. "Here's a brief sketch of each of the victims and some details on what forensics we have so far. I know I don't have to tell you that this can't be released. Don't want the killer to know what we have which, unfortunately, is not much!''

Deedra took the papers from his hand. She guessed she looked trustworthy.

''Much as I'd like to stay and get better acquainted, I must leave. Keep your doors locked. Be wary of strangers, and don't ever walk along the highway alone!''

TWO

DEEDRA SPENT the next two days cultivating Jocelyn, Harriet and the woman in the wheelchair, Emma Randolph.

It was the morning after Aaron's visit that she met Emma Randolph while on a stroll around the lake and venturing to the lower end of the swamp. Once there, she walked around the swamp on the squishy road toward the highway. When she reached the area of the crime scene tape, she took another photo of the swamp area where the body of Priscilla Dawson had been found.

The water—what there was of it under the scum—wasn't deep here—only about two feet near the edge. She found a snag and pushed a heavy layer of sludge away revealing murky water. Had the killer hoped Priscilla's body wouldn't be seen—hidden by the covering scum, or had dumping her body there merely served to place it away from the murder scene? Deedra took another photo of the swamp, the early morning light outlining old tree snags and lumps that resembled crocodiles. Later, while examining the processed photos she would discover something significant. At the moment her attention was attracted by the woman in the wheelchair's watchful gaze.

Slowly Deedra walked along—not at the water's edge

now—instead along the graveled road close to the cabins. She didn't look toward the woman, wanting to discover her at the last minute, attempt to engage her in conversation, guessing that the woman wouldn't speak first. Deedra kept her gaze on the lake, glancing back toward the crime scene area, then ahead toward the lake.

When she was opposite the woman's cabin, she glanced up, allowing a flicker of surprise to cross her face.

"Hello, there!"

The woman raised a hand to acknowledge Deedra's greeting.

"The weather is beautiful, but cold," Deedra ventured.

The woman nodded.

Deedra walked up to the porch. "I'm Deedra Masefield. I've rented the old store building for a couple of weeks. A cheap vacation, can't afford resort prices. How long have you lived here?"

The woman held up ten fingers, then another ten, bringing Deedra to the realization that the woman couldn't speak.

Deedra nodded, and glanced back at the crime scene area. "Too bad about that poor woman they found in the swamp. I heard that's the third murder around here. Scary! The sheriff warned me not to walk along the highway. Did you know any of the victims?"

The woman vigorously shook her head, and Deedra saw fear reflected in her eyes.

Deedra allowed her gaze to dwell on the welcome sign near the front door. "Melvyn & Emma Randolph."

"You must be Emma Randolph?" Deedra suggested.

The fear vanished as the woman smiled and nodded.

Deedra smiled and after a few moments of saying

how she liked the area and that the weather had been beautiful for this time of year, she bid Emma good-bye. She felt uncomfortable around the woman whose remnants of beauty told of a different life before her tragic accident. There was deep sadness in Emma's eyes even when she had smiled, a hint of pain in the wrinkles around her light brown eyes. Her body had been a lump under the heavy blanket. Probably in her late forties, Deedra mused, knowing Emma led a very lonely life.

Before Deedra reached the store, Harriet Stratton walked down her front steps and met her on the roadway. "Deedra, I'm sorry if I was rude to you. There's been criticism about our county government and your question just rubbed me the wrong way. I apologize."

"No apology needed. Since meeting your Aaron Blaine, I can tell this investigation is in capable hands." Deedra smiled. "I just had a one way conversation with Emma Randolph. Did she have an accident that caused her disabilities?"

Harriet nodded. "Yes. About two years ago now. She was riding in the delivery truck with her husband when it was struck by a state trooper's car skidding on the ice, then the truck began to slide going off into the lake. There," she pointed to the paved road leading into Percifal. "Her husband, Melvyn, managed to get their seat belts unbuckled, and the door open on his side. Another officer in the patrol car dived in and pulled Emma out. The state trooper who drove the patrol car remained unconscious for several weeks. I've never heard if he recovered or not. Anyway, Emma had a touch and go time of it. When she left the hospital she couldn't walk or speak, although the doctors think her inability to speak is psychological, not injury caused. Just trauma she can't overcome, the fear of drowning perhaps."

"How tragic! What kind of business is her husband in? I've noticed his delivery truck."

"He has a home delivery service. Refrigerated items. People up here have freezers and stock up on items like beef, pork, chicken, and eggs. And there are some who purchase ice cream every two or three weeks. He purchases the dairy products from a factory in Rufus"

"How interesting! So he has a regular customer route?"

"Yes. His delivery area extends from south and east of Rufus, to Half Town and the remote areas east and north of Brockton."

"That certainly covers a lot of territory," Deedra remarked.

"Yes. Years ago Emma often rode into Rufus with him. She was a clerk in the bank there."

"How tragic!" Deedra repeated.

"Yes. They used to live in cabin 2, but the sight of the lake where the accident happened frightened Emma, so they moved to an empty cabin at the end, and where the rent was only half what Melvyn paid for cabin 2. It isn't nearly as comfortable, though Melvyn has done his best to fix it up. The move helped Emma even though the view from their front window overlooks the swamp." Harriet sighed. "I guess most of us aren't thankful enough for the blessings we have."

Deedra nodded. Harriet was, indeed, a source of information. In her helpful way, she had filled in Deedra's curiosity about Emma.

"Who lives in cabin 2 now?"

"Neil and Marsha Landen. They run a hardware store in Rufus. Moved out here when their house in Rufus burned down. Only place they could find to rent at the time. Most days Marsha goes in with Neil, though of late she's been feeling poorly. I went to school with Marsha, we're old friends."

"Seems this area has very few strangers," Deedra ventured.

"We like to keep our own, and why would city people want to live out here? Most people want city convenience and public schools. Country schools don't have adequate funds to supply lots of books and computers." Harriet's lips formed a firm line as if she was again defending her place of residence. "Young people move to big cities where they find work and where they think there's more to life."

"That's right. I'm not certain I'd want to live out here all the time," Deedra smiled. "Let's see if I've got this straight. Jocelyn and Claude live in cabin 1, Neil and Marsha in 2, you and Dwight in 3, and Melvyn and Emma in 7."

Harriet nodded. "You've a good memory. Ivan and Sheila Wallace live in 4. Garrian and Everett Black in 5. They are brothers and long haul drivers, gone much of the time. Lance Fenton, a widower, lives in 6. Lived there as long as I can remember. His wife died two years ago. Melancholy man. Lives on a pension and just shut himself up in that cabin after his wife died. Doesn't have much to say to anyone anymore."

Deedra was amazed at Harriet's garrulousness. Without half-trying, she had elicited information about all the residents of Percifal. It was as if Harriet wanted to put any suspicions to rest. Did Harriet guess that Deedra was there on a covert mission?

When Deedra returned to the store she phoned Clete. After giving him the run-down, she casually mentioned that Aaron had told her of Clete's ties to that area of the world. "You didn't mention you're a tax payer up here. Did you know any of the victims?"

"No, I didn't. And Deedra, Aaron is a friend of mine. Try not to get…ah…any special attachment to him." Clete broke the connection.

Deedra held the cell phone away from her ear. Did Clete mean what she thought he did by that last remark? Aaron was certainly an attractive man. She was interested in him, was still looking for Mr. Right, but did Clete assume she was seriously interested in Aaron Blaine after just having met him? She hoped Clete didn't think she was that desperate. After all, she was still young, an established journalist in her own right, earning an interesting salary, and she wasn't ugly.

With Clete's departing words still ringing in her ears, she began writing up profiles on the men of Percifal. Then she added profiles on the women. Since the victims were all raped the women weren't suspects, but it wouldn't hurt to note all the information. She might even write a novel or two later and need the character studies.

Her thoughts were interrupted by a phone call from Sheriff Aaron Blaine.

"Another body has been found along the highway north of Percifal. Looks like she's been there a day or two. Probably dumped about the time we were pulling Priscilla out of the swamp."

"Is the killer speeding up attack times?"

"He could be, or just saw an opportunity and took it. There doesn't seem to be a pattern for any of these murders, no stalking of victims, just chance encounters."

"I'll be there in a few minutes."

Deedra phoned Clete. "I'm on my way to the scene, talk later."

Deedra was aware that both Jocelyn and Harriet saw her leave and tried not to speed away, not give them the idea she felt the necessity to hurry.

The crime scene was approximately one mile north of Percifal and on the right side as if the killer had been traveling north. Patrol cars, a coroner's van, and a forestry truck lined the highway shoulder. The victim had just been placed into a body bag.

Aaron strode to her side. "The body has evidently been rolled down the embankment from the pavement leaving no footprints. The victim is a young woman, probably in her late teens or early twenties, dressed in jeans and a sweatshirt with a Chico State logo. She's a bleached blonde, no identification found on her. Night darkness and early morning fogs prevented her discovery earlier. A passing forest ranger was attracted by a swarm of vultures, and a cougar who had evidently just discovered the body, there are bite marks near the victim's mouth."

To cover her distaste and shock, Deedra looked away, and saw the ranger talking to another deputy who was taking notes.

Deedra took photos of the scene, carefully memorizing it, noting that the killer had been traveling north which probably meant he had picked up the victim south of Rufus. Any woman missing from Rufus would have raised the alarm hours ago.

"We're certain she was a college student, and have inquiries out to that college, but it's difficult. College students sometimes don't attend classes for various reasons, and so far no reports of anyone missing."

"She was raped and strangled?"

"Probably. The M.E. will have to confirm that though."

"Do you think the killer might live in or around Brockton now?"

"Well," Aaron drawled, "it certainly looks as if the killer was traveling that way. However, this is the first body found this far north. Might not mean anything more than a convenient dumping place. Dumping the victims' bodies in this case seems as erratic as the victims' capture."

Deedra nodded. There certainly didn't appear to be a consistent M.O. The only confirming evidence that it was just one killer, were the minute traces of seminal fluid found on one woman's clothing, but none inside the victims. The killer had also cleaned the victims up and washed away evidence, the seminal traces found were compromised and not suitable for a DNA ID. This fact hadn't been released to the public, and Deedra had withheld it from Clete. She didn't want to throw a clinker into the investigation knowing that Aaron would never forgive it. He needed her trust…and she needed his, and it would ruin her reputation among law enforcement officials forever if she gave this vital clue away.

"You didn't find any traces of fluids on Priscilla's clothing did you?"

"No, the swamp guck eliminated any, though the medical examiner thinks there might have been, and was perhaps the reason the killer dumped her into the swamp. We'll have to see if there are any trace forensics on this victim. We might have a better chance since she wasn't found in water"

A call on Aaron's cell phone alerted him that a car belonging to Sandy Nevin, a student at Chico State, had

been found in a ravine twenty miles south of Rufus.
Home address, Rufus.

The coroner's men carried what they were now certain was Sandy Nevin up to the waiting van and drove
off to Rufus. Deedra watched it leave with a sadness
she would never be able to explain to anyone not present at the scene.

"You can follow me to the place where they found
the car. I might need some of your photo's later."
Aaron strode over to a deputy, then climbed in a patrol
car, made a U turn and roared south, siren blazing the
way.

Deedra followed at a safer speed, arriving just as a
tow truck was hoisting a small compact car from a shallow ravine. Though full of brush and boulders, the ravine wasn't as deep as many in this mountainous area
were. The road was not heavily traveled since most people used the interstate several miles to the west. Rufus
was the closest town—the junction connecting to busier
highways five miles to the south. The victim had to have
been familiar with this part of the world to choose this
road. Scattered houses dotted the area for several miles
south of Rufus. Only three cars passed during the time
Deedra was at the scene of the wreck.

She watched as the car was settled onto the pavement. Aaron and the tow truck driver looked inside, and
Deedra moved closer. On the front seat were a back-
pack, an open package of potato chips, and a soda can
that had leaked its contents onto the passenger side seat
leaving a dark stain. Testimony that the driver had probably been snacking at or just before the time the car
had gone over the edge.

Aaron put on gloves and checked the car for signs of
blood, didn't find any. The front passenger door was

jammed, but there were no signs that would indicate the woman had been injured. He gave instructions for the car to be towed to the impound center in Rufus.

Then began the search on the shoulders of the road that was graveled and left no footprints. Only a place of scuffled gravel indicated that a car might have stopped there. There was no litter, no candy wrappers, no cigarette butts, and no soda cans within a hundred feet either way of the place where the car had gone into the ravine.

Aaron shook his head. "Nothing here to tell us why Sandy Nevin was discovered raped and murdered thirty miles north of here."

"You are sure the victim is Sandy Nevin?" Deedra took another snapshot of the ravine where the car had been found.

"As certain as I can be without fingerprints. Her parents live a few miles north, closer to Rufus. They own a riding stable, and the father is a guide leading groups into the wilderness areas. I've met him several times. He headed up a group of searchers for a lost ten-year old boy a couple of years back. They found him right about where Gus Nevin reckoned they would. Nevin's kids are all resourceful. If his daughter was in the car when it went over, she would climb to the road and try to get help. Or she might have had a flat tire and was changing it when apprehended."

"And then the killer sent the car into the ravine to prevent the fact of her disappearance from being discovered for a few days?" Deedra suggested.

"Yes. Either way, it looks like this is where the killer apprehended her. Be easy, the killer offering a ride to Rufus, someone heading north toward Rufus like she was."

"You think he murdered her in his car?"

Aaron ran a hand over his eyes. "Perhaps. He's a cautious killer though, I doubt he would leave many traces for us to find."

They continued the search, a deputy going into the ravine to check for signs there. Only the tow truck driver's footprints indicated that anyone else had been down there. No footprints of anyone having left the car.

"That means the girl was apprehended before the car went into the ravine!" Aaron muttered. He gave instructions to a deputy, then strode off to his car to use the police radio. She heard him growl, "Have you got that address for me?"

"Yes, Sheriff. It's the riding stables, all right."

Aaron turned to Deedra. "Drive up the road and leave your car at that bus stop. I want you to go with me while I tell the parents. As unobtrusively as possible, get photos of the place. For a time there, we suspected Gus Nevin, thought he might have taken these women out into the woods to murder them. But his alibis all checked out, and no evidence was found in his pickup. I guess leading a group into the wilderness is as good an alibi as a person can get."

Deedra followed Aaron's instructions and was soon seated beside him in the patrol car.

The Nevin place was about two miles south of Rufus, located down a graveled lane into a clearing where a rambling house took center stage among stables and what appeared to be bunkhouses. A regular dude ranch, Deedra mused.

As she got out of the car, Deedra quickly snapped pictures of the corral where a man was training a horse, and the stable beyond. Following Aaron to the house, she managed to snap pictures of the house and another stable beyond.

A neatly dressed woman in riding habit answered the door. She was obviously surprised to see the sheriff standing there. It was as if she had been expecting someone, but the sheriff definitely wasn't that someone. A cloud seemed to cross over her pretty features and darkened her blue eyes.

Out of the corner of her eye, Deedra noted the man who had been training the horse, gave the reins to a younger man, then leapt over the corral fence, hurriedly striding toward them.

"What can I do for you, Sheriff?"

"Have you been expecting Sandy?"

"Oh, God! What's happened?" Mrs. Nevin cried, her eyes filled with fear.

Gus Nevin arrived at his wife's side. "What are you saying? Has something happened to Sandy?" The man's face had turned the color of old ashes. He clasped his wife's shoulders in a grip that must have hurt.

"We've found her car in a ravine south of here. We need you to go to the coroner's office for identification."

Mrs. Nevin appeared near collapse.

"I'll drive you there," Aaron said. When Gus started to object, Aaron gestured to Mrs. Nevin and Gus Nevin meekly obeyed.

Except for Mrs. Nevin's sobs, there was silence in the car while Aaron drove to the medical complex next to the Rufus hospital. It was a traumatizing few minutes while the Nevins identified their daughter, and learned the true facts of her murder. A loved one murdered is considerably different from one killed in an accident, and Gus Nevin's anger stampeded over his grief.

"You mean Sandy was another victim of that rapist? The one who threw Priscilla's body into Percifal swamp?" His eyes flashed in a wild sort of fury.

"Could be. We haven't had a chance to take a look at everything yet." Aaron Blaine said and threw Deedra a sidelong glance. She, too, picked up on the fact that Gus mentioned Priscilla as if he were acquainted with her.

Deedra sensed he felt it would be cruel to question these grieving parents right now, right at the moment of their greatest shock. She guessed that Aaron would question them later. By then Gus would be calmer, eager to help get the fiend who ended Sandy's life.

After the papers were signed and a mortuary selected, Aaron drove the grieving couple home where Sandy's three brothers stood on the rambling front porch awaiting them.

From her seat in the patrol car, Deedra witnessed the scene though could not hear their words of shock and grief. The older boys surrounded their parents, but the younger one slid to the floor as if his legs gave out, and wept. A teenager, perhaps only fourteen, his grief simply devastating. Deedra eyes filled with tears and a few slipped down her pale face.

When Aaron returned to the car, Deedra hastily wiped the tears away. She had a "tough" image to portray.

"You think Gus knows something about Priscilla Dawson?" Deedra asked as they drove to the bus stop where she had left her car.

"Yes. I suspect she went on one of his guided tours or might have taken riding lessons there. Since she owned a gift and fabric shop in Rufus, many people knew who she was and have probably bought something in her shop. The Nevins weren't listed among her close friends, however. Priscilla was too young to have gone to school with either Gus and his wife, and too old to have been in high school with Sandy.''

"So now you have four victims all killed in the last six weeks. Darlene Hernandez, Thelma Hansen, Priscilla Dawson, and Sandy Nevin, and no obvious M.O.''

"Well, the rapes are his M.O. Either he wears a condom or can't ejaculate and is trying to remedy that.''

"Oh!'' Deedra, slightly embarrassed, got out of the patrol car. She should have guessed the M.O. having investigated several sex crimes.

Aaron smiled in a grim way, and roared off toward Rufus.

Deedra sat in her own car pondering the few clues she knew. Could all those women have known the killer and therefore were unaware of danger? If Aaron was right about the killer residing in or around Rufus, then chances of the victims' knowing…and trusting him… were probably correct. In a small town people were acquainted with almost everyone. If the killer had grown up in Rufus, went to high school with many of the people there, he could move among them without suspicion. A fixture in their everyday lives.

She drove into Rufus and left several rolls of film at the camera shop to be developed, then went down the street to a restaurant for lunch.

Seated at a small table next to a window she was startled when a young man of about her own age said, "Mind if I join you?'' and without waiting for an invitation, plunked down opposite her. "I'm glad to see you again, Deedra Masefield. I'm Bradley Keetz, the owner of the Rufus Informer newspaper. I recognized you immediately. You were up here a couple of years ago on that missing women story.''

Deedra eyed the young man with renewed interest. ''Ah…yes. We met when I took advantage of your fax machine.''

''Right. Those women just disappeared, no trace of them has been found.''

''Yes, strange story. I believe they were from another part of the state?''

Bradley Keetz nodded, and ordered coffee from the hovering waitress. ''I was just wondering if you are here on this serial killer business? News item for my weekly.''

Deedra nodded. No sense trying to fool a colleague. ''Officially, yes. For public consumption, no. Sheriff wants it that way. I'm doing a little snooping at Percifal, rented that old store building.''

Bradley grinned. ''On vacation, I take it?''

''Yes, I must work on a novel. Soothes the native's curiosity.''

Brad nodded and sipped the coffee the waitress had set before him. She had given him an intimate sort of smile as if they had a past…or she was hoping for a future. Bradley Keetz picked up on it and a slight flush colored his features, though he allowed the incident to drift away. He was a good-looking young man with serious hazel eyes that refracted interest and mirth with friendly sparkles. There was no wedding band on his third finger left hand, increasing Deedra's interest.

''Know anything about the residents at Percifal? Anything unusual there?'' Deedra watched the play in Bradley's hazel eyes.

''Not really. I've known Harriet and Dwight for as long as I can remember. As a kid we fished out of

Percifal Lake, and bought candy and ice cream at the store. Then after the earthquake of '89, the swamp began to take over. Every year that swamp takes over more of the lake, which is gradually disappearing, soon nothing will be left but a bog. As for the residents, haven't heard of anything really unusual. After Lance Fenton's wife died, he went reclusive, sort of hugged his grief. Melvyn Randolph's wife is an invalid, has been since that accident when Melvyn's truck went into the lake.''

''They never retrieved the truck?''

''Tried to, it slipped off the chain and sank into deeper water. Since there isn't any environmental danger they didn't try again. Tight budget, couldn't get a diver to go down there and chain it up, and Melvyn's insurance company was reluctant to finance it. Bought him a new truck and paid his wife's medical expenses though. I understand she's still in a wheelchair.''

Deedra nodded. ''Appears unable to speak.''

''Well,'' Bradley drawled, ''there're several opinions about that. Doctors at the hospital say she was quite vocal at first. It was only after she had been in the hospital about a week that she developed that speech symptom.''

''Oh?'' Deedra wanted to hear Brad's version.

''They say it's psychological, that there is nothing medically wrong that prevents her from speaking.''

''Odd,'' Deedra replied.

''Strange things happen to people. I must say, Melvyn doesn't neglect her, makes sure she has her medicine and arranges his schedule so he can get her to the doctor appointments.''

''They've lived there a long time?''

''Ever since I can remember. Both born and raised in

Rufus. My father owned this newspaper so I'm familiar with much of what goes on around here.''

"You've heard about the latest murder victim then?'' Deedra saw surprise fill Brad's eyes, the hazel color hidden now by a dark stunned look.

"What?''

Deedra quickly filled him in, then he quickly excused himself and raced off to get a first-hand account. Deedra hoped Bradley Keetz wouldn't spread the word about her presence at Percifal.

News about the latest murder victim quickly spread through town. By the time Deedra had finished eating her lunch, served just after Bradley Keetz left, the restaurant was buzzing with the news.

An elderly couple sank down in chairs at the next table. Their conversation was all conjecture about the newest victim.

"If I was that killer I'd be mighty afraid of Gus Nevin. He's got a temper and he thought Sandy was just about perfect, what with them rowdy boys of his,'' the woman remarked.

"You're right about that! And if it had been one of our granddaughters, I'd be up and armed! Funny thing, they can't find no clue to that bastard! Killed four of our local women now! Sheriff is sure the creep lives around here someplace, but it's got to be a stranger! We ain't had no murders until just lately!''

The waitress arrived and took their orders. There was a pleasant exchange between them.

"You think it's someone new here then?'' the woman asked after the waitress retreated.

"Bound to be! No one in their right mind would do such a thing! And we ain't raised no crazies around

Rufus! People been living here all their lives and haven't resorted to killings like that!''

''Has the sheriff been checking on the strangers then?'' The woman seemed to defer judgment to her husband. A cultural habit of the older generation, Deedra mused.

''Yep! And he told me he's checked out the traveling salesmen, too. Aaron's a born and raised Rufus man, and he ain't likely to leave stones unturned.''

Their conversation trailed off when their meals arrived, and Deedra had no excuse to linger.

The films had been developed and she drove on ''home.'' The store was cold. She shivered as she poured pellets into the old stove, and replenished the fireplace, thankful that by the time winter really set in, she should be back in the city in her real home.

It was funny how united people were that this killer was not one of their own, but someone alien to the community, murder something they probably thought happened only in big cities where there were gangs and drugs and criminals everywhere.

While waiting for the rooms to warm, she examined the photos. Good shots of the crime scene and close-ups of the Nevin's place. The rest were pictures of Percifal, the cabins, the lake, the swamp. She was about to replace one of the swamp taken from a place on the Percifal side, when her heart gave a frightening leap. A skeleton skull stared back at her, its vacant eyes filled with sludge. On closer inspection of the photo the skull seemed to blend in, as if it was only a snag, a trick of her imagination. She hadn't seen it when she took the photo, why did it appear to be a skull now? Like the face on Sedonia, was it just a mirage? Her intuition told her it was not. This was something Aaron Blaine needed to see.

Holding the photo, she called the sheriff. "I have something interesting to show you. Meet me down near the swamp on the Percifal side."

Before Aaron Blaine could object, she hung up, made certain the fires were under control, and hurried down the graveled road to a place almost opposite Cabin 7.

Emma Randolph, seated at the front window, watched. When Aaron arrived, Emma put a hand over her mouth.

"What?" Aaron asked obviously puzzled by her summons.

She took out the photo and pointed to what resembled a snag protruding from the guck.

"I don't know, Deedra. In the snapshot it looks like a skull, from here it just looks like an old snag."

"But what if something is there? Obviously it's a really old skull, but we know the killer used the swamp as a dumping place for one of his victims. Priscilla? What if he's been using this place for years? Maybe it is his preferred location when he can safely get to it with his victim."

"Deedra, you scare the hell out of me!" Aaron's eyes narrowed giving him the appearance of only having slits. After a moment he said, "Tell you what, I'll take this film to the state police expert and have him perform his magic with it. Then we'll know whether to proceed…or let floating skulls drift away."

Deedra nodded, handing him the roll of negatives.

"You learned something else?" Aaron prompted.

Deedra sighed, trying to match his strides as they walked toward the patrol car.

"Bradley Keetz recognized me. I doubt he'll alert

anyone here in Percifal about who I am. He learned about Sandy Nevin from me.''

"I wondered what brought him to the scene so quickly. Want a ride back to the store?''

"No. It's best we don't appear that friendly.'' She would have loved to spend another few minutes in Aaron's presence. He stirred emotions that were better ignored.

Aaron roared off, a man with a distasteful mission.

Deedra gazed at the swamp with a critical eye. And then shuddered. Could that slimy old marsh hold the answer to missing persons who had never been found? The idea was ghastly, gruesome. No wonder the old swamp had such a haunting, grisly appearance.

THREE

THE EVENING TV news spread the word that another victim of the "Roadside Rapist" had been discovered. Aaron Blaine appeared on screen several times and announced that the crime unit believed the killer lived in the area where the bodies had been discovered. "We do have a few clues, though we aren't releasing that information to the public for obvious reasons. It just might help the killer evade prosecution."

"Then you do have confidence that you'll apprehend this murderer?" the anchor persisted.

"Oh, yes. Every killer leaves clues. And with our new forensic techniques, perpetrators don't have much chance of escaping detection."

Deedra settled down watching a television show, allowing her mind to roam. Often, when she didn't really concentrate, ideas formed, intuition took charge. Tonight, however, her thoughts merely roamed. She started when the cell phone rang.

It was Bradley Keetz.

"First of all, thanks for alerting me. Second, you were recognized by a TV anchor. The sheriff stalled him off by saying your presence here was coincidental, he understood that you were on vacation in Percifal, writing a novel. Aaron told them he was aware that you had rented the store building, but it was before Priscilla's body had been found in the swamp. He said he was aware that you had notified your newspaper which was consistent with the duties of your profession.''

"Oh, oh! You think I'll be getting a visit from the TV people?''

Bradley sighed. "I'm not sure. They might ignore it out of professional jealousy. After all, you've stolen their thunder several times with news-breaking stories, they might not want that to happen again.''

"Thanks for the warning, Brad.''

"Can I take you out to dinner tomorrow night?

"That's an invitation I'll take you up on only if it's for pizza.''

Brad laughed. A happy sound as if she met all his expectations. "I'll pick you up around 6:00.''

DEEDRA WAS AROUSED from deep slumber by the sound of cautious footsteps. Slipping her feet into her shoes she made her way to the front of the store and carefully pulled aside the makeshift drapes.

Someone was again inspecting her car, testing to see if the doors were open. The man didn't seem to be the same one who had inspected it that other night. This man aimed his flashlight on the license plate and copied down the numbers in a notebook. When he finished the flashlight was snapped off, and he vanished into the shadows around the old gas station.

Though she watched until cold penetrated her very bones, there was no further movement.

Thoroughly chilled she filled the stove with pellets and ran another tub full of hot water. Relaxed and warmed, she climbed back into her sleeping bag...and had a frightening dream about rats and a mutant boy named Tito. She awoke groaning—perspiration soaking her nightshirt. She struggled out of the wet gown and spent the rest of the night naked, huddled into a fetal position, the sleeping bag pulled over her head. Deedra was very glad that none of her colleagues knew how the rats of the Awful Abbey had affected her life.

She slept late and was awakened by Harriet Stratton's knock on the door.

"Deedra! Deedra, are you all right?" There was urgency in her voice...or was it fear?

"Just a minute. I need to get dressed!" She slipped into jeans and sweatshirt and ran her hand through her tangled curls on the way to the door.

Harriet was bundled up against the icy rain that had ushered in Thanksgiving Day.

"I was worried about you since I didn't see smoke from your chimney, and the weather turning colder."

Deedra ran a hand through her tangled curls. "Just overslept. Couldn't sleep earlier in the night, and had to take another hot bath. I'm not used to the quiet here. Just let me run a comb through my hair and I'll make some coffee." Deedra started coffee, filled the stove with pellets, and stoked up the coals in the fireplace adding kindling and a thick chunk of wood. Before the coffee finished perking the old store building had warmed and a feeling of comfort returned.

"Nothing like a warm house and a cup of fresh coffee," Harriet remarked as she took in the surroundings. She had watched Deedra's every move, and if she thought Deedra was out of her element, must have been disappointed. Deedra knew that Harriet would forever be able to tell anyone exactly where everything was located. Had Harriet been aware that a man had prowled about the store last night? Was it Dwight and that was the reason for her concern this morning when Deedra hadn't shown signs of activity?

"You never said what you do for a living?" Harriet prompted, eyeing Deedra over the rim of her cup.

"I work for a newspaper in Pacific Hills."

"Oh? A secretary or some kind of clerical work?" Harriet's eyes had taken on a glint as if a warning light had been turned on within.

"No, more like a feature writer. I'm not the clerical type," Deedra replied.

The glint in Harriet's eyes faded. "Is the pay for that sort of thing…ah…lucrative?"

"Just average. I'm saving up to buy a new car," Deedra gestured to her old Scout. "They don't even make those kind anymore, and finding new parts is difficult."

Evidently this pointed out a financial status to Harriet whose interest had waned.

The truth of it was that Deedra was fond of the old Scout and was reluctant to part with it, especially when she often drove a news car to fast-breaking stories around the city. It hadn't seemed important to display her middle-class wealth with a new car every year or two. Harriet's conclusion that she was a struggling workingwoman gave rise to an urge to visit a few car agencies when she returned to the city.

"You live in an apartment?" Harriet's curiosity evidently knew no bounds.

"Yes, basement apartment. It's cooler in the summer." Deedra's actual choice of an apartment in the basement of elderly friends of her parent's, was the fact that it had a separate entrance, its own kitchen, washer and dryer, was in a quiet upper class neighborhood. And the rent wasn't exorbitant. The old couple knew of her odd working hours, of days of absence when she was assigned out of town stories. Therefore they didn't worry and blissfully went on enjoying their retirement knowing the rent would be paid on time. Deedra had an arrangement with the bank so that no matter what part of the country she was in, the rent money was deposited to their bank account each month.

"Do you have boy friends in the city?" Harriet was just full of questions.

"Not any serious ones."

"Then you aren't engaged or anything?"

"No, but I do have a date with Bradley Keetz tonight, and I admire Aaron Blaine tremendously," Deedra thought her glib answer might deter Harriet's q and a session. It didn't.

"Yes, both men are unmarried and very attractive. Would you ever consider moving up to Rufus?" Harriet smoothed her perfectly ironed dress.

"I don't think so. A man would have to really attract me. I'm an independent sort of person. I like shopping malls and movies."

"Yes, I guess one gets used to that sort of thing. Do you spend time on the internet?"

Deedra felt a start of surprise. "No, not much. My spare time is taken up with my writing. Do you have access to the internet?"

"Yes. I'm quite taken with it. I like the chat rooms."

Figures, Deedra mused, and wondered where this conversation was leading. "Anyone here in Percifal addicted to the computer?"

"Oh, we all have computers. Lance Fenton spends most of his time surfing the Internet. It's probably the thing that has kept him sane since his wife died. He only ventures out occasionally, and then only to Rufus for the necessities.''

"I suppose the Landens are computer savvy with their hardware business, it's almost a must nowadays.'' Deedra remarked, wishing Harriet would go away so she could get on with early morning routine, like brushing her teeth.

"Yes. Marsha is very savvy about their business matters, but if anything goes wrong she has to call an expert. They have a p.c. at home now. I don't know how much time they spend using it.'' Was there something in this conversation Harriet was trying to convey? "I see you have a laptop.''

Deedra nodded. "It's an easy way to store information, and a real help to writers.''

"They're rather expensive aren't they?'' Harriet's eyes narrowed in speculation.

"Yes, they're a luxury all right, but credit card buying helps many of us get the things we'd like to have,'' lied Deedra, who was given the laptop as a bonus from the newspaper. Deedra realized Harriet had concluded that anyone who would rent an empty old store building for a vacation wouldn't have the funds for a laptop...unless they were computer junkies...or writers. Harriet evidently suspected Deedra had an ulterior motive for renting the old store, and probably thought Deedra was an undercover policewoman. It probably wouldn't take her long to discover who Deedra really was, but why was she so curious?

Deedra changed the subject. "Do you miss not having this old store open?''

Harriet's eyes flashed, evidently aware that Deedra was leading her away from her line of questioning.

"In many ways, yes. It wasn't lucrative the last two

years we kept it open. I miss talking to many of our old customers, but I like being able to sleep in on cold winter mornings.'' Harriet smoothed her dress and then went to the door. "I must get back and bake pies. Even though it's Thanksgiving, Dwight has to work.''

In something like relief, Deedra rushed to the bathroom to brush her teeth, comb her hair and dress properly.

SHERIFF BLAINE ARRIVED with a frown furrowing his forehead.

Deedra felt a tingle of fear. Bad news. She gestured him to a chair and handed Aaron a mug of the freshly brewed coffee.

"What?"

"It's a skull all right. We aren't going to do anything about it until Monday because today is Thanksgiving and most of the forensic people are home for the holiday, and so is everyone here at Percifal. No one knows we suspect that old snag to be skull, so we're going to wait until we have the resources to remove it properly and maintain the integrity of the site." He seemed uncomfortable. "But now I have to include the men here as suspects even though that seems unlikely. State Police don't know these people like I do and so they're not influenced by that." Aaron took a gulp of coffee as if it was needed to give him energy.

"I've told the state police you're here and why. They think this skull may be that of one of the women who disappeared a couple of years ago."

"That means this killer has been at his trade for years?"

Aaron nodded. He looked tired, the smudges under his sharp blue eyes attesting to lack of sleep.

Deedra told him about the midnight prowler and Harriet's early morning visit.

"Harriet actually woke you up?" Aaron seemed puzzled.

"Yes, said she was worried when there was no smoke rising from the chimney."

"Odd. She's usually not that bold. I wonder if she suspects someone here in Percifal?"

"She might have seen that prowler last night, or it could have been Dwight."

"I rather doubt that," but the puzzled expression remained on Aaron's face.

"What exactly do you plan on doing about that skull?"

"Monday a team from the state police will make an attempt to retrieve it. It's not going to be easy in all that sludge, and disturbing it might cause it to move and then be un-retrievable. We can't dredge out that whole swamp. No telling what's down there since that earthquake. The state geologist thinks it's wiser not to disturb things, eventually the swamp will dry up, but if we disturb it now the whole area could become unstable like the ground under that old road. It might also undermine the highway and all these cabins."

"That seems…extreme. How reliable are his predictions?" Deedra didn't take that idea seriously.

"He's been right about everything he's predicted so far, but says a complete study is needed and there's no money for that. Since there's no town here anymore, and no damage to the highway, it's not high on the priority list."

"That's not going to keep them from trying to retrieve the skull though?"

Aaron grinned. "No. You're really certain there's a connection to the present killer, aren't you?"

Deedra nodded. "I have the scary feeling that this old swamp is a graveyard!"

"Please don't say that!" Aaron took a turn around the room as if somehow that would prevent her words from becoming fact.

"Anything preventing me from spreading the word about the skull?" Deedra thought it might stir up further speculation from Harriet and Jocelyn.

"Not yet. You wouldn't be able to explain the photograph and why you gave it to me. And have Clete sit on this until Monday. That will give both of you exclusives."

"Unless someone from the state police department releases their intent," Deedra muttered.

"No, I don't think so! Those people don't want to look foolish in case there isn't anything there," Aaron replied.

"I thought their expert said it was a skull?"

"Not what kind, nor how old. It might have been in that swamp for decades or could even be the skull of an animal. None of us wants to be left with egg on our faces." Aaron took another turn around the room, stopping at a side window that viewed most of the cabins. "I've been advised by the state police to look over the men here at Percifal. With the exception of Lance Fenton, they all travel the road during the week. None of the victims disappeared on weekends. We've practically eliminated the men of Half Town, none fit the profile and no one had the opportunity. Here at Percifal, it's a different story. They all go to work at Rufus, Brockton, or points further away. Their times aren't accounted for every day though all of them seemed to have followed their daily routines. It's their proximity to the swamp. A nearly perfect place to hide a body…ah…bodies. We think the killer might have been interrupted in his attempt to hide Priscilla's body."

Deedra frowned. "But which is really his M.O.? The other victims were all found along the highway."

"Yeah, but perhaps the killer wants to confuse things, perhaps even make it look like a copycat murder."

"You don't think that though?" Deedra challenged.

Aaron shook his head. "I think this killer just kills at random. No planning ahead, just seizes the moment. Happens upon a woman alone and takes advantage. The fact that Sandy Nevin was dumped closer to Brockton may be a red herring. The killer wanting us to believe he was traveling to Brockton or points north. It's easier to track the movements of suspected men in the area for Sandy's murder than for the other victims. So far we've found no one that was in the vicinity of her car wreck."

"Any chance she had a passenger?"

"She might have, but if he was a passenger—he was without wheels, so how could he have transported her from a place twenty miles south of Rufus to a point six miles north of Percifal?"

"That means Sandy accepted a ride with someone after the wreck," Deedra murmured. "Perhaps someone she knew."

"Yeah, someone she didn't suspect. I think that explains why these women were captured. It's someone they had known for a long time and hadn't any reason to distrust." Aaron paused. "You're having Thanksgiving alone?"

"Yes and no. I'm going out for pizza with Bradley Keetz this evening."

"What? No turkey dinner?" Aaron grinned.

"I'm not that conventional with new acquaintances. Pizza doesn't have romantic overtones, just friendly camaraderie," Deedra replied.

"So, you're keeping a low profile. Is there a serious man in your life?"

Deedra sighed, she hated having to explain. "There was, but he's allergic to marriage, and I'm just old-fashioned enough to want that. I don't need a man for financial support, I'm interested in a family, stability."

"Then your options are open?" Aaron asked, a smile twinkling his blue eyes.

Deedra was startled. Was there a hidden meaning in Aaron's words?

Aaron's cell phone rang ending her moment of speculation. Aaron listened for several minutes, and after a routine "Yes, sir," hung up. He turned to her, the friendly repartee gone. "They're going after the skull tomorrow instead of waiting until Monday. The team is available then and they want someone to observe the reactions of the men here at Percifal. They would like you to cooperate in the observing part."

Deedra nodded. "They do have suspicions about someone here then?"

"Just want to cover all the possibilities," Aaron replied. "If it should be someone here, they don't want to panic him at this point."

Despite Aaron's answer, she was certain the state police had a very solid reason for wanting to keep close observation on the men living here. Police often worked on hunches inspired by their experience dealing with criminals and many times it had paid off. Every officer in the area had been working this serial murder case for weeks now. Veteran officers would have formed certain conclusions now about how this fiend worked, but would move with caution, no accusations until they had a solid case.

"I'll get in touch later tomorrow to find out what you've observed." He went to the door, then added, "Tell Bradley Keetz but only if you think he'll keep it to himself until we get proof there's something there."

Deedra watched Aaron drive away, wondering what the next day, Friday, would bring.

After a light lunch, she went for a walk taking the hiking trail behind the old gas station that led straight up the hill and from the crest looked down into a snug valley called, Shady Vale. There was a small community there, smoke rising from several chimneys. Along the hillcrest was a well-worn path traveling north and south. She walked south, the cabins of Percifal off to her right. From that vantage point she glimpsed the back of the cabins where stacks of firewood filled sheds, and attempts at gardening that told something about the residents within. There was no movement, however, people were eating Thanksgiving dinner or watching television. She walked to a place where the path separated going down into the valley, the main trail continuing south parallel to the highway and finally leading into thick underbrush. She turned back.

There was movement behind the cabins now. A man she assumed was Melvyn Randolph, was gathering up an armload of wood, and as she watched, disappeared into the house through a back door.

At cabin 4 a man and a woman stood on the back porch smoking. They waved as she passed. Ivan and Sheila Wallace, she mused, both tall and slim, the woman with a crown of dark hair like the proverbial "raven's wing." The man was broad-shouldered, wearing a plaid shirt and had a former athlete's easy grace.

When she walked down the trail toward the old gas station she was hailed by Claude Hoover.

"Jocelyn wants you to join us for dessert. It's pumpkin pie. I must tell you she bakes the best pies this side of Sacramento," he smiled, a smile that lit up his features like an inner lantern.

"Sounds tempting," Deedra smiled in return.

She followed Claude up the steps, wiped her shoes carefully on the welcome mat and stepped into Jocelyn's domain once again.

"Sit down here, Deedra. We've been waiting for you to return to have our dessert. Saw you hike up the trail and knew you were alone today."

The house smelled of roasted turkey and sage dressing, of baked pies and of wood crackling in the fireplace. A safe haven, Deedra mused. Jocelyn's sanctuary. She wondered why Jocelyn needed one.

Claude, a rustic man who fit into the surroundings as if grown there, was the gregarious type who kept Deedra entertained with tales of how Percifal "used to be." Then the talk shifted to Jocelyn's paintings.

"I keep telling her she ought to exhibit them at art shows. She's mighty talented!"

Claude shoved his chair back. "I want you to see some of her paintings." He gestured her to a room just off the living room.

The room had obviously been remodeled to accommodate her painting supplies and easels of various sizes. On one easel was a landscape, not of the surrounding area, but an original done from memory or creative vision. Jocelyn had a flair quite similar to the famous Thomas Kincaid, though distinctly her own. Deedra was no real judge, but Jocelyn's paintings struck a cord of awe, realizing Jocelyn was a very talented woman.

"Jocelyn," she turned to the shy woman standing in the doorway, "you really should market these. You have a talent for minute detail."

Deedra slowly examined the paintings while Claude watched, pride evident in his eyes and body language. Most of the paintings were of birds, of sunsets, of earlier times depicting days when Percifal was a thriving community. Then she saw a painting of the swamp slightly behind another landscape. Something about the swamp painting caused a tingle at the base of her skull. At first it seemed to depict a sludge-laden bog, snags rising from the green algae like remnants of a lost era, then the faint outline of a skull. It was camouflaged to be sure, but nevertheless there. Jocelyn had seen the skull, had painted it, but hadn't pointed it out to anyone. Why?

Deedra carefully concealed her observation and moved on to the next painting, one of the old store with people entering and leaving with full grocery sacks.

"How grand this is!" Deedra gushed knowing she mustn't let the Hoovers know she had seen the message in Jocelyn's swamp painting.

Returning to the living room where Jocelyn served more coffee, Deedra gave Jocelyn some marketing ideas, a list of galleries she knew of that might let her hang some of her paintings. "Jocelyn, your talent is wasted if no one can appreciate it. Please think about it anyway."

Jocelyn nodded, though Deedra could see her reluctance. What drama in her life had urged her to seek anonymity in a place like Percifal where she would rarely meet anyone even vaguely interested in art?

It was 4:00 by the time Deedra returned to the old store, the fire in the stove only glowing coals and the fireplace a heap of cooling coals. It took her nearly half an hour to bring in more wood from the shed at the back, and re-fill the pellet bin, vowing not to complain about the idiosyncrasies of central heating again. But she had to admit there was something comforting in a crackling fireplace where the flames danced and flickered and sent warming drafts across the room.

By the time Bradley Keetz arrived, the old store building was warm again.

THE PIZZA PARLOR in Rufus was crowded with young people and quite noisy. They decided to take pizza to Bradley's apartment where they could at least converse without having to shout. Bradley had sodas in the refrigerator and they laughed and exchanged "war stories" for a couple of hours. Then Brad brought seriousness into their discussion.

"So what's new with the investigation?"

Deedra finished chewing a pizza bite, took a sip of 7-Up and muttered, "Are you prepared for a hush-hush item?"

Instantly Brad's body language changed to alert excitement.

Nothing like a hush-hush tip to stir a journalist's adrenaline, Deedra mused. "At 8:00 tomorrow morning the state police and sheriff's people are going to try to retrieve a skull seen in the middle of the old swamp."

"They what?" Brad's eyes widened with wonder, with doubt, then with what-a-story excitement.

"You are not to breathe a sigh of it until after the fact. You are allowed to be on the scene, however. The network scoops are mine though. Understand?"

"Yes, yes. Of course. You are alerting me because…" Brad's eyes had narrowed in cautious speculation.

"Because I want to review some of your old newspaper files," Deedra challenged.

Bradley nodded agreement. "What do you expect to find in them?"

"Perhaps nothing. Perhaps something so mundane that it's been overlooked," Deedra replied.

"You're thinking that this serial killer is a resident of this area, that he has lived here always, and because he's an everyday part of things he's not under suspicion?" Bradley had the look of one who has perceived the inevitable and doesn't like it.

"Law people think so, but that isn't quotable. You might want to give thought to local gossip, someone's unusual remark, any unusual activity. A person you thought was not quite straight on." Deedra sipped the 7-Up appreciatively.

After a few minutes of discussion about law enforcement procedures, and what constituted a solid case of evidence, Deedra requested to be taken home.

"What? No time for dalliance?" Bradley grinned.

"No. We don't know each other that well, and I'm not into flings just for the hell of it. I want marriage." She laughed then blushed slightly.

"Oh, ho! The reporter who has the reputation of being very tough and sometimes living on the edge, is just an old fashioned lass at heart!" Brad eyed her with a gentleness lacking earlier, the male suddenly realizing that she was all soft female inside.

Deedra had already learned that if you competed in what was thought of as a man's profession—and you were very good at it—men treated you as a competitor rather than a woman. If you allowed your mother/nesting instincts to show, it was a completely new scenario. Deedra seldom allowed her softer nature to show. It was a tough world out there and she shielded her inner self from hurt and devastation by sheer effort. But it put men off. Deke Thomas had admired her skill and journalistic talent, but his flings were with more feminine types. Though he had never admitted it, Deke resented her competition and it had kept him on out-of-the-country assignments.

They were silent on the way to Percifal. Deedra wondering what Brad was thinking about her, and if it had radically changed his view of city reporters in general. Did she care? Yes and no. What Bradley thought of her scarcely mattered. It was what he knew about the local people that she needed to learn. Her tough side had taken over once again.

DEEDRA SLEPT in fits and starts, her thoughts cluttered with the theory that the swamp had been the killer's disposal site. How gruesome and scary that theory was! And when her thoughts weren't littered with that speculation, she dozed off, dreaming about rats streaming out of the swamp, then waking up covered in cold sweat. She had risen early, got the fires going and had taken a hot bath to alleviate the coldness that had settled within her.

After a sparse breakfast, she dressed in warm clothing, and set off toward the last cabin, the vacant cabin, at the end of the graveled road. Fortunately an early morning fog had lifted just before the police arrived to conduct their grisly task. She was standing beside the vacant cabin when the first of the police vehicles arrived.

Pretending to be surprised, she walked to the edge of the swamp and watched as Aaron and a deputy paced about, Aaron gesturing at the swamp in anger and frustration. When the police arrived in a caravan of two patrol cars, a van carrying three men in wet suits and an inflatable boat, so did the residents of Percifal.

Melvyn Randolph was first to arrive followed quickly by the two truck drivers, Garrian and Everett Black, swarthy men with dark eyes and thick unruly hair, though they sported neatly trimmed mustaches. The men muttered among themselves, words that Deedra couldn't overhear. Ivan and Sheila Wallace, a handsome couple, stood back, silently smoking their cigarettes, observing, yet seemingly detached from the group.

Lance Fenton had ventured out, a slender man with thick graying hair, glasses, and a face that looked somewhat familiar. He edged up to Harriet and Dwight, who stood next to Claude and Jocelyn, seeming to take comfort in their presence.

Soon all the residents were there, Harriet asking Deedra, "What are they doing?"

"I really can't say," Deedra replied. "Looks like they're planning to put that boat into the swamp though, and those three men are in wet suits."

Silence fell upon the group during which time Deedra covertly watched for signs of fear or guilt or anxiety. There seemed to be nothing more than the excited curiosity most people feel when they viewed unusual activity.

Bradley Keetz arrived at the scene and began taking pictures. He was gestured away from the edge of the swamp by a policeman, but edged closer every time the law people looked away. The flash of his camera seemed to define the gruesome scene, recording for all time the terrible fate of unwary victims.

Despite the need to observe the men's reactions, Deedra was fascinated with the drama played out on the other side of the swamp—at this point less than half a block away—and couldn't pull her gaze away.

"Where is Neil?" Deedra asked Harriet who had sidled up beside her.

"He had to go in early and open their store. They're only closed on Sundays."

Harriet's attention was obviously not on Neil's absence.

The wet-suited men inflated the boat and put it in the water. They slowly rowed through the thick goo toward the middle of the swamp, and on arriving at what looked like a snag, reached out with some sort of clamp-like hook and dragged it toward the boat. After a few moments of tugging on the object, they lifted a skull and part of a skeleton from the sludge. Even at that distance the residents could tell that it was a skeleton, and their reaction was swift and shock-laden.

Harriet cried out in distress and Jocelyn smothered a scream, hiding her head in Claude's shoulder. Dwight began to curse. Melvyn stared in open-mouthed wonder.

The truck drivers began to run down the unstable road toward the police, but were waved back, and reluctantly returned to stand in the group that watched as the skeleton was placed in a black body bag and lifted into the van. The three wet-suited men climbed in with it and the van roared away. The boat was left alongside the swamp.

Aaron and the state policemen talked and gestured and put up fresh crime scene tapes. The inflatable boat was deflated and placed in the trunk of one of the patrol cars.

Bradley Keetz stayed around taking pictures, his camera pointed at the Percifal group a time or two.

"What do you think of that?" Harriet remarked. "Looks like that old swamp holds more secrets than any of us know!" With that she marched back to her cabin, Dwight still staring at the swamp as if what they had just witnessed couldn't possibly have happened. His face was pale, a sick look pulling down the corners of his mouth.

Strangely, Melvyn Randolph was watching Dwight, reminding Deedra of a cat stalking a mouse. What was Melvyn thinking? Did he suspect Dwight of something dreadful?

Ivan and Sheila carefully lit fresh cigarettes and then strolled back to their cabin.

They hadn't exchanged even social greetings with the others.

It was Jocelyn who brought Melvyn into the present. "Emma is waiting on the porch, Melvyn. She probably wants to know what's going on."

Melvyn glanced at his cabin, evidently saw Emma sitting there in her wheelchair, and strode up to her side.

Deedra saw them in conversation, at least Melvyn was talking. She turned her attention back to the group still standing beside the swamp. Did any of them harbor dark secrets about this place? Was she standing in the company of a vicious fiend? It suddenly seemed depressing, like a place of desolation, a grisly, ghastly, carnal place.

Deedra shuddered.

"Yes, it's cold out here," Marsha Landen remarked as she moved to Deedra's left. "Isn't this a spooky place? I've been wanting to move back into town for quite awhile now. Maybe this will persuade my husband to do that. He thinks it's neat living out here where no one from town bothers us, and heaven knows the rent is cheap enough. I like living in town though. I've always felt just a little…ah…hesitant about this place. Never liked it as a child either. It has the aura of being sort of…ah…desolate.''

"Yes, I think you're right about that. But I think the fact that the lake is dying is what gives it that sort of glum feeling. The swamp encroaching on what used to be clear water. I'm Deedra Masefield, and you are Marsha Landen?''

"Yes. Sorry about not introducing myself. We own a hardware store in Rufus. We moved out here two years ago. It was supposed to be temporary. Our house in town had burned down and this was the only place for rent at that time.''

"You haven't seen any unusual activity around the swamp then?'' Deedra watched the men as they stood around discussing the latest find in the swamp.

"No, but I'm gone most of the time. I'm not very well acquainted with the rest of them here. Of course, our close group of friends live in town.''

Well, that explained a lot about the Landens. Not given to socializing with neighbors, their interests more self-centered.

The men still huddled in a group and Deedra felt it wise not to intrude on their man-to-man discussion even though she would have liked to hear what they had to say. Gradually they drifted back to their own cabins, though Dwight and the Black brothers lingered.

Back in her abode she phoned Clete with the exclusive, and promised to phone as soon as an identification of the skeleton could be made. Then she went to the side window and watched the men of Percifal who still stood around talking. Only Melvyn Randolph was absent, and she could see that he was on the porch with Emma who seemed upset. Even as she watched, Melvyn put a hand on Emma's shoulder. Emma seemed to flinch, but Deedra wasn't sure of that. It might have been a sob for the poor woman was weeping as if she had lost someone near and dear.

Dwight and the Black brothers parted, each going to their own cabins.

Though Deedra had hoped to meet all the men there, the opportunity hadn't been just right. She mustn't even hint that she wanted to learn what made them tick. If the killer were here in Percifal, she would have to be extremely cautious. Killers often had a sixth sense, a radar-warning instinct to protect them from impending danger.

Later, Bradley Keetz appeared at her door.

"Cold out here," Bradley greeted and edged up to the fireplace. "Nothing like a wood fire to get warmed up." He sighed. "The police haven't a clue to who this skeleton might be. It's old from the look of it, but who knows what the water in that old swamp might do to a skeleton? Aaron said they'd have to wait on what the M.E. has to say."

Deedra nodded. "Do you suppose the killer is using this swamp as a place to dump his victims?"

Bradley started. "What a thought!" He paused. "You might be right though. There's been six or seven disappearances in this part of the world in the last few years."

"Were they all women?" Deedra asked.

"No. That sort of eliminates this killer doesn't it," he muttered.

"Yes, unless he's just into killing for the thrill of it. Killers get a taste for it, you know. He might just find it easier to victimize women. Men are strong and not easily enticed into situations where they could be kidnapped," Deedra ventured.

Bradley nodded. "Guess I need to go back into the files and find out who and how many people are missing from around here."

"I'll go with you. Besides, I wanted to look at articles on the victims found in the last two or three months. It's a good day, your office will be closed so the word won't leak out about what I'm doing there," Deedra remarked.

"Let's go. I'll even buy you lunch." Bradley grinned as if he was bestowing something very special on her. He had a fetching grin that sneaked up on a person. "By the way, your Clete Bailey bought some of my photos. Thanks!"

The newspaper office and plant was like many others Deedra had seen, not as up to date in equipment, of course, but well organized and very neat. Bradley took her on a tour of the plant. In the basement was an old morgue where newspapers hadn't yet been scanned and put into computer files. "It's an on-going project with me, and I'm doing it myself. Can't afford to hire the help."

For the next few hours they searched through files for missing persons who had never been found. There were several from the Rufus/Brockton area. Most of them just small items as if their disappearances were of their own choice. The most recent was of the two women who had disappeared two years earlier and hadn't been heard of since. Deedra read the account of the husband's assertion that his wife would never have gone off without saying something, that she was definitely not the "lesbian" type. It was obvious that he remained dissatisfied with the official conclusion that the women had simply disappeared by their own choice.

On an ancient machine in the basement Deedra photocopied several articles for study later.

Bradley took her out to lunch at a popular restaurant down the street from the newspaper. While there, she had a glimpse of Bradley's popularity and esteem among the citizenry. She and Bradley had scant time for discussion between the cheerful greetings.

Deedra did get something of an assessment for a possible suspect.

"Claude Hoover," Bradley commented, "is sort of an enigma. He keeps Jocelyn home though not pregnant. They have three daughters, all in their twenties now, who left home at early ages. Someone told me they live out of state. Never seem to visit home, though Harriet told me that Jocelyn receives letters from them. I've always thought it odd that they never returned for even a brief visit. There's been hints that they are afraid of Claude. Whatever that means," Bradley answered in a glum tone.

"That could explain why Jocelyn is so shy," Deedra ventured, knowing that Bradley had hinted that incest might have been involved. If true, that placed Claude Hoover right up there at the top of the list of suspects. "What does Claude do? Where does he work?"

"Manages a string of apartments and a couple of rental store buildings. Takes care of all the complaints, sees to the repairs, collects the rent each month. He deposits the rent money in an account at the bank. Has an office in one of the apartment buildings. If the repairs are simple, he does the work himself, things like plumbing are hired out.''

"Then his time isn't necessarily on a certain schedule?''

"Right. He can't always be reached at his office.'' Bradley grinned. "I'm sure Claude is one of the reasons Aaron Blaine wants you to …ah…oversee Percifal.''

Again they were interrupted by Bradley's fans and left soon afterwards for the privacy provided by the newspaper office where Brad prepared fresh coffee.

"What about Dwight Stratton? Anything in his background?'' Deedra felt a sense of comfort in the surroundings. No doubt about it, she had writer's ink in her veins.

"He's apparently just what he seems. A friendly guy, knows the grocery business with a skill born of years of dealing with the public. Employees all respect and like him, no rumors of straying.''

"You think this killer is a ladies' man?'' Deedra asked.

Bradley looked surprised. "Don't you?''

"Not necessarily. Rapists aren't necessarily popular with women. Rape is more a need for power or revenge, perhaps rage even. Profiling cases show they tend to be sort of unassuming males, often very shy. Some have histories of sexual deviance's in their childhood, things hidden from their spouses.''

Bradley looked glum. "That certainly doesn't narrow the list.''

"That's why serial killers go undetected for years before being caught. Neighbors and friends just can't believe them guilty of such things.'' They were silent a moment. "Now, what can you tell me about the others?"

"Nothing much about the Black brothers. They're gone most of the time and were on the east coast when Darlene Hernandez and Thelma Hansen were murdered. I doubt they had the opportunity to commit any of them."

"Yes, and if it had been one of them, the bodies would have been discovered far away from Percifal," Deedra remarked. "Anything on Melvyn Randolph?"

"Nothing concrete. He does travel about, but never seems to vary his route, and on the days in question appears to have been in opposite ends of the county. He's been delivering foodstuffs around here for over twenty years. Never heard a complaint against him, and his truck is inspected periodically according to county regulations on food carriers."

"Dwight appears to be quite busy. No rumors there, I suppose?"

Brad shook his head. "No, though he knew Darlene Hernandez and Thelma Hansen who clerked in the grocery in Brockton for a time a few years back. I'm sure he knew Priscilla and Sandy, too. But that proves nothing. Everyone goes to grocery stores, and the store in Brockton is a supermarket offering lower prices and more variety. Many from Rufus go there to shop."

"Of the established Percifal men, only Claude has anything suspicious in his character then, and that might not mean anything," Deedra sighed.

"Quite frankly, Deedra, I doubt the killer is among the Percifal people. I still think it's someone from another state or at least a different part of this state. Someone who travels this way on occasion or deliberately seeks out victims here."

"You may be right, Brad, but I have to take experienced law officers' hunches seriously. Law men have a lot of savvy about the criminal mind, and since Aaron requested my presence here for that express purpose, I need to follow through."

Bradley nodded, his eyes reflecting acknowledgment and alert interest. "Do you have any romantic commitment in the city?"

"Is this leading to something?" Deedra grinned.

"Well, I'm not married, I like intelligent women, interesting dinner conversation, and movies with a female companion. Are you free to indulge?"

"Yes," Deedra smiled, "I keep my life clutter free. Are you suggesting dinner and a move tonight?"

"Movie tonight, dinner tomorrow night?" Bradley smiled in his particular fetching way. There was something about the man that intrigued her, something humble, but self-assured. He wasn't the least taken with his status in life, a guy with simple tastes who just enjoyed being alive.

"Yes, I'd like that." And from that moment on, Deedra and Bradley Keetz were an "item." Deedra needed a man in her life, not a really serious relationship, but someone to make her feel like a woman. Bradley had already glimpsed the person she was behind the tough exterior. She wouldn't have to pretend with him.

After Bradley took Deedra home that afternoon, she discovered that someone had gone through her writing materials, and had tried to access her laptop, but was denied entry. The search had been careful, but Deedra had placed things in a way that would detect any intrusion. Somehow she had been expecting it, though the evidence of it caused shivers along her spine and reinforced the suspicion that the killer was, indeed, a resident of Percifal. It should have been expected anyway with the close access to the swamp.

Her cell phone rang.

Aaron's angry voice reaffirmed their suspicion that the skeleton was one of the missing women who had vanished two years earlier. Dental records on file at the state laboratory had confirmed it.

"Let me guess. It was the wife of the man who never accepted the "lesbian" theory that she had run off with the other woman?"

"Right. We've notified the husband who is on his way up here."

"Aaron, someone searched my place while I was in Rufus today. I think my real identity as a reporter has been discovered," Deedra muttered.

"Well, it was bound to happen after this morning's events. State police have taken over this woman's case for now. It was their lab that matched up the dental records and made a positive ID, and the woman was from another part of the state. Just as well, I've enough on my plate with the other four murders."

"Do the state boys know what killed the woman?"

"Not yet. And they haven't determined the cause of death nor how long she has been in the water either. It will take time for that." Aaron paused. "I hear you and Bradley Keetz are "chummy?"

"Chummy? He took me to lunch and on a hunt through ancient newspaper files, if that's getting chummy."

"Well," Aaron drawled, "that was the rumor I heard. And just when I was about to ask you out to dinner, too."

"Oh! Dinner when?"

Aaron laughed. "Sometime. Just checking for Clete

who seems concerned that you might need protection up here.''

"Hm. What gave Clete the idea I'd need protection after he sent me to reside in a rat-infested store building?"

Again Aaron laughed, an infectious laugh that caused her to grin until he answered, "Said you were afraid of rats and might want to move into Rufus."

Anger replaced Deedra's repartee and she retorted, "He did, did he? Just tell him that rats aren't what's threatening up here, that a vicious rapist/killer is, and that he threatens women not editors in cozy offices back in the city!" She slammed the receiver into place, immediately repenting her outburst. Having her digs searched had upset her more than she had realized.

FOUR

BRADLEY KEETZ ARRIVED promptly at 6:30. When she got into his car she found sacks of freshly popped popcorn.

He grinned. "They charge too much, and put too much butter on it. Besides, it's cheaper this way so I can handle the cost of sodas."

Deedra laughed. "Am I having a cheap date or what?"

"I'm not cheap, just economical. I always pop my own popcorn, get a sort of heart burn if I don't."

Deedra was attracted to his "I'm gonna do it my way," style. It was refreshing after dating some men who tried to impress her by extravagance. Bradley was a small town guy and wanted her to know it. No pretenses.

"Hear anything new on the murders?"

Bradley shook his head. "Only inquiries from all over neighboring states. Did you find anything in those old files?"

"Not yet, haven't finished. I had to fax a story to the newspaper. Brad, do you know where Clete Bailey's property is located?"

"Clete Bailey? That must be the old Bailey place just this side of Rufus. Grand old house with an old barn and a couple of sheds. After Clete went out on his own, his parents moved into Rufus. I don't think anyone has lived on that property since. I heard Aaron say that Clete intended to live there when he retires. It's a scenic place. Has it's own pond and creek.''

"Hm. Clete has never mentioned it to my knowledge. I wouldn't know about it if Aaron hadn't told me. I wonder why Clete is so reticent?''

Bradley laughed. "It's no secret around here. Clete doesn't want a lot of visitors. He plans to stock the pond with fish and have his own private hunting and fishing domain. Told Aaron that city folks don't know how to treat the land, that he didn't want hunters making camp-fires and cutting down his trees for firewood. When Clete visits he stays out there. Hasn't been up here for a couple of years though. The man who rents his Rufus house checks on things for him.''

"Guess I'll take a look-see before I go back. Clete seems to have a whole history none of us know any-thing about,'' Deedra murmured.

"Is it important that his employees know?'' Brad's tone was rather stern.

"It is to me. I like to know who I'm working for... and with.''

"Oh!'' Bradley lapsed into a thoughtful silence caus-ing Deedra to wonder where those thoughts were lead-ing him.

The theater was the only one in Rufus, and always had a crowd. On this night it was packed with a teenage crowd, the feature a thriller scary enough to cause Deedra a few shivers. When the killer pounced on a woman who thought she was alone in her house, Deedra jumped.

From that moment on through the rest of the movie,

Brad had his arm around her shoulders in a protective, comforting gesture.

After the movie, Brad drove to the river located a few miles east of Rufus. The campground was deserted, but the moonlight shimmering off the water spectacular.

"This is one of the more scenic places around here. It's a popular fishing area, and usually filled with tents during summer. The RV Park is back up the road a bit. Didn't have such things when this park was created, and no room for them now."

Deedra drank in the sight of moonlight, of hearing the rush of water over boulders, of listening to the slight breeze rustling through the evergreens. An owl hooted from a tree somewhere down river.

Brad took her in his arms, their first kiss more thrilling than she had imagined. Here beside the river in the moonlight they spent several romantic moments though nothing that involved real sex. Their relationship was way too new for any heavy involvement. They didn't know each other that well, and both were old enough to be cautious.

On the drive back Brad pointed out the graveled road that led to Clete's property.

"There are two places down that road. Clete's is on the south side, and a man named Harvey Harrison's on the other. The Harrison place is empty now, too. The old man is in a nursing home in Brockton. I understand it's going to be put up for sale in the spring."

Deedra had a glimpse of heavy pines lining a narrow roadway, and mentally marked the place so she could go there before returning to the city. She was a bit perturbed with Clete. He knew so much about her life, and she knew practically nothing about his. Nor had she bothered to ask, she recalled ruefully.

Bradley's car lights silhouetted the old store building as they drove up. A stripped cat skittered away when they pulled up in front.

"I hope that cat likes to catch rats!" Deedra muttered.

"What?"

"Never mind," she replied as she got out. "I'll see you tomorrow?"

"Yes. I'll pick you up about 6:30. We'll go someplace special for dinner."

"Right. Thanks again."

Brad waited until she was inside the building before turning the car around and heading out toward the highway.

Deedra held her breath as she stepped within the dark house. She waited a moment, her intuitive sense seeking out another presence, but received no vibes of danger.

She took a long, relaxing bath, the water warming her. The cold weather had caused a chill to settle. The thought of the swamp as a disposal site had her nerves and imagination on edge. Deep within her "knowing sense" she knew the killer lived nearby, that the police theory about that was correct, and that now the killer would be on alert, even suspecting her motive for renting the old store building. Perhaps even watching her every move. He could without leaving his home tell when she left, and when she went to bed just by looking out his front window. But the killer would be especially cautious now with the police in the area. He would simply watch and wait, try to learn who the police suspected.

The scary part was how long had he been killing women? It could have been going on for over a decade, perhaps two. The profile indicated that the killer was between 40 and 50 years old, that these kinds of sex crimes usually started when the killer was in his early 20's. And that once they had killed without detection or capture, they got a taste for it, seemingly unable to stop.

These thoughts were interrupted by a noise outside the store building. Cautious footsteps on the graveled road.

She grabbed her terry cloth robe and shoved her wet feet into fuzzy slippers. Without turning on a light she scurried to the front window. Although no one was in sight she was certain someone lurked in the darkness, someone who needed to know her whereabouts, perhaps even stood in the shadows of the old store listening, trying to over-hear any phone conversation.

A fog was beginning to rise from the lake and swamp, a gauzy cloak enclosing Percifal in a wet shrouding mist.

Deedra shuddered, made certain the door was bolted and hurried back to the tub of hot water. At the door of the bathroom a large rat stared at her with a menacing look in its bright beady eyes before scurrying into some hidden shelter near the back porch.

Deedra's scream tore at the night quiet. Her breathing shallow gasps, ineffective at stopping the heavy thumping of her heart. After a moment and another shudder, she sheepishly returned to the comforting warmth of the bath water.

"I've got to get over this fear! I'm bigger and stronger than any old rat!" she muttered.

Outside the fog had closed in, the stalker smiled to himself having heard her scream and learning that the young reporter was afraid of rats. A thing he would put to use later.

It was nearly half an hour before she relaxed enough to crawl into the sleeping bag again.

The old store grew cold during the night, but Deedra didn't get up to replenish the fires. Memory of that old rat kept her huddled inside the sleeping bag. At 7:00, fearing another early morning visit from Harriet, she donned the heavy bathrobe and fuzzy slippers, rebuilt the fires, and sat in front of the fireplace with a mug of freshly made coffee.

It was Saturday so everyone but the Landens was at home. Saturday was the busiest day of the week at their hardware store. There was little movement around the cabins, but smoke swirled from every chimney.

Clete called and after bringing him up to date and committing notes to the laptop, she went for a morning walk. She wanted the residents to know that walks were part of her daily routine. On this morning she was joined by Jocelyn who was taking a freshly baked pie to Emma and Melvyn Randolph.

"I bake one for them a couple of times a month. Poor Emma was such a good cook and Melvyn has no talent for it. Harriet and I are practically the only ones that ever visit Emma. She had lots of friends before the accident, but they drifted away after several months. She still gets cards from them, but it's very difficult to talk to someone who can't."

"You say she was a bank clerk?"

"Yes. Knows practically everyone in Rufus. Harriet and I often thought Melvyn was jealous of her popularity. He can be quite dour at times, doesn't have her gracious ways. Of course, he is a man and they sometimes have different sets of social standards," Jocelyn remarked.

Deedra threw her a sharp glance, noted the stern line

on her lips, the slight clench of her jaw. Jocelyn, it appeared, had negative notions about the male gender. Was her marriage to Claude as placid as she let it appear?

Melvyn opened the door for them with a special smile for Jocelyn when she handed him the pie. "You and these pies are always welcome, Jocelyn! Emma and I are most grateful." He ushered them into a living room where a cheerful fire burned in a fireplace hewn of native rock with a mantel of polished oak.

Emma was seated near it, her face a smiling thanks to Jocelyn, but a slight hint of distrust...or was it fear shadowed her eyes as she nodded a greeting to Deedra, and gestured them to a sofa.

Melvyn took the pie to the kitchen and called out, "Coffee, anyone?"

"No, thanks," Jocelyn and Deedra replied in unison.

Jocelyn kept up a non-stop conversation with Emma who listened carefully, occasionally allowing her gaze to fasten on Deedra.

Deedra allowed her own gaze to wander about the room as guests do, though covertly studying Melvyn. A man trapped in a marriage where he was his wife's nurse, where conversation was sparse and blunt. A thing that caused many a man despair and deep frustrated anger. Melvyn did not appear angry, however. A friendly type, like the next door neighbor who aroused only positive feelings, now relaxed and interested in Jocelyn's chatter about people they knew in town, about the murders, the weather, and Claude's trip to the dentist.

Deedra slowly became aware that Melvyn was sizing her up, a male's interest in the new female on the block? It was an uncomfortable sensation, and one Deedra hadn't experienced since spending lots of time on the beach and at swimming pools where bathing suit-clad females were the objects of ogling.

Fortunately, Jocelyn had decided they had visited long enough and stood up, still talking as she headed toward the door where Deedra gratefully joined her.

Jocelyn continued talking as they went down the stairs and walked toward the south end of the swamp. "My that old swamp gives me shivers and quivers!" Jocelyn muttered. "Just to think that skeleton they pulled out of there yesterday has been in there for two years now. I wonder if the other woman is in there, too?"

"Goodness, where did you hear that news?" Deedra pretended surprise.

"On the TV news this morning. There's bound to be media people here soon though Bradley Keetz has supplied them with the main photos. I understand the state police are in charge." Jocelyn shook her head as she surveyed the swamp. "I guess my nervousness living here had basis in fact, after all."

"You've been anxious about living here for a long time or just the last couple of years?" Deedra asked.

"Actually, for several years though the last couple of years I've been really upset. I guess it increased when I painted that skull. I always thought that snag looked like a skull, to have it turn out to really be a skull was shocking. I knew you took notice of that in my painting. Thank you for not bringing it to Claude's attention. He would just scold me for letting my imagination frighten me. Claude is very realistic, doesn't understand artistic concepts."

"Yes, most men have to see, feel, or touch something to acknowledge it," Deedra agreed.

Jocelyn stopped walking and turned to Deedra. "I know you are a reporter, Deedra. I remember seeing you on TV two years ago when you were in this area on the story about those missing women. I study faces, you know, part of a painter's prerequisite. That's why I remembered you. Harriet hasn't tumbled to that yet, but she will. She's very interested in why you're here. Why are you?"

Deedra couldn't help grinning at this remarkable woman with her unexpected insight.

"Your Aaron Blaine contacted my editor, Clete Bailey, when Priscilla's body was discovered. I was sent up here pronto. I would appreciate it if you kept that confidential. Since Aaron and Clete are old friends, the media or someone up here might make that connection, but we'd rather not have that fact publicized."

Jocelyn nodded. "I won't tell, and it gives me great satisfaction to know something Harriet doesn't. She's my best friend, but it's helpful to know that she doesn't know everything about everything."

Deedra's cell phone rang. It was Aaron.

"Just called to let you know that Sandy Nevin's car had an empty gas tank. She didn't have any money on her so her father thinks she thought she had enough gas to get home. The gas gauge didn't work. Might have been walking along the road."

"Oh, oh! Listen, can I call you back? I'm walking alongside the swamp with a neighbor, and it's cold out here."

Deedra wanted to talk to Aaron, but she didn't want Jocelyn to know they conversed often. The less the residents knew about her the better. Especially since they were almost convinced that the killer resided among them.

Jocelyn evidently thought the call was from her boss. "I'm acquainted with Clete Bailey, you know. Knew his parents quite well. It's something of a pity when our local young people move away. Leaves a vacancy that the newly arrived don't quite fill."

They were slowly walking back toward the store and Jocelyn's house, passing the place where the swamp ended and the sluggish water of the lake began.

Jocelyn stopped in her tracks. "Oh, my! I really feel that other woman is there, in that old swamp!" Her face had turned the color of native stone, ashen, her features pinched with fear.

Deedra nodded. "Probably, but you mustn't fret. It can't hurt you. I don't know whether they plan to drag the swamp or not. I understand the local geologist thinks it might cause water to seep under the highway like it has that old road."

"My goodness, that old earthquake really upset things, didn't it?" Jocelyn stared around as if the area had changed without her noticing. And noticing was Jocelyn's stock in trade. As an artist she took in everything from color and landscape to object and location. Had she unconsciously noted a slight change in the swamp, a disturbance that had registered, now just recalled?

On returning to the store Deedra phoned Aaron. "Sorry, I was walking with Jocelyn. She's very observant, wouldn't surprise me if she's noticed changes about the swamp for several years now, and is the basis for her fear."

"She's afraid of the swamp?" Aaron sounded surprised.

"Yes. She's got a painting showing a skull covered with algae. Claude probably told her she was imagining things. Jocelyn told me she never looks at the swamp when it's foggy. Of course, if it's a heavy fog she can't see it anyway.''

"Yeah," Aaron grunted. "The state police aren't decided what to do about the swamp. There's only a chance the other missing woman is in there, and there's danger in really disturbing things. They've received another analysis of the area and it shows a great degree of instability, possibly danger to the highway and shifting of the earth under the cabins. At this point, I think they've agreed to postpone any action.''

"I suppose that is the most sensible plan," Deedra agreed. "My bet is that the other woman is in the swamp. In two years nothing has been heard from her, and the other woman's dead. They were together when they disappeared, and were probably together when something happened.''

"Yes, I'm sure we all have that theory, but caution has to be taken otherwise the headlines would read, 'despite a geologist report,' sort of thing. None of us in law enforcement can take chances with adverse publicity. Hampers a lot of our ability to do our job. And there's always the budget consideration.''

"Have they learned how the woman met her death?''

"No, just her identity. No link to the other murders here. And the M.O. is quite different. Two women together and no evidence they were on or near the highway. Their car has never been found which is something of a mystery in itself. Could have been shipped off to some foreign port, I suppose.''

"What do you really think?" Deedra challenged.

"I think there might be a connection, perhaps in a different mode, but right now I'm glad the troopers are handling it." He paused. "Anything new about our people there?'' Deedra told him what she had gleaned. ''I haven't yet gone through all the old newspaper files on missing persons' during the past ten years.''

''Still plan on having dinner with Bradley tonight?'' There was an odd resonance in Aaron's tone.

''Yes.''

''Perhaps I'll see you tomorrow.'' Aaron cut the connection.

Deedra spent the afternoon going over the articles about missing women during the past ten years. Two from Rufus, two from Brockton, three women who vanished somewhere north of the junction at the Interstate and the highway to Rufus. All three of those women were traveling alone, had stopped for gas at a station just off the highway and two had purchased snacks at the small grocery there. A high school girl had vanished, supposedly with her boy friend who had also turned up missing, a total of nine.

Deedra fed the information into the laptop. The two Rufus women were not friends, but may have known each other. One, a woman who worked for an advertising company regularly traveled about the state to check on accounts. Her permanent home was in Rufus, though she was on the road approximately three months of the year. She had never been heard from after leaving her home on a planned trip to Sacramento. Her car had been found several months later in a wooded area south of Rufus. There had been no sign of foul play, her clothing and handbag gone. She and her husband had agreed to a divorce, but had postponed action on it until she returned from the business trip. A man she had been seeing for several months and her husband were carefully checked out, and no indication that they had anything to do with her disappearance. She was still on the missing person's list, though since she hadn't been heard of for over seven years, now legally dead. Her husband had collected her insurance in the amount of $5,000, not enough, the insurance company concluded, for her husband to have done away with her.

The policy had been in force for many years, and the husband had not been having an affair, and according to Bradley Keetz, had not remarried.

The second woman had disappeared after visiting her parents living in Half Town. She had gone there on a Friday in mid-December, spent a few hours helping her mother decorate the tree and bake Christmas cookies. In the afternoon the weather turned cold and it began to rain. The woman left her parents with the promise to return and take them to her house for Christmas. The woman, aged 35, was anxious to get home before dark and assured her parents that she would get home safely, not to worry. Her car was found in a ditch alongside the highway a day later. Her handbag was missing. She was never heard from again.

"That fits the M.O." Deedra muttered, and typed the woman's name into the laptop in capital letters. MARIAN MOSNER, wondering if she had been this killer's first victim.

The two Brockton women had been in their early 30's, both brunettes, both living alone in apartment houses in Brockton. Neighbors had not seen any men go into their apartments, didn't think they had any steady male friends. Both women had daytime jobs, one a grocery clerk, one a waitress. Both worked weekend shifts, the clerk off Mondays and Tuesdays, the waitress off Thursdays and Fridays. They were not friends though acquainted, the waitress buying groceries where the clerk worked. There their similarities ended.

The grocery clerk loved music and often attended local musicals, and played in a local orchestra. She had just disappeared one Monday, her usual day off, and was never heard from again. Her apartment was left intact containing all her possessions including her handbag, though a heavy jacket she usually wore was gone. She never picked up her last paycheck. That was over five years ago. Her mother still lived in Brockton, an older brother in Sacramento. Her missing person's file still open.

The waitress had disappeared almost a year later on a Thursday afternoon. She had told a friend she was going to an early movie, and indeed, her car was found parked in the cinema's huge parking lot two days later. When questioned, ticket sellers said the car had been there since early Thursday evening. Investigation led the Brockton police to believe the woman had a male friend and had learned from another waitress, that he was married though she did not know who he was, nor if he lived in Brockton. Evidently the man had never visited her apartment, and the woman's neighbors had never seen a man there. The woman's sister, her only living relative, lived in Half Town, where she, too, earned her living as a waitress. When interviewed, the sister confirmed the fact that the woman had a secret male friend, that all she knew about him was that he was married. Her sister had been very secretive about it.

This woman had also left her apartment intact, her clothing and possessions still there, and had not picked up her last paycheck. The Brockton police still carried an open case file on her believing she had met with foul play.

The two youngsters from Brockton, the girl 16, the

boy 17, were last seen walking south on the highway going toward Rufus. It was assumed after weeks of investigation that the couple had run away though both sets of parents refused to believe that explanation. The girl's mother was quoted as saying, "She wouldn't go away without taking at least some of her clothes. She was particular about her looks, always needed clean and neatly pressed clothing. Why, even her favorite CD's are still here!"

The boy's parents stated that he would not leave without money, and he hadn't closed his savings account nor taken over $200 found in his room. That alone, mused Deedra, indicated that something ominous had prevented the teen's return. If this was another of the serial killer's deeds, the M.O. differed. As far as had been determined, there had been no male victims, but what if the killer couldn't get the girl without eliminating the boy?

Deedra sighed. There was no evidence that this killer had been active that long ago. Still, her gut feeling quivered with suspicion. Serial killers were obsessed with the act of killing. In this case it didn't seem to be the thrill of seeing blood spurt from his victim's bodies because they had all been strangled, only the skeleton from the swamp undetermined as to cause of death.

On the laptop she created a chart starting back ten years and bringing it up to the present. Four bodies recovered along the highway, one skeleton pulled from the swamp, nine missing persons counting the skeleton's missing companion. And chances were heavy in favor of her remains resting in the swamp. Fourteen in all including the teenage boy. Perhaps others in places as yet undiscovered.

Bradley Keetz arrived at 6:30. It was already dark, a

chilling drizzle caused the pine trees to drip and mud puddles to expand in both depth and width. There was an eerie mist shrouding the lake and swamp. Old snags rising from the swamp water were like giant tentacles held high from slimy creatures skulking below the surface.

Deedra shuddered.

"Yeah. Spooky damn thing!" Bradley remarked.

"Especially if the skeleton of that other missing woman is in there!" Deedra muttered, trying to ward off another shudder. Mustn't let Bradley know how deeply it affected her.

"If you're…ah…uncomfortable staying out here, I have a guest bedroom. No strings attached."

"Thanks, Brad, but no thanks. I'm not afraid and am committed to helping Aaron in this."

Bradley nodded. "I'm taking you to a special restaurant just north of Brockton. It's not spectacular though the food is, and the mood relaxing. No loud music."

"Thank, God! Have you noticed how twangy and annoying the music is in movies and lately some TV programs? It's as if they don't want the audience to hear the dialogue, want to cover up the words so that the audience doesn't realize what poor actors they are."

The restaurant was charming, set back off the highway, surrounded by tall pines, a replica of a Swiss chalet. The parking lot was nearly full. Bradley had made reservations and they were immediately escorted to a secluded table where pine-scented candles provided a soft glow though still light enough to read the menu. It was definitely a romantic setting and Deedra began to wonder just what Bradley had in mind.

Their conversation was about their lives, the places they had vacationed, the movies and books they liked, and TV news. After the meal they danced in a dimly lit ballroom, went for a stroll in a landscaped area behind the restaurant, and then Bradley drove her back to Percifal.

If Bradley had planned a romantic encounter, he had changed his mind, perhaps realizing that Deedra wasn't ready to let her guard down. She hoped it wasn't because he found her unattractive. Did the fact that she was an investigative reporter for a big city newspaper give him a sense of professional inferiority? Big city journalists were apt to put down small town weeklies.

Fortunately, Deedra had left a light burning in the old store or she might have clung to Bradley instead of going inside. The cat had scuttled under the porch at their approach to the steps, and again Deedra prayed the cat caught rats.

FIVE

BRADLEY ACCOMPANIED her inside and helped get the fires going again.

"It's amazing how cold this old place gets in just a few hours," Deedra muttered, once again appreciating her central heating system at home.

"Yeah. Just think what a tough time the pioneers had, no electricity, no running water. Afraid I'm not made of such sturdy stuff. I like comfortable chairs and hot showers." He roamed about the store going through to the back porch, checked the door lock, looked into the bathroom and bedroom. "All clear."

"What made you check?" Deedra asked.

"Just an urge. Don't know who has been in and out of this old building since it was vacated. I don't think Dwight and Harriet store things here anymore though."

Deedra grinned. "If they did, I haven't found anything."

"I didn't mean upstairs here. There's a storage basement where they kept emergency supplies just in case of foul weather."

"I haven't seen a basement entrance," Deedra challenged.

"I'll show you. It's covered up with all those empty crates and boxes." Bradley led her to the back porch where he moved a few plastic crates and revealed a padlocked door in the floor. "Doesn't look like anyone's been down there for several years."

Deedra was relieved to see the padlock firmly in place. At least it kept the rats constrained to the cellar.

They went back to Deedra's makeshift living room. Deedra had made fresh coffee on arriving home and the aroma was inviting. They settled on the sofa, her chair filled with the copies of newspaper articles and her own notes.

"You've been working, I see," Brad gestured to the clippings and notes in the chair, at the laptop resting on a plastic crate, at the old barrel placed in front of the computer that Deedra used as a chair.

"Yes, and like you, I like comfortable chairs," she smiled.

"You think there's a pattern in those disappearances?" Bradley's hazel-colored eyes looked dark in the uncertain light shed by the ceiling bulbs. There were no light fixtures just bare bulbs refracting the light from a gray ceiling.

"Yes, I do, but unless their remains are found locally, there's no proof. The only case that puzzles me is that of the missing teenagers. All the victims have been women."

"You mean all the victims we know about. There might have been some men along the way," Bradley reminded.

"Yes, there could have been, which would, of course, louse up the M.O. Throw the authorities off the scent."

"You don't suspect anyone here?" Brad gestured toward the cabins.

"Not at this time. Their lives all seem to mesh, nothing suspicious in their movements, though I haven't really talked to the men. Whoever this killer is, he's very clever, probably suspects why I'm here. Jocelyn knows who I am, remembered seeing me on TV when I was up here two years ago. They're all connected to the Internet so could learn from it.''

Bradley nodded. "Yeah. Modern technology, no privacy. Makes one wonder if it will balance out."

"Are you getting philosophical, Brad?" Deedra teased.

He grinned, a charming thing that highlighted the humor in his hazel-colored eyes. "You know what I mean, and don't tell me you haven't wondered about the consequences to peoples' lives!''

"No one in their right mind hasn't been a little nervous about the prospect of having someone snoop, really snoop, into their private lives, yet no one has pinpointed the ultimate danger. It's all too fascinating. Eventually huge law suits will curb much of it, like it has on wire tapping.''

"Law suits?" Bradley challenged.

"Yes. Eventually a smart, courageous lawyer will take a case and win, and then the chain reaction will follow.''

"Any attorney in mind?" Bradley's eyes betrayed serious interest.

"No. Haven't heard of any gutsy enough, though with millions, perhaps billions of dollars at stake, there's bound to be someone. This would earn twice what the tobacco suits have settled for because it involves authorities that let it happen or instigate it. The ramifications are tremendous. Just think about it. What judge authorized such a thing, who put it into action? Who knew about it and did nothing to stop it?''

"I see why you're a very skilled investigative reporter," Bradley remarked seriously. "Have you ever run across a case that could make such a splash?"

Deedra nodded. "Suspected case. The newspaper backed away. Too many high-ups involved."

"So big city journals have a strict precautionary rule?"

Deedra nodded. "Of course. You don't go after big game without considering loss of revenue. What's the squelching of one reporter compared to the big picture?"

"I see. Justice deferred or ignored, the public apathetic."

"Right. Now let's get back to these murder cases. Have you any background info on Percifal people that I don't know about?" Deedra refilled the coffee cups.

"Can't think of anything. Besides, this is a date, and I'd like to practice kissing you." Bradley drew her into his arms, a rather uncomfortable position until she moved closer and settled against his shoulder. His kisses were soon flames that ignited an emotion she usually guarded quite fervently.

What the heck, she mused, melting into his embrace, his kisses sending an unusual warmth through her.

Her cell phone rang.

"Damn!" Bradley muttered as he released her.

It was Clete. "Deedra, I need you to do me a favor while you're up there. I hired a guy to wrap the outside faucets, one in front of the house and one near the cellar door in the back on my vacation property. Just check to make sure that's been done, will you? Aaron can tell you where the property is, and kind of look around, make sure no vandalism is happening."

"Okay. What brought this on?"

Clete sighed. "Well, the person who rents my house

in Rufus usually does that for me, but he and his wife are spending a few months in Florida this year. Got a postcard from him reminding me he wouldn't be able to do that this winter. Hate to ask Aaron since he's busy with those murder cases." Clete paused long enough to catch his breath. "What are you doing?"

"Well, Clete, as usual you've interrupted a romantic interlude. Do you have radar or sonar or some special antennae that focuses in on these special moments of my life?"

"Oh, sorry!" Clete spluttered. "Who's the lucky fellow, Aaron?"

"No. Bradley Keetz has just taken me out to a scrumptious dinner and we were having a cozy fireside chat."

"Oh. Don't let it interfere with your reason for being up there!" Clete abruptly disconnected.

Their romantic moments lost, Bradley prepared to leave. "Guess we were moving along too rapidly anyway," he muttered ruefully, and gave Deedra a long goodnight kiss.

"Let's try again sometime."

Deedra watched as Bradley strode to his car, gunned the engine in evident frustration, then drove off in the hovering fog. While turning the car, the headlights caught the silhouette of a man alongside the old gas station.

Deedra moved behind the tattered drapes and though she watched for several minutes, saw nothing else to indicate that someone still lurked in the night shadows.

It was still early, not quite 10:00, so she decided to watch TV, and abandoned her thoughts to the movie, relaxed and was half asleep when she became aware that someone was leering through the window. Only a small movement had alerted her, she didn't react, instead kept her gaze on the television. A tingle of fear touched the base of her skull, icy tentacles skimmed down her back. She remained very still, staring at the TV, and was finally rewarded when the man went away.

She scurried to the back porch and was just in time to see Claude Hoover enter his front door and disappear within the lighted interior.

About to return to her "living room" when she noticed a movement alongside the old gas station. A man in a heavy hooded jacket lingered there a moment, then moved up the hill toward the path behind the cabins and melded into the shadows cast by the pines.

Deedra rebuilt the fires and though the television was still on, her thoughts were on the night prowlers. They didn't fit the killer's profile who kidnapped victims in daylight and left their bodies along the highway...and in the swamp. It was frightening to know that men stalked the night, moved about near that scummy old swamp with its weird-looking snags and heavy mists. What grisly secrets did it hide beneath that greenish sludge?

It wasn't easy to fall asleep, the vision of the skeleton being pulled from the swamp, the skittering noises caused by what she hoped were mice and not rats, eliciting a rapid pulse and a nervous alertness.

The old store cooled as the night grew colder. A wind from the north suddenly began banging loose hinges and shutters and causing an eerie whine down the broken gutter pipes. Before daylight the wind ceased, but had carried in snow clouds, the ground now covered with an inch of the white stuff. Without the wind sounds it was very quiet, the stillness that follows a snowstorm.

After Deedra roused, got the fires going, and with a

steaming mug of coffee in hand, peeked out the window saw fresh footprints leading from her place to the old gas station. Evidence that someone had again prowled about her abode. Why? Curiosity or peeping tom?

Since it was Sunday, everyone seemed to be at home. Winter had set in, Thanksgiving over, and now they awaited Christmas and a new year. Funny, she mused, how rapidly time in this new millennium was passing. It seemed like just yesterday instead of years ago that people were preparing for Y2K, the main topic of conversation and concern at the turn of the century.

Smoke rose from every chimney, reminding her to gather more firewood. The aroma of cooking bacon and eggs wafted through the cold morning air as she gathered an armload of wood from the shed. Suddenly she was very hungry.

During breakfast, which consisted of bacon and eggs, she decided to investigate the old gas station. Since she'd seen several mysterious movements around it and fresh footprints in the snow that led from her front porch to the abandoned station—the need to snoop was urgent. By the time she had washed the breakfast dishes rain had descended and obliterated the prints. Nevertheless, she was determined to look around it.

As she walked down the front steps, Harriet and Jocelyn drove up in Harriet's car.

"We're going to church in Rufus. Our men don't seem to find it their duty!" Harriet flicked her fingers at Deedra in a gesture of good-bye and drove away.

Deedra watched until Harriet's car turned south on the highway, then strode up to the gas station. Despite its long abandonment there were lingering smells of gasoline and something else, something old and musty. The door to the station was unlocked and surprisingly opened quietly and smoothly, evidence that it was kept oiled, the hinges in good repair. Evidently someone visited regularly though there were no cigarette butts, no candy wrappers, the floor fairly clean. Shelves were either empty or contained neatly stacked cartons. The storeroom was stacked with large cardboard cartons, the kind car parts and heavy objects were shipped in, otherwise clean and containing nothing of a personal possession. The washroom was clean, though had no running water. The back door was unlocked, and it, too, opened and shut quietly on well-oiled hinges.

Deedra wandered back to the front where one of the wide windows overlooked the lake and swamp. The station was located a few leagues higher on the knoll than the old store, and had its own advantages. From there anyone wanting a good look at the tiny lake and swamp could get a clear view, could note any activity.

Even as Deedra stood there two young boys emerged from the woods on the far side of the graveled road and began meandering along the lake, throwing rocks into the water, as youngsters are wont to do, continuing to walk until they reached the highway where one boy stopped, obviously reluctant to continue. The other boy gestured toward the crime scene tape at the far end of the swamp, the other boy shook his head. They seemed to argue for a few moments, then the boy who had gestured toward the crime scene tape began walking toward it. For a few moments the other boy hesitated, then with lagging footsteps, began to follow. When he caught up, they halted for a few minutes, throwing stones into the swamp. The more venturesome boy picked up a long broken limb and gave it a toss into the swamp. It landed with a muted splash, then suddenly the sludge seemed to move. Something popped up out of the slime, then quickly vanished.

The boys took off running never stopping or looking back until they reached the woods, where they stopped a moment, glanced back at the swamp, then quickly disappeared into the woods. Something had obviously sent the fear into them.

If the situation had been different, Deedra would have laughed. Now, she was anxious to find out what that something was, and began striding down the graveled road toward the highway. When she reached the place where the boy had thrown the long tree branch into the swamp, she halted. The branch, now covered with thick algae, had settled into place as if it had always been there. There was nothing else to see, the swamp still and unmoving. She walked to the place where Priscilla Dawson's body had been found, covertly watching for movement around the cabins. Indeed, she saw Claude Hoover go to the back of the gas station and assumed that he went inside. Probably checking to see if she had disturbed anything, or perhaps to watch her activities from the wide window that afforded such an unrestricted view.

She stopped at the crime scene noting how unmoving the swamp water was, the algae like a lid covering the roilings beneath. What stirred in that sludge? What ghastly things lurked beneath that thick slime?

Aaron's patrol car slid to a stop beside her causing her to start. She had been so immersed in grisly speculation that she hadn't heard the car's approach.

"You shouldn't be out here along the highway, Deedra! Don't tell me it's broad daylight as an excuse! Those women disappeared during the day!"

She smiled. "I know, Aaron, but never on a weekend.

This is Sunday. Which means the killer is a family man who is expected to be home weekends.''

Aaron nodded, a grim look settling on his not quite handsome features.

Deedra felt a sudden attraction to this stern man with his intense blue eyes that seemed to probe a person's thoughts. He represented a profession Deedra had deep respect for, often an overlooked value to a community's stability. Their work often behind the scenes, seldom praised, many times criticized. And there had been a few who had taken advantage of the uniform and badge to disgrace it, leaving the brethren to cope with the bad press.

"Well, what are you doing out here?" Aaron's eyes were narrowed as if he disapproved.

Deedra explained what she had observed from the window of the old gas station.

"The boys ran as if another skeleton had risen from that goo and disappeared into the woods. Right now, Claude Hoover is in the gas station watching.'' She told Aaron about the footprints in the snow.

"Suits Claude's character. He keeps a sharp looked out on strangers. Always has in all the years I've known him. Don't know if it's anything other than curiosity though.''

"He and Jocelyn get along all right?''

Aaron nodded. ''As far as I know, and Harriet would have mentioned anything out of the way, I'm sure. She and Jocelyn went to church?''

"Yes. Harriet expressed disapproval of their husbands 'lack of duty' as they drove off.''

Aaron grinned. ''Harriet can always be counted on to do her duty. Take care.'' Aaron drove off toward Brockton.

Deedra continued circling the swamp ending up at the abandoned cabin. There was something about that old cabin that intrigued and repelled her. The fact that it might have rats kept her from trying to enter it.

Though almost everyone was home no one ventured out for a morning greeting, and Deedra arrived back at the store in time to refuel the fires.

She couldn't get the scene of the young boys running away, obviously frightened, out of her thoughts. Wondering who they were and where they lived. The lake and swamp were bound to be magnets for young boys.

After a light lunch, Deedra walked up the knoll past the gas station to the crest and then turned north going parallel to the highway, reckoning that the youngsters lived somewhere to the north of Percifal and hoped to locate them.

She glanced over her shoulder in time to see Claude Hoover watching her from his back porch.

''That man is going to give me a permanent case of paranoia!'' Deedra muttered, and waved at him in what she hoped was a defiant manner.

The trail was not well-traveled going through thickets whose tendrils laced across the path trying it seemed, to obliterate it. Nature trying to reclaim itself, she mused. Here and there in the more shady places were patches of snow, the underbrush glistening with wetness. She reached a place where the trail began to climb, and after a few minutes arrived at what appeared to be a viewpoint. A forestry sign indicated that this was Look-out Hill.

There the trail branched off into three different paths, one leading into the valley on the east side, one going down toward the highway where she could see several houses tucked among the trees, and a faint path continuing north. She spent several minutes there, taking pictures and resting. She really needed to take up hiking again, startled by the fact that she was somewhat winded by the climb.

On impulse she descended on the path leading toward the houses and highway. If it hadn't been for the pine needles that covered the trail it would have been muddy, and Deedra wasn't into mud. She hated having to clean her shoes of it, avoided muddy places wherever possible. She was so intent on avoidance that when she almost ran into the man standing in the middle of the path, she jumped sideways with a high-pitched squeal.

"Scared you, didn't I?" the hulking man sneered. His dark eyes glittered with a malicious excitement.

When Deedra didn't answer, he commanded, "What are you doing way out here alone?"

Deedra was too stunned to reply. She hadn't seen the man from the viewpoint nor any sign of movement in this direction.

"Must have scared you bad, since you can't speak now. Seems kind of stupid though for a young woman to wander around these parts with that serial killer loose. What are you looking for over here?"

"I was just out hiking," Deedra replied, astonished to hear that her voice was like the squeak of a drawer in her bathroom. And home was just where she wanted to be at that moment, not staring into the dark eyes of a threatening stranger, a man who's right hand rested on the hunting knife strapped to his belt.

SIX

Suddenly the sounds of someone approaching sent hope through Deedra who had found herself breathing in shallow gasps, pulse racing.

"Oh, there you are, Deedra! Thought I'd never catch up with you!" Bradley Keetz nodded at the man. "Howdy, Travis."

"I'm very glad to see you, Bradley. How did you know where I went?" Deedra tried to still the tremors that shook her.

"Long story, tell you later. Right now I want you to say good-bye to Travis Tucker. He lives down there, but this land here belongs to him and he really resents trespassers."

"Oh, sorry, Mr. Tucker!" Deedra grabbed Bradley's hand and they hurried back up the trail, Deedra feeling the intensity of Travis Tucker's stare all the way to the viewpoint.

"Whew! What would have happened if you hadn't arrived?" She asked.

"Travis would have insisted that you pay a visit to his cabin, listen to stories of what happened to people who trespassed on his property, given you a cup of tea, and insisted that you stay for an hour or two, perhaps half a day, depending on his mood."

"Really?"

"Yep. Old Travis doesn't pretend to be sociable. Several people have tried to press charges against him for holding them sort of hostage, but since he never threatened them with a weapon and they were on his land, he said that meant they wanted to visit.

That he was simply being hospitable. Won every case that ever went to court. No one around here ever trespasses on his land now."

"How did you know where I was?"

"Claude Hoover called me, said you'd headed in that direction and that you might run into Travis. Thought I ought to know since we were sort of…close, as he put it. Are we close?" Bradley turned laughing eyes on her, and they both laughed relieving Deedra's sense of anxiety. What was there about Travis Tucker that had frightened her like that?

"Why did you hike that way?"

Deedra explained about the boys and how they had left in such a hurry, and how she wanted to question them.

"So you think they might have seen…what?" Bradley's eyes gleamed.

She threw him a sidelong glance. "You know as well as I do, Brad, that the other missing woman is probably in that old swamp, and that perhaps the boys disturbed it."

Bradley nodded. "We've been getting a lot of questions about that possibility at the paper, too. I guess Aaron's office is swamped with inquiries. He says he just refers them to the state police, that there isn't the manpower for such an undertaking."

"Any new clues on the other cases?"

"Nothing that I know about. People are really upset

about the Nevin's girl, and her father is keeping the pressure on to find the killer.''

They had reached the place where the trail led down to Percifal, and Deedra saw Claude on his front porch. They threw him a thank you wave. He turned and went inside without an answering gesture.

"Funny old coot," Bradley remarked. "Takes in all the activity, but somehow just observes. Makes a person wonder what he's seen here, and if any of it is a clue to our killer."

"Seems to keep a close eye on Jocelyn," Deedra remarked.

"Yes. Harriet thinks he's too possessive."

"She's a very talented artist. Did you know she painted a picture of the swamp with a skull's head covered in algae, rising from the surface?"

Bradley halted. "You saw it?"

"Yes. I'm not sure Claude has noticed it. Jocelyn painted it in so smoothly, one has to really be inspecting her painting style to notice it. She's afraid of the swamp."

Bradley resumed striding down to the old store, a frown bringing his dark brows into a straight line.

"Time for a cup of coffee?"

"Not now," Bradley declined. "I have a newspaper on hold. How about tonight, though it will be near 9:00 before I can get here?"

"Fine. Dinner?"

"No. I'll have something sent in. I usually do when I'm working late."

Claude was on his front porch when Bradley drove away.

Deedra phoned Clete, told him of her encounter with Travis Tucker and that Bradley had been sent to rescue her. Clete knew of the man's reputation, and grunted something that sounded like, "Just like the old reprobate!"

"Did you get any vibes that Travis could be the killer?"

"He's frightening in his way, but I'm sure Aaron has checked him out," Deedra replied.

"Have you checked on my property yet?"

"Going out there right after lunch."

Aaron Blaine phoned right after her call to Clete.

"Hear you met our Travis Tucker! Anything you observed about the man?"

"Clete just asked me if I'd received any vibes that he might be the killer. No, I didn't."

"And?"

"I wouldn't want to trespass there again!"

"You don't think he has murdering tendencies?" Aaron persisted.

"No. The killer we're looking for kidnaps the women. He made no attempt to do that, only stood on that trail preventing me from going further."

"Yeah. We've checked him out and there's no links to the women, though he has an ideal place there to hold them captive. No near neighbors, several outbuildings and a barn. We've no cause for a search warrant, but when Travis went to his sister's funeral in Denver, a volunteer civilian did us a favor. There was no evidence that the victims had ever been there."

"Oh!"

"I'd appreciate it, Deedra, if you would alert me of your activities. Don't want you suddenly turning up missing, and if you did, we'd like to have a clue about where to start looking."

Hesitantly, because she resisted having anyone telling

her what she could and couldn't do, "I'm going out to Clete's place this afternoon. He wanted me to check on some things."

"You haven't mentioned it to anyone in Percifal?"

"No, of course not."

With Aaron's warning tone ringing in her ears, she drove away from Percifal with a sense of driving into some kind of danger, and admonished herself for such an active imagination.

The rain clouds had disappeared, the sky that hazy blue of winter, a hesitant color when it isn't sure how long the clouds are going to stay away. The mountain air was invigorating, and Deedra hummed to herself as she drove slowly south. The turn off to Clete's property was on the east side nearly a mile this side of Rufus. The narrow lane leading into the property was well-graveled though brush from the roadside was beginning to attest to the fact that no one lived down that narrow road now. Someone was going to have to do some trimming there soon.

Clete's two-story gray house sat behind a circular driveway. It was an old house, circa 1930's, with a wide front porch and tall narrow windows. A balcony off an upstairs room was balanced by two dormer windows on the other side. Two large chimneys dominated the roof where newer roofing of a green color had been installed in the not too distant past. A grand house in its way, and probably notable at the time of its construction. Huddled in the trees, it was a house Clete would find acceptable.

After parking her car, she tried the front door, found it locked and no signs of any attempt to gain entrance either there, at the windows, or the side door leading from the garage. The garage was locked though a wood shed at the rear was not. Wood was stacked neatly against the far wall, a cutting stump, an ax, and a wedge were leaning against it. Spiders had taken up residence there.

She checked the faucets, found them wrapped against damage from freezing weather, then checked the back door. It was locked though she noticed scratches in the paint around the keyhole as if someone had tried to get in, though nothing she had seen so far indicated that. She glanced around experiencing a funny tingling sensation, a paranoid sensation as if someone secretly watched, then shook her head to banish the feeling. Sometimes her imagination just went into overdrive.

Despite her uneasiness, she went to the barn where the door opened by sliding it along an overhead railing. Her gaze traveled first to the loft where broken bales of hay were scattered about. Off to the side a hay elevator leaned against the loft and two pitchforks stood against the wall. An old tractor with an attached hay wagon, numerous saddles, bridles and reins hung along the other wall. Stalls for horses and perhaps a cow or two were located along the sides and back wall.

She was about to leave when the sight of a round, orange-colored spool of baling twine caught her eye. It had been opened part way, the plastic wrapper pushed down about half-way, and part of the twine cut into three or four foot lengths. A chill enveloped her as she examined the twine. It certainly looked like the twine that had been used to strangle Priscilla Dawson. Without touching the twine she carefully examined the area and the empty stalls. Though she found nothing to indicate that anyone had been there recently, one of the stalls had a layer of hay scattered about the floor and a harness hanging from a nail in the wall. The other stalls were clean.

The chill she experienced became a tremor as it occurred to her that this place might have been where the first victim, Darlene Hernandez, had been held captive for those four missing days before her body had been discovered along the highway. What better place to hide someone?

She carefully shut the barn door, deciding to tell Aaron of her suspicions though in private. No sense stirring up something that might not prove out. She was still shaking when she drove out the circular drive.

The house across the road was also vacant, a real estate sign indicating it was for sale. An imp of curiosity caused her to drive up its narrow drive into a parking area at the back of the house. This place was definitely unkempt, emphasizing the fact that the owner hadn't been able to perform the chores that had in younger years been quite easy.

Deedra found the doors and windows locked, no signs of entry or vandalism. The barn and woodsheds were empty. Weeds were beginning to choke out the flowerbeds.

She walked around the house, found nothing to indicate intruders, and experienced sadness for the owner who had grown too old and feeble to care for this place.

It was almost 4:00. With the shortened daylight of the winter months, she drove the darkened lane to the highway with the headlights on, and a sense of having escaped something. A movement at the side of the road caused her a start. A deer loped along in front of the car, then leaped away into the woods.

"Got to get control, girl!" She muttered.

Aaron wasn't in his office. She didn't leave a message. The fewer people who knew of her suspicions the better. And Clete would have a fit if she started gossip about his property. This was a thing she didn't intend to share with Bradley Keetz either.

When she drove up to the old store, it seemed to crouch in the evening shadows. The dark skinny cat scooted from under the porch and raced across to the old gas station vanishing in deep shadow. She idly wondered who's cat it was, and if they ever fed it.

The store building was cold, of course, and she spent several shivery minutes getting the fires going. She was huddled against the fireplace, a blanket over her shoulders when Aaron arrived. He had not driven a patrol car, but a fairly new Ford Explorer. He wasn't in uniform either, dressed in jeans and blue sweatshirt. He seemed to have taken on a different personality with the change into casual clothing.

"I hear you stopped by to see me?"

"Yes. I like the Explorer. Hope you've changed the tires?" she quipped referring to a scandal involving defective tires a few years earlier.

He grinned. "Of course. Have you any coffee?"

"It's perking. Had to get the fires going first. Have you had supper? I can cook up a fast tuna fish or toasted cheese sandwich."

He gave her a lopsided grin as if his face hurt. "A woman after my own heart! Yes, I'd like a couple of sandwiches and some serious talk. Isn't that coffee ready yet?"

Deedra heard the hoarseness in his voice and knew he was in the first stages of exhaustion or at the least a nasty cold. Aaron was cross and out-of-sorts like a man who had missed many hours of restful sleep, and obviously needed chicken noodle soup and TLC. She scurried to the kitchen, delivered a cup of steaming coffee, then scuttled back to the kitchen to heat soup and toast sandwiches on the grill.

Her cell phone rang. It was Bradley begging off for the evening. "Ran into a snag here with some of the equipment. I'll have to work late. A rain check?"

"Yes. Talk to you later," Deedra replied.

When she returned to the front room, the fire had burned low and Aaron was sound asleep, his head against the back of the sofa. He was snoring lightly, the indication of a stuffy nose or exhaustion. The sight of him there caused her an unexpected warm feeling. The dim overhead light etched the weary lines of his rugged face, and outlined a scar near his right ear that she hadn't noticed earlier. Exhaustion knew no boundaries, it brought down the toughest of men, taught them the whining ways of sick children, and twisted their manly pride. She grinned. It was obvious that Aaron was going to sack-out on her sofa that night, and she experienced a sudden affection for him.

Deedra ate the cheese sandwich alone, listening to Aaron's irregular breathing, drawn ever closer to this rugged man as he slept. How long had it been since he'd had an eight-hour night's sleep? Probably not since the murder of Darlene Hernandez. Watching the sleeping Aaron, she wondered what it would be like to be married to such a man. Would his lovemaking be gentle, careful, or would he just be demanding, lack the tenderness that created deep love? Many courageous men with stress-filled lives lacked the romanticism most women craved, the thoughtful little gestures and words that sealed the fractures of love.

Deedra sighed. Would such a man ever fill her life? She had always hoped that Deke Thomas would be that man, ruefully learning he wasn't the commitment-type. Then there had been Brent with whom there was commitment. Only Brent had been sent off to Bosnia and lost his life there. Deedra had struggled through that grief without letting on how shattered she was, once again showing the world her tough image. Now she dated Bryce Paxton on occasion and a couple of news reporters, though the chemistry just wasn't there. And the media guys she dated just wanted to pick up tidbits of news to enhance their own ratings. Life never seemed to measure up to a person's expectations.

Aaron snored on, and Deedra placed an extra blanket over him, and replenished the fires, warming the house against the storm that had arrived in full force with its strong gusts and squalls of pounding rain.

A reflection at the window suddenly told her that someone had peered inside, and had quickly stepped back into the shadows. Probably Claude Hoover, she mused.

Instead of watching television, she read a paperback novel she'd brought along to take up slack on sleepless nights. Near midnight, Aaron awoke, seemed disoriented, staggered to the bathroom, and on returning, sank onto the sofa again with a groan.

Deedra fixed tea, coaxed him into eating hot soup, then gave him Tylenol PM and ordered him to remain on the sofa until morning.

"You aren't good for anyone or anything until you get at least twelve hours of sleep. I've got your car keys hidden so you can't leave anyway. Even if the killer deposits another body in this county, you can't do anything about it until daylight. So just go back to sleep and let me finish reading this exciting book, will you?"

Aaron threw her an enigmatic look as if he didn't

quite comprehend or couldn't believe she would tell him what to do, moaned softly, and closed his eyes again.

Deedra stood guard, replenishing the fires, listening to the wind whine creating eerie sounds that echoed through the old building, and to the rain whose sound-effect noises on the roof and against the windows were reminiscent of the annoying noises heard as background in late movies and television.

She dozed, then awoke to the chill of the house cooling, added fuel to the fires and huddled in the chair, dozing again. She awoke at 7:00, her first thought, "...do I always have to be the strong one?" Ending a dream in which she had battled the elements and saved several strangers from an unknown fate, the men frowning in disapproval at her.

Aaron was awake. His eyes were clear, the symptoms of exhaustion gone.

"So, you're still among the living. You snore, do you know that?" Deedra grumped as she headed for the bathroom. "I'll make breakfast while you take a bath."

"Are you always so cheerful when you wake up?" Aaron remarked.

Deedra closed the bathroom door quite firmly in answer.

The bacon and eggs, toast and fruit seemed just what Aaron needed as he sat opposite her, his hair still wet from bathing.

"Thanks," he muttered. "I needed to crash like that, didn't plan on being here all night though."

"Good nurse, aren't I?" Deedra grinned. "Last night I didn't think you'd be up and feisty today. You're tough!"

"Like you," he answered. "You stopped by my office yesterday. Something I need to know about?" Aaron's blue eyes glinted.

"I'll pour more coffee and tell you."

Aaron was dubious about her hunch that Clete's place might have been the place where Darlene Hernandez had been held captive those four days before the discovery of her dead body. But he did not rule out that possibility.

"I'll take a run out there myself. I don't want word of this to get out. There's enough speculation going on as it is, and it might not prove out."

Deedra nodded. "Just a hunch, that's all. And, of course, I won't alert Clete. He'd be up here before the next edition could hit the streets."

"Tell me what made you so suspicious?

Deedra sighed. "A shudder when I saw the twine, the sensation of...being watched. A sort of certainty that the victim had been held captive there. Might just be my imagination which at times leads me into realms of...ah...dark speculation."

Aaron eyed her in the manner of a man who needs evidence to form suspicions.

There was a timid knock on the door.

Deedra found Harriet standing there with a plate of fresh cinnamon rolls. She pretended surprise to find Aaron there.

Aaron tried to explain, but Harriet gushed, "No explanation needed, Aaron. Claude checked a time or two and reckoned you were 'plumb tuckered out.' His words not mine. He noticed that Deedra kept the fires going, and that your car was here all night. No harm in being friendly. Those are your favorite breakfast rolls as I recall, Aaron. Now, I've got to get back to my own business."

Harriet went out the door and scurried up the knoll as if afraid something would chase her.

Aaron and Deedra burst into laughter.

But before leaving, Aaron took her into his arms and kissed her quite thoroughly, a kiss that sent thrills of emotion surging through her, like a wave at high tide.

"Just to let you know our night together could have meant something more...serious, and because I can kiss you now that I'm out of uniform. I have to control my urges when I'm wearing it, but I can't squelch my feelings." He kissed her again, a long lingering kiss that aroused them both, and only the fact that they knew Claude Hoover and Harriet Stratton kept an eye out, caused their immediate parting.

Deedra watched Aaron drive away, her heart beating rapidly, her face flushed with desire.

"Whoa, girl," she muttered, "let's not get too involved here. Aaron may not have any futuristic plans that include me."

Clete phoned. "You went out to my place?" Clete was always so abrupt, he had no time for things like "Good morning," or "How are you today?" No wonder he'd been married and divorced twice. Deedra overlooked the fact that both women had found other men and left Clete, and that he'd become morose and sometimes rude in the wake of those marital fractures.

"Yes. I went out there yesterday afternoon. Everything seems to be in order. The faucets are wrapped for protection against freezes."

"Um. Thanks. Any news on the murders?"

"No."

"Aaron's following up all the leads, I suppose?"

"Yes."

"You aren't very talkative. Something wrong?

Aaron's all right?'' Like most newsmen, Clete had picked up on the wavelength of her hesitancy.

"Aaron's fine this morning.'' She told Clete how Aaron had crashed on her sofa and spent the night, and of Harriet's delivery of freshly baked cinnamon rolls.

"Hm. So those people know Aaron spent the night with you?''

Deedra sighed. "Aaron spent the night on my sofa, he did not spend the night with me!''

"Deedra, I don't care if he did spend it with you, might rid you of that remote coolness. He's my friend and I don't want anything to happen to him. You've reassured me about that.'' Clete cut the connection.

Deedra held the cell phone away from her ear. "Sometimes I just don't understand that man!''

Though she was tired from her night of vigil, Deedra went for her usual morning walk. Mustn't give the natives reason for more speculation.

The rain had subsided, leaving a damp chill and mud puddles. The lake was cloudy-looking, gray and murky. A mist hung over the swamp, its algae surface a thick goo, the snags daunting extrusions in the morning light. An unexpected shiver slid down her spine. What a dismal place this was even without the murders. The dying lake threw out a miasma of gloom, causing her to wonder how much the dreary, decaying lake influenced the killer's psyche.

Melvyn Randolph was just leaving in his delivery truck and she waved as he drove past. A glance at their cabin showed Emma at her usual place in front of the window. Again thought of what the woman might have observed crossed her mind. Surely if Emma had seen anything suspicious she would have written it down. Her arms weren't paralyzed, only the lower portion of her body. Unless, like Jocelyn, she hesitated to mention untoward things pertaining to the swamp. Having been a bank clerk meeting the public each day and suddenly unable to speak confined to her wheelchair here in this semi-remote place must be very difficult to accept and immensely frustrating.

Deedra waved as she strolled past the Randolph cabin on her way to the edge of the old road noting that the rain had caused the ooze to spread further under the old roadbed. There was really no doubt about the ground there being unstable.

She walked around the squishy place to the far side of the roadbed then carefully made her way to the highway. No vehicles had traveled that route for many months.

The crime scene tape was still in place.

She scrutinized the surface of the swamp looking for anything that might have frightened the young boys the day before. The many snags and unidentifiable objects made the surface a mass of floating flotsam. Returning, she walked along the side of the road where weeds had grown into thick mats of vegetation. Moisture from the swamp kept the vegetation growing though there was the musty odor of decay and rotting weeds.

She walked to the back of the vacant cabin and once again gave the place a cursory inspection. Only tire tracks at the rear gave indication that anyone had been around the decrepit place. She suspected that rats had taken up abode there, and quickly descended to the graveled road in front of the cabins.

She waved at Emma Randolph and was about to climb her steps for a polite one-sided conversation when Melvyn drove up in his delivery truck.

Emma put a hand over her mouth.

Melvyn climbed down, very pale and holding his stomach.

"Flu," he muttered and hurried up the stairs as if vomiting or diarrhea hastened him along.

Emma shook her head, the look in her eyes dark and worried. After a hurried gesture to Deedra, she wheeled herself away from the window.

Deedra sighed, another opportunity to talk to Emma lost. She relied on talking to the women to get a read on the men since they all went to work each day with the exception of Lance Fenton who appeared to be something of a recluse. On sudden impulse she walked up Fenton's steps and knocked on the door.

The man was a surprise. Though she had glimpsed him earlier, hadn't really taken stock of the man. He was of medium height, though wiry, all muscle. No fatty cells had settled around his waist, his hair thick and wavy with the grayness of his advancing years melding its darkness to a lighter shade. Bright blue eyes gleamed from a face with few wrinkles. A man, she mused, who took care of himself. A much more intelligent person than she'd been given to understand.

"Yes?"

"I'm Deedra Masefield. I'm temporarily residing in the old store building. Just wanted to get acquainted."

"I know who you are. Investigative reporter for the Daily Spokesman. You here to investigate those murders?"

Deedra, looking into those shrewd unclouded eyes, "Yes. I prefer not to advertise that fact, however."

Lance nodded. "Step in, we might as well get to know each other."

Deedra found herself in a living room filled with books, comfortable chairs, an overloaded desk, a TV, and an elaborate radio, stereo, CD, and DVD combination. A stack of old records, vintage 40's and 50's, filled a tower next to it.

Lance Fenton noticed her interest. "My wife's collection. She often played them. I can't seem to get rid of them."

Deedra nodded. "Collector's items now. I have mementos I'd rather my colleagues knew nothing about. It isn't 'cool' to be sentimental in this New Age."

He laughed. "You aren't as tough as you're portrayed."

"Well, I do have some feminine characteristics," she quipped. "You are obviously retired. Harriet said you have lived here for as long as she could remember. Only didn't know what you did for a living."

"She didn't tell you? I thought Harriet knew everything about everything. I have a private income... ah...investments. I've recently made another million or two by selling out my NASDAQ stocks at their peak. Any thinking person would have seen that crash on the way. Grab and run is my policy."

Deedra laughed. "Whatever works. Not many have your...wisdom."

"Get too greedy. What goes up like a balloon eventually falls. Everything was over-rated."

"I don't see a computer?" Deedra glanced around.

"Nooo. I have a computer room. I don't usually allow anyone in there. In your case, I'll make an exception."

He led her down a hall to a room with high windows placed above eye level. "Around here, one needs to have windows above Claude Hoover's curious spying. I can't abide a snoop like that, but no one else seems to mind."

"Yeah. I've caught him peering in my windows a time or two. You really have a setup here, you must spend a lot of time in cyberspace."

"Not as much as you think. This is confidential, but I'm sure you'd ferret it out anyway. I'm an author. Write under a pseudonym. I think you've read some of my stuff."

He confessed to being a quite popular and prolific author.

Deedra felt surprise, then excitement. "Yes, I have read your books. How do you keep Harriet from learning of it?"

"Because she hasn't been that interested in me. I've lived here a long time, pretend to be reclusive, and shred and burn everything."

"Has Claude always snooped around?"

"He has ever since I've known him. He means no harm, and no, I don't think he's the serial killer."

His words stunned Deedra.

Lance grinned. "You certainly aren't here on a vacation, and I doubt you're really dedicated to finishing that book. And I am aware that your boss and Aaron Blaine are old friends. Aaron needs all the eyes and ears he can get right now. I suppose you've been posted here to fill that capacity?"

Deedra grinned. "How long did it take you to figure that out?"

"The minute I saw you with Aaron. Got the rest off the Internet. I've followed your career with interest. One of my best sellers was written after your sojourn at the Awful Abbey. I just used some of your personality traits, not your career, for the protagonist in my novel. And, by the way, Deke Thomas is the son of a very dear friend of mine who passed on a few years back."

"Deke and I are ancient history. I wanted marriage and family, he didn't."

"Aaron Blaine?"

"What? Oh, you noticed his car there all night! He hadn't slept in many hours. He simply fell asleep, and didn't wake up for hours and hours. No rendezvous, if that's what you want to know."

"But you're available, aren't you? No fella's panting on the sidelines?" Fenton grinned.

"I don't think anyone has ever 'panted', over me. And no, nothing of a serious nature."

"Good thing I'm older, because I too, am now available!" He tried to make a lecherous leer, but it turned into a smile, his bright blue eyes sending a message of approval, a rapport of empathy and understanding.

After a moment of silence Fenton asked, "What's your take on these murders?"

"Don't really have one, although I think there's another skeleton in the swamp, the woman who disappeared at the same time as the one they recovered." She explained about the young boys and how they raced away in what appeared to be a panic, and how she had decided to talk to them and ran into Travis Tucker.

"Strange old geezer, isn't he?" Fenton remarked.

They discussed books and authors and Deedra was surprised to find it past 11:00 when she glanced at her watch.

"Oh! I must go. What will the neighbors think!"

Their meeting ended with laughter, and Deedra went back to the store building in a lighter frame of mind, arriving just as Bradley drove up.

"I hear Aaron spent the night?" Were the first words out of his mouth.

"And?" Deedra experienced a spurt of anger.

Bradley sensing discord, grinned. "Just thought I'd drive out and see if you needed rescuing."

The anger receded, but an imp of doubt lingered. "No rescue needed. Aaron was exhausted and crashed on the sofa, and I've just spent almost two hours with Lance Fenton."

"Fenton? You actually entered his sanctum?"

"Yes, he invited me in, and we had an exceedingly interesting discussion. He has a computer room Claude Hoover can't peer into. High windows."

"Ah, the reason we know very little about our famous author."

"So you know who he is?"

Bradley nodded. "He keeps a low profile, and who can blame him? My father knew him well, and swore me to…ah…secrecy."

"Time for lunch?

"For coffee anyway. Sorry about our dinner date last night."

"No apologies necessary since Aaron was conked out here."

"He's really got his plateful with these murders, all right, and not the man-power needed. Have you gone through all that material from the newspaper yet?"

Deedra shook her head. "No, plan to finish it this afternoon."

Bradley finished his coffee and went to the door. "It's raining." On the porch he gave a searching glance down the row of cabins. "I see Melvyn's delivery truck is at home."

"He drove out earlier, came back a few minutes later clutching his stomach and looking quite pale. Said something about the flu."

Bradley stared toward the Randolph's cabin and muttered, "Hm."

He turned to Deedra. "Can we re-schedule our date For Thursday night?"

"Fine. Dinner, movie, what?"

"Dinner and dancing," Bradley smiled.

"Hey, I didn't bring any formal clothing with me," Deedra objected.

Bradley grinned. "Don't need it, barbecue dinner and Western style dancing. I know this place north of Brockton. Casual clothes."

The rain settled into a heavy thudding, not exactly a downpour, but acting as if it was going to last awhile. She savored another cup of coffee by the fire before settling down with the information on each of the men living at Percifal...and finding nothing except Claude's peeping tom inclination to indicate anyone with the characteristics of a serial killer personality. The men's alibis had all been thoroughly checked. She entered the statistics into the computer: the times, opportunities, motives. The computer had no answers either, spit out the conclusion that someone in Percifal was the killer because of access to the swamp.

The killings appeared to be random opportunities with no planning ahead. There seemed no real M.O., just chance happenings. Travis Tucker seemed to have more of a motive than the men of Percifal.

Rain had ceased during the early evening and a reluctant moon appeared between scurrying clouds. A fog began hovering over the lake and swamp. She sat in a chair pulled up close to the window and stared at the dismal old swamp. After a few moments the fog lifted for an instant, outlining the figure of a man across the swamp near the place where she had seen the young boys. An icy chill enveloped her. Then the fog closed down again shrouding the man.

Deedra quickly donned a heavy jacket and scarf, placing a flashlight in one of the wide pockets. She slipped out the front door, scurried around the upper end of the lake, a lake that was not much bigger than a tennis court, her feet making whispering sounds on the wet graveled road. In a few minutes she arrived near the place where she had seen the man, and earlier the young boys.

The fog was as thick as if the rain had been crushed into unmoving mist. She held quite still for several minutes. Noise, she reflected, sometimes echoed in fog making distorted, disoriented sounds, but now there was no sound. A chilling shudder swept over her.

Hesitantly she moved forward, veering too close to the edge of the swamp, quickly side-stepping in time to avoid the full force of the blow aimed at the back of her head. It felled her, and she sprawled full length on the soggy ground.

The man grunted, lifted her slight body and heaved her into the swamp, where she slowly disappeared into the slimy green sludge.

The man grunted again, turned, and hurried toward the highway.

SEVEN

THE ICY GOO revived her and instinctively she clutched at a jagged limb beside her. Her feet floated down through layers of algae and at last touched the bottom. Gagging, she tried to wipe the algae from her face, spitting and coughing, repulsed and nauseated by the taste. The pain in her head peaked in bright spots behind her eyes, then began a throbbing that shook her whole body. Goo dripped from her face and hair, hitting the sludge with soft plops. She was shoulder deep in terrible, stinking, guck.

The fog prevented sight of the shoreline, and disoriented she dared not move in fear that she would slip into a deep chasm. So she waited, trembling with fear and an icy chill, allowing her common sense mind to overcome her terror. And an eon later the fog began drifting away. There was no one at the swamp's edge or on the road. Suddenly moonlight appeared between the floating clouds illuminating her perilous situation.

Carefully, steadying herself with the limb, she began moving toward the edge. It was like walking through thick cream, each step an act of slow motion, an effort to put one foot on the bottom and lift another. She spit and gagged, and finally vomited, her head a hurting thing that caused exhaustion. She leaned against the limb, resting. But the cold was penetrating and warned her to keep moving, knowing she needed to get warm...and soon, very soon. Her body trembling like a leaf in a passing wind.

Walking proved slow and vexing, her foot hit an object, and she tried to kick it out of the way. It seemed stuck, she stepped sideways, then forward again. Her feet suddenly slipped out from under her, and she went into the goo again. Clinging to the limb she pulled herself upright, spitting and gagging, frantically trying to rid her face of the slime. Overhead a nighthawk uttered a raucous call as if mocking her.

The object below had broken loose and began a slow rise to the surface. It brushed against her. She pushed it away. Panic seizing her again. As she moved toward the edge, the object followed along having caught on her clothing. Deedra tried to push it away again, but it held in a stubborn clinging. Deedra experienced deep fear as if something dreadful was about to overtake her. Time seemed to drag, her urgency to reach the edge was like trying to catch a moving target.

At last she reached the edge, heaved herself onto the wet ground with a heavy groan. The object, hooked into her clothing, trailed along with her. When she reached around to unhook it from her jacket to push it away, her screams echoed across the swamp.. A partially dressed skeleton with an algae-covered skull grinned up at her in the moonlight.

For long moments her heart thumped heavily robbing her of breath, then with the realization that the skeleton could not possibly harm her, she began a slow deep breathing that brought back a sense of reality and of extreme coldness. With shaking hands she finally unhooked the skeleton from her jacket, pulled it fully onto the ledge, then as fast as she could get her legs into motion, raced off to the old store, algae flipping and dripping off her sodden clothes.

She stumbled on the steps, fell and hurt both knees, got up and slammed into the house where she sank to the floor. After a moment of sobbing and deep breathing, she stripped off her clothing, raced to the bathroom where she bathed her face several times, intermittently blowing her nose, and spitting into the toilet. The sight of the greenish stuff made her feel nauseated and unclean. She ran hot water into the tub where she washed off the worst of it, drained the tub, and refilled it again. She had to wash her hair twice, then ran out of hot water.

Before refueling the fires, she phoned Aaron.

"What?" he answered in an anxious voice.

"I need you out here now," and she hung up, afraid the screams she held back by sheer effort would seek release over the phone.

She knew Aaron would see the skeleton as he drove up the road into Percifal. It was necessary for him to get there before anyone else did, and in a few minutes the patrol car that sped up the road, suddenly braked to a stop. She saw a man get out, and knew it was Aaron. He examined something on the ground, then returned to the patrol car. Within a few minutes another patrol car arrived. There was discussion between the men and finally Aaron drove on to her place.

When Aaron opened her door, she was huddled next to the fire, drinking coffee and nursing a throbbing headache.

"Tell me!" He rushed to her, held her closely before examining the head wound.

"I'll get a doctor out here!"

"No, it's all right. I'll go in the morning."

"No. I'll take you now. I don't want you driving. Now, you ready to tell me how the hell you found that skeleton?

Though Deedra tried to quell the tears, she ended up sobbing it out in Aaron's arms.

He had few questions at the moment, but she knew he would want specifics later, and agreed to let him to drive her in to Rufus to see the doctor. He helped her into a jacket and out to the car. She was amazed to find how weak she felt. Outside, moonlight spilled across the lake and swamp as if the fog had never existed.

The scene was etched forever on Deedra's mind as they drove toward the place where the skeleton lay.

When they reached it, Aaron stopped, instructed his men to have the M.E. take the skeleton away, to mark the place with a wooden marker only, and to clear out before daybreak. "I don't want the media here if we can help it. And I don't want anyone talking about this!"

Aaron notified the state police. "Might as well meet us at Dr. Carron's office, get the whole story then," he said to the trooper on duty. He turned to Deedra. "Do you think you can cope?"

Her tough trait had returned. "Yeah," she muttered.

Dr. Carron's office was a division of his home and alerted by Aaron, he had lights glowing, and was awaiting them in his office.

"Now, young lady, let's find out what that head wound looks like!" He parted her tangled hair, still damp from washing. "My, my! You are fortunate. Looks like some heavy pointed object did that damage, kind of slantwise though as if he didn't hit square on."

"I was near the edge, and had just stepped back," Deedra muttered.

"Lucky thing. A square hit and you would be dead." He x-rayed her head, then did an overall check; blood pressure, pulse, heart, eyes and ears.

"Your heart and blood pressure indicate trauma and pain. I'm going to give you an injection for protection against whatever bacteria lurks in that old swamp. That will hold you until I see you again at 11:00. I'd prefer that you rest sitting up. I don't think the cold hurt you, nevertheless, keep warm and as quiet as possible."

Aaron took Dr. Carron aside, and they spoke in low tones preventing Deedra from overhearing.

Dr. Carron turned back to Deedra. "On second thought, Deedra, I'm going to admit you to the hospital for observation. That head wound is serious, and you have a slight concussion. You need to be observed by professionals for the next few hours. I'm having Aaron run you over to the hospital, I'll phone instructions, and this will all be done as quietly as possible." He patted her arm, and Deedra knew that between them, they would allow no objections.

"Yeah, Clete might set up quite a disturbance should you suddenly disappear!" Aaron grinned. "You really need to do this, Deedra. If the killer learns he didn't kill you, he might try again and right now you're vulnerable. We can't take that chance!"

Deedra realized that vulnerable was the right description for how she felt, and relaxed. In the hospital she wouldn't have to replenish the fires to keep warm.

Her admittance was scarcely noted, and she was taken to a private room near the nurses' station on the second floor, "for observation."

Though her head was elevated, she went to sleep almost immediately, assured that the creatures from in and around the swamp could not invade her space there.

At 11:00, Dr. Carron arrived. "Ah, you've had a beneficial rest, looking much better, I see." He made another examination. "Aaron will be by to pick you up when you're released about 6:00. Usually we get patients out of here by 3:00, but the county has you under protective custody, so we've bent the rules a bit. Unless the nurses report any change in your condition, I won't see you here at the hospital again. If you need anything feel free to call me at my office."

A nurse arrived later to give her another injection and check blood pressure and pulse.

The phone beside her bed rang. It was Clete.

"Deedra, what the hell were you doing alongside that ghastly old swamp in the middle of the night?"

"Clete, I'm in no mood. My head really hurts, and I'm very cranky. If you want to hear my story just listen. No questions until I'm through."

"Dazzle me," he growled.

Deedra told him how and why she had gone out to the swamp.

"This was on the road side leading into Percifal?" He asked when she finished.

"Yes. Where I saw those young boys the other day."

"The skeleton got caught on your jacket, eh?"

"Yep."

"Sometimes you do have scary encounters!" Clete muttered as if he found her adventure incredible.

Deedra didn't voice the thought, "You send me on scary investigations.." Instead she said, "I'll write up a feature on my...ah...discovery. You can run it as a sidebar to the news story whenever Aaron gives the okay."

"Right!" Clete sounded pleased, and hung up.

Bradley stood in the doorway. "All right if I come in?"

"How did you find out I was here?" Deedra asked.

"Harriet phoned me. Said Aaron had arrived at your place in the night and took you away. You didn't seem to be at home this morning. No smoke from your chimneys."

"And so you called Aaron?" She wondered what else Harriet had observed last night.

"Right. He tells me that you found something... ah...interesting that I can't print about yet."

Deedra nodded. She felt tired, actually didn't want company at that moment and hoped Bradley wouldn't stay long. "Sit down, Bradley. You don't happen to have a cup of coffee, do you?"

A look of compassion crossed his handsome face.

"Sorry. Won't they let you have any?"

"Haven't asked. I'm just grouchy."

"I understand headaches can do that! Can I get you anything else?"

"No. I'm just recuperating and letting off a little steam. Clete just called wanting to know why and how like he wasn't the one who sent me here to find out!

Bradley grinned. "Well, it is a bit disconcerting to have one's special reporter get conked over the head and thrown into a swamp, and then drag up a skeleton belonging to a woman whose been missing a year before Clete sent you up here two years ago."

"What did you say?"

"The woman has been missing for three years. She isn't the woman's companion whose skeleton was found last week."

"What about this woman?" Deedra felt her pulse speed up.

"This woman's car broke down just north of Brockton. She was leaving her husband. Evidently she got a ride with someone, and hasn't been seen since. The husband was at work in Brockton all day. Found his wife gone and a note telling him she was leaving him. So she wasn't reported missing until the sheriff of our neighboring county impounded her car. The first her husband or anyone else knew of her disappearance."

"No lover waiting?"

"No indication that she had someone she was interested in. She told co-workers that she just couldn't stand to live with her husband any longer, drew out her last pay check and that was the last they saw or heard from her."

"And that woman wasn't included in the ones missing from this county," Deedra remarked. "So the killer may not live in this county, just uses the swamp as a disposal place."

Bradley nodded.

"And that might eliminate the men here at Percifal as suspects."

Bradley nodded again. "The media is bound to descend on you. My offer to stay at my place still stands."

"Thanks. I might take you up on that offer. Don't think I can cope just now." She fought back tears and looked at her hands to keep Bradley from noticing.

"Do you have a ride when you leave here?"

"Aaron is picking me up about 6:00."

"Do you think he'll bring you over to my place?" Bradley frowned, and Deedra knew he didn't really like the idea of Aaron picking her up when he wanted to do it himself.

"I don't know. I really don't want to go back to that old store tonight, and I don't feel like having to replen-

ish the fires to keep it warm enough. I've been cold
ever since I got tossed into that nasty old swamp. Just
thinking about it sends ice into my veins!'' She leaned
back against the pillows. Her head had ceased paining,
but she felt an unusual lassitude and grouchiness.

After Bradley left she phoned Clete with the news of
the skeleton's identity. "A victim out of Aaron's jurisdiction. How many skeletons are going to surface in that
nasty old swamp?'' Deedra muttered.

"Is there someone you suspect there at Percifal?''
Clete asked.

"I hardly know them. I think we can rule out Lance
Fenton though. And perhaps Melvyn Randolph since he
was ill earlier that day, and I doubt he was the man out
there in the fog who threw me into that brine.''

"You're sure he was ill?'' Clete's voice held a note
of doubt.

Deedra told him how Melvyn had returned looking
quite peaked and had rushed into the house after mut-
tering something about having the flu.

"You haven't been able to get any kind of assessment on the other men?''

"Well, there's always Claude Hoover who has a penchant for peering into windows which seems harmless
enough. However there're rumors that his daughters
never go home though Jocelyn hears from them regularly.''

Clete sighed. "Yeah, I heard that. He was mighty
strict with those girls.''

"I just can't seem to connect with the men here to
get a conversation going with them. Their whereabouts
and alibis all checked out for the approximate abduction
times though. Aaron and his men and the state troopers
did a thorough investigation. The real problem is mo-

tivation. This killer just leaves things to chance, no specific timing, planning or stalking. Just takes advantage of the moment."

"He also has to know that part of the state very well," Clete reminded. "How many strangers would know about that old swamp and be able to dispose of bodies there without being noticed? The swamp can't be over half a block long near the highway. Access to it is somewhat limited."

"Yeah, right. The lake part is only a few leagues wide at the upper end now, though I understand it's very deep."

"I'd say the lake's size has been reduced to about one fourth of its original size since that earthquake. Someone with easy access has to be able to be seen around there without arousing suspicion," Clete ventured.

"The killer could take advantage of the heavy fogs to dispose of the bodies. When that fog rolls in you can't see the highway from the cabins at Percifal."

"Too bad Emma Randolph can't talk. Might be interesting to find out what she knows and has seen." With that suggestion, Clete rang off.

Aaron arrived later than planned with instructions that she was to remain in the hospital another night, and would be picked up in the morning by a deputy and returned to the old store. Later in the afternoon Bradley would take her to dinner and then she was to spend the night in his guest bedroom.

"I think by Friday you can stay at the store if you feel up to it. I've had new dead-locks put on the doors and special latches on those back windows, and Bradley is going to lend you a gun!" He stared at her with a don't-challenge-this look in his eyes.

She chose to ignore his last remark. "Bradley says the skeleton is that of a woman who disappeared up around Brockton, out of your jurisdiction?"

Aaron nodded. "We made a cursory search all through this county during the initial investigation. Of course, we didn't search the swamp. At that time it didn't seem feasible." Aaron sighed. "I went out to Clete's. I see what you mean about that twine and one of the stalls. We're trying to get some prints out there, but don't know if we can find anything usable."

"Clete was asking me about the men at Percifal. I just don't know enough about them to make any judgments."

"Dwight's an open book. Goes to work, arrives home on time, never been a breath of scandal, no secret affairs, no gambling problems. Harriet would have found out anything like that anyway. He was upset about having to close the store at Percifal. Had those earnings planned for retirement purposes. Kind of went around in a daze when they finally had to give it up. Harriet acted as if she thought he'd self destruct at the time."

"Hm," Deedra muttered, wondering what Aaron said that caused the tingle at the base of her skull. "Dwight works in Brockton, drives there every working day. And with this new skeleton that means there were three missing women from the Brockton area, not two," Deedra remarked.

"Yes. The odd fact is that this woman, missing over three years, is found partially clothed. The other skeleton missing two years didn't have a scrap of clothing on her."

"Must mean the other skeleton was nude when she went into the swamp," Deedra ventured.

"Or that the skeleton you dredged up drifted into the

swamp from the lake. Cold lake water wouldn't deteriorate clothing like the swamp does,'' Aaron suggested.

Deedra nodded. "Who gets this latest find?"

"Cooperation between both our sheriff departments.

Had it been the other skeleton's companion, it would go to the state troopers since those women were from down state."

"So that means you still have Darlene Hernandez, Thelma Hansen, Priscilla Dawson, and Sandy Nevin all in your sphere!" Deedra sent him a look she hoped conveyed sympathy and understanding.

"And the attack on you!" He reminded, his eyes glittering anger.

"Oh!" Was all Deedra could think of to say.

"Clete released the news this evening, and Bradley has it for his Friday edition. That's one reason I'm keeping you here tonight. The media can be overwhelming. You'll have to deal with them tomorrow though."

Deedra sighed. It didn't help to know it was her own kind who were going to plague her, make her life hectic for the next few days. Her head began to ache.

Aaron held her hand a moment before leaving. She was alerted by the glint in his eyes that he wanted to kiss her goodnight, but being in uniform prevented it.

Later, Bradley called and when Deedra asked him if he knew who owned the cabins at Percifal, she learned quite surprisingly, that Emma Randolph had purchased them two or three years before her accident. The rent money, Bradley said, was deposited to Emma's account at the bank where she had worked as an executive and part-time clerk. Emma had completed the purchase and made arrangements at the bank for the rents to pay for the property, the income taxes, and the insurances. It was to be her "security" she had told co-workers, "in case Melvyn ever walked out on her."

"My father was on the board at the time and he thought her remark unusual. Her real estate transaction was to remain confidential, and Melvyn had not signed any of the legal papers. The bank has respected her wishes all these years, and the bank president visits Emma once or twice a year to have her sign various legal documents."

"The papers are kept at the bank?"

"Yes," Bradley sighed. "In a safety deposit box. I understand her sister is to inherit should anything happen to her. She doesn't spend the money in event she will ever require professional nursing care."

"And you're sure that Melvyn doesn't know anything about it?" Deedra had serious doubts about Melvyn's ignorance of the facts.

"Well, he's never inquired about it, and he pays their rent on time. None of the bank employees have informed him, and the general public was never made aware of the transaction."

"Her sister lives near here?"

"No, in the mid-West. There's a younger sister no one has heard from in years."

"The twists and turns of kismet," Deedra muttered.

"Remember, I'm taking you out to dinner tomorrow night. Aaron said you'd be at the store. I aim to pick you up before dark."

"Right. Only I'm not really up to dancing, so that part of our date is on hold, but the barbecue sounds great." Actually, it didn't. Deedra's appetite had dwindled, and she felt slightly queasy. The nurse had told her it might be the side affect of the medicine, but Deedra was certain it was something she picked up from her dip in the swamp. She still shuddered each time she thought of it, of the slime that clung tenaciously to her face and body, how it had filled her ears and nose. She dreaded having to return to the old store where glances out the window would be a constant reminder.

Because of the security of just being in the hospital, Deedra slept like a young child, curled up with her knees drawn toward her chin, and had no dreams of the gooey swamp nor of the dreaded rats.

WHEN THE DEPUTY left her at the store after he'd started the fires and had checked to make certain things were not disturbed, Deedra made tea and with a plate of cheese and crackers, went to work faxing Clete the feature story she'd promised. Since she had been thinking about it for several hours, the words spilled out and the chore was completed in half an hour.

The weather had regressed into a winter rain, then turned to an icy rain, and that to sleet. By noon icy tendrils hung from the pines, and caused a glitter across the graveled road. The lake had a dull, dark looking surface, almost an ominous look, and where it merged into the swamp, a greenish tint that faded into that thick sludge.

Despite the weather, Harriet and Jocelyn made a visit just before lunchtime.

This time Harriet presented her with a slice of chocolate cream pie. The two huddled next to the fireplace, holding their hands toward the flames to get them warm.

"Deedra, dear, I saw Aaron arrive here in the middle of the night and help you into the car. You weren't at home all yesterday, and then I heard that you were ill and in the hospital! If you were ill, dear, why didn't you call one of us to help you?"

Deedra was aware that Harriet probably knew the whole gruesome story, but out of politeness, went ahead and explained anyway.

The women stared at each other, speechless it seemed, after she finished telling them about her grisly adventure.

Harriet had obviously been clued in. "I understand This skeleton is that of a woman who disappeared from Brockton three years ago, and not the companion of the woman who visited Rufus two years ago?"

Deedra nodded. "So I've been informed."

"Do you think that means that the other woman is still in the swamp?" Harriet threw Jocelyn a nervous glance.

Deedra stared at them and decided to be blunt. "Probably. Not only that, there are other persons missing besides the four whose bodies have been recovered. Two missing women from Brockton, three women have vanished after stopping at that grocery and gas station at that junction south of Rufus. And a teenage girl and boy from up near Brockton."

"Oh, my goodness! Surely they're not all in the swamp?" Jocelyn whimpered, her face pale, her lips trembling.

Deedra shook her head. "No, I don't think so."

The women appeared stunned though Harriet's eyes had narrowed as if she was recalling things from the past. Harriet, more than anyone at Percifal, was the most knowledgeable, knew the families, their habits, where they lived and worked…and perhaps the scandals that had surfaced about them many years earlier.

Vaguely, Deedra entertained the notion that Harriet had the solution to this ghastly puzzle, that given a hint in the right direction, she could provide a vital clue.

Outside, the rain turned warmer, and the iciness melted causing rivulets of water to rush toward the lake. A winter wind began flailing tree branches and rattling gutter troughs.

"This weather is certainly mercurial," Deedra remarked, throwing another log on the fire. She filled the other stove with pellets. With her back toward the women, it gave them an opportunity to view her head wound.

"Oh, my!" Jocelyn gasped. "We didn't realize how hurt you are!"

Deedra turned to them with a grimness they hadn't witnessed earlier. "He isn't going to get away with it! There's no statute of limitations on murders, you know. And this damn creep tried to kill me!"

Her tone frightened Jocelyn who got up and scurried to the door. In times of fear and stress, Jocelyn retreated.

Harriet reluctantly joined her at the door. "We hope you'll feel better soon, Deedra. It might be wise not to go out at night now. The person who did this to you will be very disappointed that his attempt has failed." Harriet ushered Jocelyn out ahead of her and quietly shut the door.

EIGHT

BRADLEY ARRIVED AROUND 4:00, just before the darkness of that winter day. By 4:30 on this cold Thursday between Thanksgiving and Christmas headlights were needed. The rain had turned into a steady drizzle, the road sloppy with puddles.

Deedra had packed an overnight bag and her laptop, Brad carried them out to the car. Since it was still too early for dinner, Brad took her to his home, the home he had inherited from his parents, a large rambling house with comfortable furniture and the latest in appliances. Bradley's study was filled with books and the paraphernalia of a journalist, a computer setup with fax, scanner and two printers.

"I've got to go back to the office, need to see to a few things for tomorrow's delivery. I think you'll be comfortable here. Feel free to make coffee, whatever."

Aaron phoned to make certain she had arrived. She told him about Harriet's and Jocelyn's visit, and of Jocelyn's fearful reaction.

"You think she might suspect Claude?" Aaron asked.

"I'm not sure. I just know she is afraid. I realize people get uneasy about things like finding skeletons close to home, but her fear is basic, like someone who has been threatened."

"That so? Guess I need to pay more attention to Claude's alibis at the times those women disappeared. Didn't find anything the first time though, and believe me, we tried."

Deedra sighed. "What about the truck drivers? I haven't seen them around lately."

"No, they're on long hauls to the east coast. There's no way one of them could have thrown you into the swamp, and they weren't in the vicinity when the four latest victims met their fates. I doubt they know anything that goes on here. They don't take a newspaper, aren't here longer than two or three days at a time. They live here because the rent in cheap, expenses at a minimum. It's a place to hang their hats and receive mail."

When Bradley got home at 6:30, Deedra was ready to go out to dinner. Being in a different environment had eased her fears and suddenly she felt hungry.

The restaurant was located fifteen miles north of Brockton in a mountainous area where the scattered homes were nearly half mile from the nearest neighbors. A junction leading to the interstate was just north of Brockton, and it was where Bradley turned off the main thoroughfare onto a country road. Trees lined the road making it shadowy and slightly mysterious in the early darkness.

The restaurant, however, was well lighted, the parking lot crowded with vehicles, mostly of the SUV type. Western music thrummed from a loud speaker and even before entering, Deedra wanted to tap her feet to the steady rhythm. Spicy smells wafted from the swinging doors as patrons entered and left. There was life and laughter here. Deedra felt her spirits lifting, the depression dropping away. An evening out was just what she needed to bring her thoughts back into focus.

Bradley had reserved a table in a far corner with a modicum of privacy, where they could talk and still hear the music, see the entertainers. And they avoided mention of the murders and her dip into the swamp.

Deedra was alarmed at finding herself suddenly exhausted, weaker than she had imagined and though he didn't mention it, Bradley took note, and they left earlier than planned. Deedra could scarcely stay awake on the ride back to Rufus.

If Bradley had thought there might be a romantic interlude, he was surely disappointed. Deedra collapsed on the bed in the guest room after taking off her shoes and dress. She didn't hear Bradley's "goodnight" from outside the bedroom door.

She awoke remembering it was Friday, and that she was to return to the old store that day. Bradley had already gone to work, leaving her a note that he would return around noon to take her back to Percifal.

She felt uneasy about returning to that dismal place though knew she couldn't object, couldn't let Aaron and Brad see her fraidy-cat side. She shook her head wondering once again if the reputation she had earned as a tough reporter was really worth the extra bucks in her paycheck. Then recalled the fact that she just might have need of all those greenbacks if she had to grow old alone.

"Damn Deke Thomas anyway!" she muttered, knowing he had robbed her of self-assurance, that she was now afraid she might never get married and have a family. She tried to analyze her feelings about Deke. Was she still in love with him? No, she reflected, she was not, she was merely angry with him, and when she tried to bring his face into focus, she failed. "So much for that!"

She checked in with Clete, learned that the media had descended, and that they had replayed her part in solving the murders at North Ledge and the Awful Abbey. A top ten magazine was offering her big money for an article about her experiences.

"They want an exclusive, of course, but can't prevent your appearance on the talk show circuit," Clete informed her.

"Damn disgusting how one gets to be a celebrity!" Deedra muttered.

"Well, it's five minutes of fame, then some other tragedy will occupy the media. I am sending Bryce Paxton up there with a cameraman. We want some exclusives taken from inside that old store, shots of the old store and the cabins of Percifal. The lake and swamp, of course. You know the drill...and please, you and Bryce try to act like colleagues, try not to maim each other!" He hung up before Deedra could object.

Aaron phoned to make certain that Brad was going to take her home. "Make sure that he gives you that protective item! I don't want you out there without one, and I can't give you one!" The tone of his voice told her not to object, that he would make certain Bradley did as instructed, and that Aaron was taking a chance by advising her to obtain a gun. Aaron was going out on a limb for her.

Brad arrived with hamburgers, fries, and milkshakes that they consumed before going to Percifal. Just before they left the house, Brad gave her the gun. It was an older Smith & Wesson, but would suffice if the occasion presented itself. Deedra was certain it wouldn't, at least not while she was inside the old store anyway. The killer would scarcely bring suspicion on himself by limiting the suspects to those living in Percifal...unless he was dumber than she imagined. However, people did unexpected things, sometimes without rhyme or reason, and her surviving his attempt to kill her might cause the killer to do something drastic.

The drizzle continued, swollen, bruised-looking clouds hung low overhead as if slowly sinking. It was a dismal day, a gray day, the lake smooth and the color of slate, the swamp the texture and color of decaying weeds.

Deedra shuddered as they drove past the place where she had dragged the old skeleton from the murky depths.

Brad noticed, and gave her a sympathetic look. "If it really gets to you, remember you can always stay at my place."

"Thanks, Brad. It's reassuring to know there's someone I can depend on."

"Hey, look there! A car right in front of your steps, and a couple of media vans parked in front."

"Just what I needed to add spice to my dull life!" Deedra muttered.

Deedra stepped from the car just as camera flashes streaked into the dismal mist. Bryce Paxton stood on the porch awaiting her arrival. He gave her a scowl, "Do you always create stories?" As if she had made up the scenario to fit some script. He gestured the cameraman into action.

Deedra introduced Brad to Bryce who simply nodded as one does when meeting a delivery person, or a passing stranger. Deedra was aware that Bryce felt himself somewhat superior to men of what he considered lesser stature. Raised by wealthy parents in a house full of four sisters, he had developed a swagger of male pride. It was his egotism that made Deedra gnash her teeth.

Deedra threw Brad an apologetic look, and turned to the media people who had waited for her to give them an interview. An NBC anchor from a local affiliate asked for a photo of her wounded head, and she answered his direct questions. Then after a few minutes begged off with, "The concussion has given me the nuisance of a headache, so I hope you'll excuse me now?" She waved to the cameraman and scurried into the old store through the open door Brad was holding for her and quickly shut, but not before Bryce slipped inside.

"Give me a cup of coffee, Deedra, and we'll be on our way back," Bryce demanded.

"I'll make it," Bradley hurried into the kitchen. "Perhaps Bryce can start the fires, it's very cold in here."

Bryce obviously resented the order, but dared not object. He was honestly shocked by Deedra's pallor. "Damn cold in this…ah…hovel," he snarled.

"Just be glad you don't get these kind of assignments, Bryce. It's big bonuses for a lot of scut work, and sometimes you have to live on the edge of…ah…doubtful shelter."

Brad returned with a cup of coffee for her, and indicated Bryce was to fetch his own.

Bryce spent only a few minutes downing the coffee, grunted thanks, and went away. The sound of the departing news car echoed around the room.

They looked at each other and laughed.

"Can you imagine Bryce pulling a skeleton out of that swamp? You'd be visiting him at the psychiatric ward," Brad said.

"He just isn't right for real investigative work, though Clete seems to think he might develop a knack for it in time. He might manage it doing virtual reality though," Deedra couldn't help adding the snide remark.

Brad wasn't up on virtual reality computer stuff, and Deedra knew he was puzzled by her last remark.

"What type of news does he cover?" Brad asked

"Mostly business, politicians, local crime. He likes to work from 8:00 to 5:00, stop at the club for a drink with the boys on his way home. He wants to be a news anchor for one of the networks, I must say, he does have the looks for it."

"Is he married?"

"I think he and his second wife are still married, but separated."

Brad replenished the fires, made certain she had food for her evening meal, and reluctantly left her there.

Clete phoned at 4:30. "Just making sure you're all right. Bryce tells me your head wound looks serious. Explains your hospital stay. I thought Aaron was just trying to keep you out of harm's way."

Deedra frowned. Surely Clete wasn't going to protest the hospital costs? "I still have a bad headache if that's what you mean, and I'm working on another human interest thing. It's dark here and that damn fog has sneaked in again. Aaron put new locks on the doors and I'm in for the night."

Clete must have picked up on her grouchy mood for his tone softened, and he wished her a goodnight. She guessed that he would probably call Aaron later.

She settled down in front of the fireplace with fragrant candles burning on either side. Their fragrance helped cover up the smell of damp vacancy...and the rats. Though she had only seen that one, she was constantly on the lookout, suspected they had taken up residence in the basement. That they scuttled between the old gas station, stealing garbage from the large dumpster there, and then back to the store. "Rat haven," she muttered. The dumpster was emptied once a month and evidently the residents shared the costs for she had seen Neil Landen empty garbage there.

Hearing a noise near the back door, she cautiously went to find out what caused it, never remembering to take the gun Aaron had insisted she have. The back porch light didn't reveal the cause though she noticed that the stack of cardboard boxes had been moved again. Probably the men who had replaced the locks. The cellar door was still padlocked and nothing else seemed disturbed. Could have been old Claude up to his spying tricks again, she mused.

She was about to turn out the light when she noticed a dab of mud close to the cellar door. The mud looked damp as if it hadn't been there long. On closer examination, she saw a faint imprint of a shoe or boot. It, too, was still damp.

Brad had checked out here, but only long enough to make certain the back door was locked. He didn't go near the cellar door, and since he'd been at the newspaper most of the day, probably didn't have any mud on his shoes.

Perhaps it had been one of the men who changed the locks, but that had been three days ago, and the mud would have dried by now.

She studied the lock. The light wasn't bright enough to detect any fresh scratches, and she couldn't tell if it had been unlocked in the last few hours. She would have to inspect it again in the morning when there was better illumination.

With a cup of tea she again settled in front of the fireplace. Her head ached in a dull monotonous way that prevented reading the new novel, and tried concentrating on a TV program. Though her gaze was on the screen, her thoughts were not, busy instead assembling myriad bits of information on the murders. Were the two skeletons victims of the same serial killer as the latest four? Had the skeletons been accident victims, a car gone into the lake that no one knew about? No. Marian Mosner's car had been found alongside the highway. Somehow her body had been transported and deposited in the swamp. Again the notion that all the missing persons had ended up in the swamp seized her. An involuntary shudder shook her. No wonder Jocelyn was a nervous, anxious person. Was Emma Randolph's psychological trauma caused by fear of the swamp? Had Emma witnessed something quite dreadful, something other than her own near drowning in the lake?

The program ended and the news suddenly attracted her attention when a picture of her getting out of Bradley's car showed on the screen. There was a brief glimpse of her head wound, surprising her with its look of vented savagery. The killer was very angry with her.

A shiver slid down her spine as she realized why Aaron insisted that she have a gun. The killer, if the opportunity presented itself, would make certain next time.

Instead of going to bed, she huddled close to the fire, arranging pillows behind her against the hearth, and a heavy quilt over her. She kept the fire going through the night, alert to any sound, the gun under one of the pillows. Inner vibes warned her of the killer's anger, she could sense it, almost feel it, and she was certain he feared her. Why did her presence pose a threat to the killer?

Through the night the mud and faint trace of a shoe

print kept recurring in her thoughts, even when she had started to analyze her feelings about Bradley...and Aaron.

Brad was a colleague, understood the workings of a news reporter, and therefore understandable about the rapport. Aaron excited her, intrigued her. He was not as handsome as Bradley, probably not as wealthy because Brad had received a substantial inheritance. They were both respected in this part of the world, both dedicated to their professions. But if anything developed, could she abandon her career to live up here in this mountainous area and be content? Only, she mused, if the prospect of a family was more conducive than years and years of chasing after the "big" stories. She could always write novels and non-fiction articles, her files were filled with ideas and research on sometimes little-known subjects. She wanted a home and children.

And without conscious thought, she was once again thinking of the mud around the cellar door, the notion lingering after daylight was long gone. Instead of getting dressed, she took the flashlight and with the overhead light on, studied the padlock on the cellar door. Proximity to the cellar brought back images of rats, and she began to experience a creepy, tingly sensation.

There were fresh scratches in the grime on the padlock. Someone had unlocked that padlock in recent days. She glanced up and caught Claude peering through the window near the back door.

She waved at him and stood up.

Claude immediately retreated.

Not wanting Claude to become too interested in the padlock, she turned off the light and went into the bedroom where she dressed in jeans and sweatshirt.

Wondering where the key to the padlock was she

returned to the porch. A search of the rooms met with failure, but some imp of curiosity drove her to search the rest of the old store for the key. It was strange that it wasn't there, strange the cellar was locked like that. Surely the cellar hadn't been padlocked in the days when the store was open, the stairs inside the building.

She didn't find the key and decided to ask Harriet about it sometime.

Aaron phoned. "No visitors during the night?"

"Claude checked a time or two."

"I wonder if he has insomnia?" Aaron muttered.

"Does seem strange, but everyone thinks he's harmless enough." Deedra recalled Claude peering into the back porch window.

"Everyone home today?"

"Dwight and the Landens went out earlier, and I think the Black boys are gone."

"I've been checking on Dwight, but he seldom goes anywhere other than the grocery store. Does his food ordering by phone. We've been checking on the salesmen who travel this territory again. Only one of them was even in the area when Darlene Hernandez vanished, and from his appointment schedule, didn't have time to kidnap her, and deposit her body along the highway four days later. None of them were in this county when you were heaved into the swamp. That perp had to be from Percifal or a place nearby. We've been kind of watching the highway with some special surveillance cameras and haven't seen anything unusual or any strangers. Trouble is, we didn't have it set up near the swamp so it didn't catch a glimpse of whoever attacked you. It's tricky anyway, has to be installed on a power pole or traffic light. There isn't a place to do that out there at least not without being noticed. We don't need any invasion of privacy lawsuits. People like to watch candid camera, but they sure as hell hate it when they're the objects being watched. Can't say I blame them, gives a fella paranoia. Besides, its too expensive.''

"I don't think this killer is into technology, isn't actually seeking out victims, just lets them cross his path," Deedra remarked.

"Yeah, and that's what makes apprehending him so difficult. He just goes about his usual way letting chance present itself.''

"Any chance Neil Landen could be the perpetrator? He has the opportunity to meet these people, could hold them hostage somewhere in that hardware store. I understand Marsha only works part-time and some days doesn't go in at all.''

"Yeah, we've taken a look at that. Could happen, but the conditions would have to be just right. Neil would have to be at the store alone, have to be able to conceal the victim for a few hours. He parks his car in the alley behind the store. Wouldn't attract any attention by that. There's a basement storeroom, an upstairs break room and an office where Neil talks to salesmen. I haven't been up there in years, but I recall an office, storerooms off to one side, and a bathroom. Perhaps another small room. He could conceal a person there, I suppose, with no one the wiser.''

"Well, whoever did this had to have kept Darlene Hernandez hidden for those four days," Deedra reminded.

"I thought you had Clete's place picked out for that?" Aaron teased.

"Yes, I think she might have been there part of that time. It would have been simple for Neil to deposit her at Clete's on his way home.''

"Then," Aaron sighed, "dispose of her on his way home from work another time."

"Yes. The opportunities fit. He might even have left Marsha at the store while he ran an errand, whatever. None of the victims disappeared on a weekend, a time when the hardware store is the busiest and Marsha there with Neil there most of the time."

"Makes sense. Try to get Harriet's take on Neil. Harriet went to school with Marsha."

"Really? I thought Marsha was several years younger?"

Aaron laughed. "Having no children Marsha has spent a lot of time on her looks. Had a face-lift and the works. Harriet can probably fill you in on the details since being a man, I don't fully comprehend."

After warning her to keep her doors locked, Aaron rang off. He didn't tell her to use the gun if necessary, but his tone of voice implied it. She realized he thought the killer considered her a danger to his freedom.

She was standing at the wide front window overlooking the lake and swamp when Clete phoned.

"Just checking on your state of health."

"Slight headache and still grouchy. Otherwise, okay. Aaron and I have been kicking a theory around that Neil Landen could be the killer." She went on to explain. "What do you know about Neil?"

"He went to Rufus High with the rest of us. Serious-minded, not into sports. Worked in that hardware store after school. Man named Simmons owned it then. After college, Neil returned and bought that store. Remained a bachelor for about ten years, then suddenly married Marsha."

"Did Marsha work in that store at that time?"

"Don't know. I was down here working on this newspaper. Only made sporadic trips to Rufus."

"You think Neil is a good candidate for serial killer?" There was a pause on Clete's end. "Might be. He's not the type to stand out in a crowd. Polite but aloof. Right age. A loner in his younger years. Dwight would also fit that profile though the opportunities would be very limited. The same could be said of Melvyn since he does travel the area every day. Has Aaron checked out his schedule?"

"Yes, and he's double-checked everyone. Melvyn has a regular route and the times don't seem to jibe, he made his deliveries as scheduled." Deedra paused. "Ivan and Shelia don't seem to fit in around here. Very reserved, together all the time,"

"I don't know anything about them. New to the area, I suspect. Aaron has undoubtedly checked them out. What has Harriet to say about them?"

"I don't recall that she's said anything. They're a handsome couple. Wave when they drive by."

"Well, find out!" Clete hung up.

Not wanting to give the residents the idea that she was now afraid to venture out, she put on a heavy jacket. Then suddenly realized that her swamp-wet clothing was missing. She checked the washer and dryer. Empty. Aaron must have disposed of them or taken them as evidence of the attack on her. She hated to part with that particular jacket, it was warmer than the one she wore now, and of a style she preferred.

The weather had turned colder, the sky clear and a crystalline blue. Ice crystals crunched under her feet as she strolled past the cabins. Smoke drifted upward from all the cabins except the Black brothers'. They were gone again.

When she reached Lance Fenton's house, he stepped onto the porch.

"Been looking for you. I have fresh coffee and conversation."

Deedra nodded, climbing the recently installed stairs. "Just what I need. Weaker than I thought."

"I suspected that. Your step was a mite slower and less energetic."

Deedra gratefully sank onto the sofa. The room was warm and comforting.

"You're quite pale. Sure you should be out expending all that bravado?" His eyes probed hers.

"Probably not, but I mustn't let the residents know I'm afraid of one of them." Deedra sipped the coffee gratefully.

"So you and Aaron have narrowed it down to Percifal?"

"Or nearby. I don't rule out Travis Tucker."

Lance raised his eyebrows, then they slid into a slight frown. "Travis? Really?

Deedra nodded. "He lives on that side of the swamp, and walks as softly as a cat. Never heard a thing before I was hit. And sound echoes in heavy fog. He's also strong enough to have thrown me into the swamp."

Lance nodded, obviously considering if Travis Tucker fit into the role of serial killer.

Deedra let the pause lengthen before asking, "What do you know about Ivan and Shelia Wallace?"

"Harriet hasn't given you a run down?" Lance grinned.

Deedra shook her head.

"They run an accounting business. Both are C.P.A.'s. They have a small list of clients and spend the required eight hours at their offices. Live out here because they don't want to get involved with clubs and community groups in Rufus. Ivan said in a few years they'd take a world tour and decide where to put down roots.''

"Their business can't be that lucrative?''

"It can if you've invested in solid stocks and sold when the market was way up there. In fact, it was at Ivan's suggestion that I sell and get out. I was planning to and he told me not to hesitate. So I'm okay, and they are very rich.''

"And they still live out here?'' Deedra received the impression that Shelia would like the good life, demand it, from resorts to the latest fashions.

"Ivan said it was better and wiser these days not to flaunt it.. At first I thought he was referring to clients or the possibility of robbery, then I realized he might have been referring to the I.R.S., and I decided against further questioning. What I don't know, I don't write about,'' he grinned.

"Though it leads to speculation,'' Deedra suggested.

"Sometimes. It's the spice of life that hints of danger in novels. People want to live on the edge in their reading habits, but stay in the safety zone of reality.''

"Yeah, right,'' Deedra laughed. Lance knew as well as she did that some people lived out their fantasies and sometimes those ideas sprouted from books and movies. Long gone were the days when youngsters played cowboys, all wanting to wear the white Stetson, not the black.

"Tell me about your worst ever adventure the other night,'' Lance asked.

Deedra described the dreadful time in detail, knowing Lance wanted to know how she felt, what it felt like with that awful ooze around her, the difficulty of walking in it…and her terror at finding the skeleton hooked onto her jacket. All details for the grist of Lance's writing skills.

They spent another half hour talking about writing, plots for stories, and at Lance's request, the pursuit of the "big" stories.

It was when Lance asked her to tell him about her dreams that Deedra hastened away. No one had the right to know about her dreams, and she was not about to share them with a famous author like Lance Fenton. He tried to apologize, but she was still unhinged by the latest trauma, and was not about to let Lance Fenton witness her tears of fear and distress. Her internal battles were her own, to share them would mean to give away part of her inner self and give other people the advantage of knowing her weaknesses. It was not a wise thing to do for a "tough" reporter. Besides, she had a headache and felt really grouchy.

Harriet waylaid her, stepped off her porch to intercept her before she could reach the store.

"I see you're out on your usual morning walk. Lance Fenton seems to have taken a shine to you. He seldom bothers with the rest of us." Was there disapproval in her voice?

"Yes, he's quite friendly. Knowledgeable about the stock market."

"Has he any theories about the murders?" Harriet was definitely suspicious.

"We really didn't talk about the murders, more about my being heaved into the swamp and what that was like," Deedra muttered.

Harriet evidently picked up on her cross vibes and after a sharp glance, changed the subject. "Dwight is home this morning, or I'd invite you in for coffee. He has the afternoon and evening shift today. Doesn't often have that shift, thank goodness. I like having him home evenings.''

"Thank you, anyway. I have a headache and really need to lie down. Why don't you visit me this afternoon? I'll have fresh coffee." Deedra recalled Clete's order to find out what Harriet knew about Ivan and Shelia Wallace.

Harriet arrived at 2:30, almost bursting with curiosity, with a plate of fresh baked cookies.

Deedra wondering what had stirred Harriet's curiosity now, opened the door with a smile, graciously accepted the plate of cookies, placing them beside the coffee things set out on a makeshift plastic crate table. She apologized for her crude furniture.

"I'll bet you'll be glad to get back to your real home, Deedra. Isn't your vacation over?"

"Yes, Sunday, but I may have to extend my visit to get the legal papers about that attack on me signed, and get the doctor's release. The swamp water may have infected my head wound, they want to make sure it hasn't before I leave."

"My, how long do they think it will take to know?" Harriet seemed perturbed at this news, though whether it was concern about Deedra or the fact that she wouldn't be leaving very soon was debatable.

"Probably fourteen days. They've given me protective doses of antibiotics, of course, and I suspect that's all I'll need, but no one knows what bacteria thrives in that old pond."

"Makes me shudder just to think of it," Harriet remarked.

"I haven't seen much of Ivan and Shelia...ah.... is their last name Wallace?"

"Yes. Wallace. They aren't the sociable kind, and

don't feel the need to be real friendly. Declined our invitations to barbecue get-togethers here at Percifal earlier in the summer. I do understand they've become very rich with some stock market investments. Wouldn't surprise me if they move away soon. Shelia's never been happy living here. Her parent's live in New York so naturally she thinks of Percifal as the end of the world. I could never understand why people from there thought all places should copy them. If they did, then why would New York be so special?''

Deedra grinned. Harriet, the unintentional philosopher. "Yep. If every city copied New York, that big old apple wouldn't radiate like it does now."

"Anyway, I suspect the Wallace's will be moving on very soon. Finding those skeletons has been upsetting enough for those of us who have lived in Percifal for eons, but to a fidgety couple like Ivan and Shelia, it probably is very difficult to cope."

"I imagine so. Is Ivan from this part of the country?

"Oh, yes. I thought you knew. His mother died when he was a young lad and his father hanged himself a year or two later. He stayed with an uncle in Brockton until he went into the military. Then he went to college, married Shelia, and resettled here. Shelia once said he'd wanted to be a stockbroker, but there wasn't enough interest in that in Rufus. What he meant, I'm sure, is that there isn't the wealth needed to support that type of investment. Rufus isn't a poor town, but it certainly doesn't have residents of considerable wealth either. Those that have it have moved away."

"I'd think the Landens and the Wallaces would be close friends, both in business in Rufus and neighbors here."

"Well, Shelia just isn't used to our country ways,

she's not the 'exchange recipes' type. Guess when you've grown up sophisticated you miss some of the folksy stuff!'' Harriet smoothed her perfectly ironed dress.

"What do you think about all these murders, Harriet? You've so savvy about this part of the world, know about people here and where they're from and going. Do you ever get a hint that you suspect a special person who fits the profile of killer?''

Harriet blinked, then as the notion settled in, her eyes darkened with a flash of insight that she quickly masked, but not so quickly that Deedra missed the indication that Harriet did have her suspicions. Harriet opened her mouth to say something just as Jocelyn knocked on the door. She clamped her mouth shut with a slight audible sound.

NINE

WHEN DEEDRA OPENED the door, Jocelyn gushed, "Would you tell Harriet that Dwight called and said he'd be about a half-hour late. Something about overseeing a late shipment."

"Won't you come in and have coffee with us?"

"Can't. Claude is home and this is our day on the Internet." With that Jocelyn skittered hurriedly back to her house like something was chasing her. Claude, Deedra mused, was the type of man that decided young women against marriage.

Harriet left rather abruptly, almost as if she was afraid Deedra would pursue the question of whom she thought might fit the role of killer, as if there would be danger in even hinting at it.

She watched as Harriet quickly covered the space between the store and her house, and wondered if Dwight had really phoned or if Claude had sent Jocelyn to break up their conversation. All the residents were now aware that she was a newspaper reporter and wouldn't want Deedra to learn of their eccentricities...or of their secrets.

Deedra replenished the fires and as she carried in enough wood to last through the night, glanced again at the padlock on the cellar door. After filling the wood box, she went back and once again examined the cellar

door and the padlock. There were definite signs that the
door had been opened recently. Could it have been
Dwight, who might have left personal items stored
there?

Suddenly she needed to see what was in that cellar.
Even visions of rats receded under the need to find out
what was down there. She would need a bolt cutter and
a new padlock and that meant a trip to Brockton, not
wanting to purchase them at Neil Landen's hardware,
not wanting to alert him that she needed a cutting tool
like that.

But it was getting dark, and she dared not leave the
store building now. The next day was Sunday, would a
hardware or rental place be open? She would just have
to wait, but an unexpected urgency nagged at her. She
paced about restlessly, unable to concentrate on the
novel or television, though left the television on for anyone to hear who snooped about outside. She checked
the doors and windows again, put an extra towel over
the bathroom window screened by a thin tattered shade,
and continued to wander about like a boat adrift in a
swirling current.

When Bradley arrived with chicken dinners she was
shaky and had to calm herself by clenching her teeth
and pinching her arm.

"You seem nervous this evening, Deedra. Did something happen?"

"No, nothing unusual. Just shaky from my wounds,
can't seem to get warm enough. Just reaction. This meal
will certainly help."

"My offer still stands, you know. You can stay at
my house as long as you're here." Brad reminded.

"Thanks, but I can't have the neighbors gossiping,
might ruin my reputation," she smiled. "Seriously,

Brad, I can't run from this, and I'm sure Aaron would be disappointed if I did, and I know Clete would be. Clete expects a story and if I don't get it he'll send someone else. Reporting isn't without its risks, you know.''

Brad nodded and changed the subject. ''Do you intend to stay here until Aaron arrests someone?''

''Not sure. Depends on if and who, I guess. If he has a suspect in mind, I don't have a clue to who that is.''

Brad frowned. ''Funny. I thought Aaron had evidence against someone.''

''Did Aaron say that?'' Deedra felt a tingling at the base of her skull.

''Not in so many words, just a hint that he was following up on a lead.''

The tingle subsided. ''Oh. Forensics might have learned something from one of the dead women. The reports weren't all in last time I heard. Sandy Nevin's body might have produced something for DNA. Do you know if they found the murder weapon?''

''Haven't found it, but think it was baling twine like found on Priscilla's body.''

Again the tingle of the hairs on her neckline, the sensation that she had already viewed the source of that twine in one of the stalls on Clete's place. She did not, however, tell Brad about it. Later, she wondered about that omission.

Harriet told me that Ivan's mother died when he was quite young and that his father had committed suicide. I didn't read about that in the old newspaper articles.''

''What?''

''Ivan Wallace. There wasn't any mention of his young life in the files.''

Brad frowned. "Strange. And this is the first I've heard of it."

"I guess he went to live with an uncle in Brockton, so he probably went to school there, too."

Brad continued to frown.

"Is there," Deedra asked, "a chance that he changed his name, took his uncle's name?"

"I don't know, but I intend to find out." Brad only stayed a few minutes after that statement, leaving her with the impression that he was troubled by something. Brad was secretive in a way, probably a characteristic of the news reporter, she mused. Had her question about Ivan Wallace reminded him of something that happened long ago?

Aaron phoned around 9:00. "I hear you're having some shaky reaction. You all right now?" There was a hint of worry in his voice.

"Yes, of course," she lied.

"Um. Tell you what. I'm off duty now and I need to get away from my phone for awhile. Is it too late for a visit?"

Deedra smiled. "Not for someone who has already spent the night here!"

"Is that another invitation?" Aaron hung up before she could reply.

Despite her anxiety Deedra found herself humming, excited at the prospect of seeing Aaron again…out of uniform. He seemed much more compassionate, unrestrained by professional ethics, a regular guy. She debated whether to tell him about the cellar door and padlock and what she intended to do about it. She was still undecided when Aaron arrived.

The weather had turned colder, a light rain spattered

the cars and buildings and with no moon or stars, the night was dark and dreary.

"Let me look at you?" Aaron turned her toward the light after shutting the door behind him. "Hm. Pale, dark circles, lovely mouth. A kissable mouth." Aaron followed through on that statement, and for several moments they were locked in a pulse-racing embrace.

"I think you're going to be okay," he said, leading her toward the sofa where they sat with his arm around her in a comforting way, the smell of his after-shave a tantalizing aroma that aroused nesting instincts.

For several minutes they just huddled against each other, not talking, just taking strength and comfort from the moment.

"Have you ever thought of marriage?" Aaron asked when the chemistry began to sizzle.

"Yes."

"And?"

"I want a home and family."

"What, no husband?"

"Of course, that first. A man who understands who I am and what I am, and that at times I will feel the urge to write, write, write."

"That's all the man needs to be eligible?" Aaron began running his fingertips across her face, over her lips, down her neck.

"Not all, of course. He needs to have all the qualities of a certain law enforcement officer I know."

Aaron's fingers played a tune of desire on her face and lips. "Could this tough investigative reporter give up the career that makes her special for this man?"

"Depends on the offer of when, where, and how many children?" she quipped.

"Since when did children get to be a negotiable factor?" Aaron teased.

"Because that has to be in the final agreement," Deedra sighed.

The moment had aroused them and probably would have led them into actions beyond their control if Claude hadn't slipped and fallen down on the front porch causing a loud crashing noise then a muttered groan into the midst of their privacy.

"Damn!" Aaron muttered as he released her and stomped to the front door.

Claude was lying face down on the front porch though he was not seriously hurt for he began to struggle to his feet. Aaron helped him inside, quite against Claude's wishes.

"No, Aaron, I don't need any help. Just slipped. Damn porch is wet from the rain. No need for you to see me home, would just upset Jocelyn."

But Aaron was just as insistent and walked Claude back to his cabin. Their romantic mood had been destroyed, however, and Aaron was obviously annoyed and disappointed.

"I DON'T KNOW HOW that murderer disposed of all those victims around here without Claude's observation. Unless Claude is the killer." Aaron paced around the room. "I suppose it's not appropriate to spend another night here!"

"It seems rather awkward now. We'd know people knew and it would take away the sweetness of discovery," Deedra murmured.

Aaron stared at her. "Yeah. Right. It has to be a different time and different place." He replenished the fires, kissed her a long time, and departed.

The sound of the car's engine was a lonely sound echoing through the dark night.

It was midnight, the mysterious witching hour.

Instead of seeking her sleeping bag on the bed, Deedra again huddled close to the fire, dozing and waking, keeping the fires going and longing for the central heating of her own apartment. In a dozing state it occurred to her that Claude might have staged the fall on the porch to prevent the inevitable between she and Aaron. Why? He did seem to have appointed himself as protector with his call to Brad about her wandering toward Travis Tucker's place, his checking around the old store, and now this. She wondered what had started Claude in his snooping ways. Had he witnessed something he didn't understand, or was it from something he noted in Jocelyn's paintings? Was he trying to learn if Jocelyn had just used her imagination, or had actually seen scary things in and around the swamp? There might be earlier paintings, more explicit ones, pictures that were kept out of sight. Was it possible that Claude and Jocelyn held the clue to the vile events that were held secreted in the swamp?

Despite these ponderings she drifted into a deep sleep, roused only when the room began to take on a damp chill, and was filled with early morning light.

Rebuilding the fires again, she ran a tub of hot water. She was still in the tub when Aaron arrived.

"Just a minute," she called out, scrambling into a bathrobe and slippers.

"Hope I'm not too early to take you out for breakfast?" Aaron eyed her with gleaming interest and she wouldn't have been a bit surprised if he intended to follow her back into the bathroom.

"Sounds great. Just let me get dressed."

"Don't take too long, I'm very hungry."

Deedra heard him putting wood on the fires, then the sound of footsteps as he went out to the shed and re-filled the wood box on the back porch. She half-expected him to enter the bathroom for a morning kiss. He did not. Evidently he'd decided not to pursue any romantic moments for the time being, causing her poignant regret. Lost moments, lost memories, lost beginnings.

"Anything new?" Deedra asked when she joined him.

"Nothing to point to your assailant. Since it was night no real way of telling who was where. There didn't seem to be any cars in the vicinity, though I'm convinced that the man was a resident of Percifal."

"You're certain of that now?"

When Aaron nodded, she asked, "Who? Claude?"

"I'm not sure, though he certainly roams around and could have seen something important. It might depend on his loyalties, whether he's willing to think of a neighbor and friend as a vicious killer or not."

"You think he'd really protect a killer?" Deedra felt a start of surprise.

"Not sure, just certain that at some time in the past few years he or Jocelyn saw something significant, whether they think it's significant or not is the question. Jocelyn is more apt to consider the consequences of small actions or words. She's rather like a frightened rabbit, hiding out, not showing people her paintings, not exploiting the opportunities to put them on display when she has real talent. Artists usually paint so people can view the beauty of things the way they see it. Just like writers who want people to read the words of their stories. Creativity is a way of expressing to the world the beauty and dark places of the human psyche."

"And how many years of psychology did you take at college?"

"My major. Only went into law enforcement as a...." Aaron stopped, grinned, and turned away. "You ready for a sumptuous breakfast?"

The restaurant was tucked away in the trees close to Rufus. It couldn't be seen from the highway, though the parking lot was filled and there was a feeling of bustling activity.

Away from the old store, Deedra's appetite returned and the breakfast of bacon, eggs and hash browns was as sumptuous as Aaron had promised. The restaurant catered to the breakfast crowd, and did not serve lunch. It opened again at 6:00 for the dinner patrons.

"I don't think I've ever heard of a restaurant that closed for lunch," Deedra remarked, pursuing thoughts of writing a feature story about this popular place.

"No, there aren't many, I suppose. Though this gives the owner and manager here the opportunity to prowl the highway during certain hours of the day. We've been checking it out."

"Oh," was all Deedra could think of to say. Aaron wasn't overlooking anything or anyone, and he was clearly observing both men during their meal, causing Deedra to realize that this just wasn't a "date." She sighed.

By the time they left the restaurant, the crowd had thinned out.

"They're closed between 11:00 and 6:00," Aaron said as he held the car door open for her. "Of course, it's Sunday and some of the regulars weren't here. I don't think any of the victims were regular customers though.''

"What about the working staff?"

"Mostly women. If any of the victims were friends or neighbors we'd at least have a place to start. This random selection is a puzzle.''

They were silent on the return to Percifal, few cars on the road. The trees looked refreshed from the cleansing rain, the atmosphere of a quiet forest scene seemed to change when they turned onto the road leading to Percifal.

There was a hushed, dismal look pronounced by the stark snags protruding from the goo-thick marsh. It was, Deedra decided, like suddenly driving into a "lost world," a time before man walked the earth. The swamp was a gray-green color under the morning's drab sky. Dense clouds had rolled in during their absence, eclipsing the sunlight, causing Percifal's dingy, dreary mien. Smoke rising from the cabin chimneys simply added to the gloomy atmosphere.

"What a bleak place this is,'' Deedra muttered when Aaron braked to a stop in front of her somber abode.

"You afraid to stay here? If you want, I can drive you into town?" Aaron frowned.

"No. Just commenting on the general landscape.''

Aaron checked the rooms to make certain no one had entered during her absence. Then after a quick kiss, drove off to his policing business, making Deedra realize this was the life he led, the life she would have to adjust to if their relationship developed into marriage. And Aaron had hinted at that, hadn't he?

After warming the house and watching Harriet and Jocelyn drive off to church, Deedra drove to Brockton. It was a town of 20,000, the county seat of Brockton

County, therefore the local government offices provided employment that kept the city surviving. The two sawmills that had thrived in the last century had long since shut down, the loggers and millwrights moving on or changing vocations.

There seemed to be three main streets that formed the downtown core with only a few open for business. At the far end of Pine Street she located a rental business…a business that seemed quite busy with its lot full of cars. Across the street was an open-for-business hardware store. She pulled into a space in front of the hardware store where her presence was less apt to attract attention.

A middle-aged man and woman were seated behind the counter, the man going over the accounts. The woman greeted her with a pleasant smile and showed her the bolt cutters whose price exceeded her expectations, and an array of new padlocks. She charged them to her own credit card, wanting no hassles about destroying other people's property, breaking and entering, etc., against the newspaper. People did like to sue businesses like her newspaper that they assumed had deep pockets.

"You a new resident around here?" The woman asked.

"No, just passing through."

Deedra purchased milk and fresh fruit from the grocery she reckoned was the one Dwight Stratton managed. A large, bright store with attractive displays and large over-head signs indicating the aisles where certain foods were located. It was a bag-it-yourself store featuring lower prices, and the aisles were filled with customers. Dwight, Deedra mused, probably earned a handsome salary here. Why didn't they move into

Brockton closer to his work? They didn't own the Percifal property, and with the dying lake, the former beauty of the place had diminished.

The stores in Brockton were decorated for the holidays, Christmas trees alight in wide storefront windows. The approaching holidays caused Deedra sadness. She was alone now, had been for several years. An only child, she'd taken care of her mother for a few years after her father's death. When her mother died she had sold the house that had been home all her life because it echoed with loneliness and haunted memories that kept her edgy and depressed, and moved into the basement apartment she now called home. Part of her tough image was her necessity to financially meet all the obligations of her mother's final illness, and to provide for herself without help. She desperately wanted a family, especially at this time of year with its carols and messages of family gatherings, and that song about "to grandmother's house we go." She wanted to create a secure home, a place of comfort for her children like the Christmas cards of old. However, she didn't want to marry someone she wasn't in love with and the holidays were poignant reminders that she hadn't found her soul mate.

The drive to Percifal was just another obligation she had to live through, if she'd had her druthers, she would have just driven by the swamp and straight back to her apartment where no one would know of her unrequited nesting urges.

Even though the drive was scenic it didn't lighten her spirits, and thought of returning to that dismal place she believed was the bone yard for the killer's victims brought on a cold chill, certain there were victims beneath the thick slime that would never be recovered.

What had caused a human being to turn into a grotesque monster?

On this Sunday there was no fog lingering over the lake and swamp, and under other situations, the area might have appeared as an interesting freak of nature. Never the less, the word "swamp" would forever cause Deedra the same type revulsion that the word rats did.

Entering the old store was a teeth gritting experience. Inside the door with her hand still on the doorknob she held very still and listened to that inner voice that had almost always alerted her to someone else's presence. But that vibe-thing merely hummed a vague restiveness. She replenished the fires and carried in more wood from the shed. She was about to make use of the bolt cutters when Lance Fenton knocked on the door.

"Lance! What a surprise! And here I've been led to believe you are something of a recluse!" She held the door open for him.

"Had to check on your writing facilities. Ah yes, a laptop, and top of the line, too." He laughed. "You aren't as remote from communication as I had feared."

"Yeah. The newspaper gave me the laptop as a bonus last year."

"I saw Aaron drive you off early this morning. Anything new on the murders?" Lance ambled about the room, glanced at the title of her novel-in-progress.

"No. We went out to breakfast."

"How's your head? Still have headaches?" Lance sat down next to her on the sofa.

"Not really. A twinge now and then."

"You're not making any progress on your novel, I see. Well, a writer can only tolerate so many interruptions and very few traumas. I am here to invite you to dinner this evening. At my house. I am a very good cook.''

Deedra experienced surprise. ''I accept with thanks. I, on the other hand, am a very poor cook. I do not really like to cook, I like to eat. My mother was the cook and I was my usual self by resisting learning her capable skills. I shall also try to glean bits of your story writing skills. Perhaps a visit with you will spur my creative urges.''

''It's not often I entertain guests, and it will no doubt irk Harriet. She wants to see how I've arranged the house and my life since my wife died. I shudder at the thought of her invading my domain.''

''Oh?''

An expression of distaste crossed Lance's usually placid features. ''It's just that she doesn't need to invade my space.''

Though Deedra was aware that there was more behind Lance's derision, she didn't quite fathom it, and let the remark pass. Perhaps, like Jocelyn, he resented her knowing everything about every thing.

Lance took another turn around the room. He emanated nervous twitches, rather like a bird undecided about which branch to perch on. It was a characteristic Deedra hadn't noted early on, an uneasiness he emanated that distracted her.

''Deedra, should you need help, signal from the back porch window. A light or white flag, something. I feel very uneasy here. Are you sure this old store isn't haunted?'' His serious look thawed into a rueful grin.

''Please don't even suggest that!'' Deedra muttered. Then to avoid letting Lance glimpse her own uneasiness, ''It could be the setting and plot for another novel though.''

Lance held perfectly still. She could almost see the gears of his thinking process mesh. "I think you have given me the plot for my next book. I must commit it to paper before the thought vanishes into that hinterland of the forgotten."

Lance hurried away without a good-bye and Deedra watched through the back porch window as he hustled along giving Harriet a "can't stop to talk now" wave.

Harriet, who had hurried down her front steps to intercept him, stood there smoothing her dress as if it needed ironing again. After a moment of indecision, she shrugged, and went back into her house.

Relieved that Harriet wasn't planning on a visit at the moment, Deedra made certain she had locked the door after Lance left, and went back to use the bolt cutters. It wasn't difficult to cut through the padlock hinge.

The door opened with a chilling creak—a squeak like a mouse caught in a trap. The steps leading downward were covered in dust-undisturbed dust-evidence that no one had gone down there recently. She played the flashlight beam down the steps to the cemented floor, then around the large room, illuminating crates and boxes stacked against the walls. It seemed reasonably clean with everything in neat order.

Seeing no rats, she ventured half-way down the steps, leaving her prints in the dust, shining the light one way then another. Nothing seemed disturbed, no rat droppings.

At the foot of the stairs she hesitated. Why spend her time here since it was obviously just a storage place. But her innate curiosity wouldn't be stilled until she had really looked at everything. She examined empty crates which had probably been used to ship vegetables and fresh fruits. The heavy cardboard boxes were another matter, sealed with packing tape. When Deedra tried to move one from atop another, found it unusually heavy, obviously containing something. Unable to resist her snooping on her own, she cut through the tape with the cutting tool.

An ancient musty smell arose from the opened box. Inside something was wrapped in a heavy plastic tarp.

A funny tingling sensation started at the base of her skull followed by a paranoid feeling. She glanced about then made a hurried trip upstairs to make certain no one was there. Funny, she mused, almost certain someone had sneaked inside. She paused to put wood on the fire—pellets in the stove—then returned to the cellar carrying a kitchen knife to cut through the heavy tarp.

At first glance she thought the box contained old clothes, but another slit by the knife revealed two mummified bodies, one on top of the other. Her heart tripped, then began a heavy beating that shook her body. She caught back the screams that would have brought Harriet on the run.

As she stared at the bodies, her numbed mind took in the fact that one was wearing male clothing, the other a female outfit. Her mind leaped...the missing teenagers? Rooted there, like in the child's game of Statue, her body weighted down with terror, her gaze seemingly hypnotized by the mummified bodies and immobilized by the horror of it. What did those other boxes contain? Unable to move, for long seconds her mind grasped at calm control, knowing she needed to notify Aaron right away, knew he wouldn't want her touching what was evidence of a ghastly crime.

Finally, her body fluids seemed to thaw and gradually the circulation returned to her legs. She slowly climbed the stairs, almost she mused, as if she had suddenly grown old. Carefully closing the cellar door, she stashed the cutting tool and new padlock in a drawer on the porch, then phoned Aaron.

Fortunately he was in his office. He sensed something wrong from her husky tone of voice and the tears she was determined not to shed.

"What?"

"I've discovered something you need to see. No questions now. Please arrive in your own car so you won't attract undue attention." Her body trembled, her hand shaking when she replaced the receiver. The headache had magnified into a really hurtful thing.

Before Aaron arrived Brad phoned, wanting to take her out for dinner.

"I can't tonight Brad. Lance Fenton has invited me to supper at his house. Can I have a rain check?" Her voice must have sounded normal for Brad didn't question her state of health.

"I suppose," Brad grumbled. "Fenton is too old for you!"

"Brad, he hasn't asked me to marry him, just to dinner. Probably gets tired of eating alone."

"Yeah, well, he'd better not make any passes!" Brad hung up.

At least Brad's call had allowed her to regain control, and the inner shaking had subsided by the time Aaron arrived.

As requested Aaron had driven his own car, and was not in uniform.

"What?" He stepped inside, a worried frown causing his eyebrows to mesh above his eyes. "You're pale as a ghost!"

"This way," she clenched her fists and fought the inner shaking that had commenced again. When she opened the creaking cellar door, the sound resonating through the house, alerting whatever wraiths lingered there.

"What the hell?" Aaron muttered, as she led him down the cellar steps and over to the box. A sort of groan escaped Aaron's lips, his face took on an ashen hue, he glanced at her and then back at the bodies. "The missing teenagers?"

"I think so," she nodded. "I haven't touched anything except to open the box and cut the tarp. What I'm worried about is, what's in those other boxes?"

Aaron grimaced, gave her a long I-hope-not look, and sliced open another box. It too, held a mummified body, that of a woman who had evidently not been young when she died. The other boxes were empty and unsealed.

The cellar had provided a dumping place for three of the missing person's-now confirmed victims-bodies and they had been there long enough to mummify.

"Do you think this means Dwight is the killer?" Deedra asked.

"I don't know. I can't, at this point, fit him in that role, but who can figure?" Slight perspiration covered Aaron's forehead and after a moment formed droplets that dripped into his eyebrows and down his cheeks. He wiped his face with a large white handkerchief.

"This is very difficult to accept, Deedra. What the hell do I do now?" He shut his eyes as if asking for guidance. Finally he said, "First we've got to get you out of here long enough to remove the remains. I want to do that without arousing panic. I'm going to arrange for a television company to bring out a new television, bringing in an empty television box and taking out the box with the bodies. Then I'm going to enlist the aid of the electric company. They will finagle the other box out by some means. A man will tinker with the antennae as if something has gone wrong with the reception. I know it's Sunday, but only the killer will be edgy about anything going on here.''

Aaron stared at the body of the woman. ''I wonder who she is? Doesn't fit any of the known missing persons, and how long has she been here?'' He turned to Deedra. ''This must be hell for you. Do you have someplace to go for the evening? Should I call Brad?''

Deedra let out a pent-up sigh, unaware until that moment that she had been holding her breath. ''I'm having dinner with Lance Fenton. He claims to being a very good cook.''

''Okay,'' Aaron replied reluctantly. Was he pondering whether Lance had placed the bodies here? ''Just be very careful about what you say. We'll remove the bodies while you're gone, then I'll return around 9:00. Plan to be home by then.''

''I hesitate to call this home,'' she muttered, glancing at the box containing the two bodies. ''However, this might answer the question about why the killer wanted to get rid of me.''

Aaron nodded. ''Let's get on with it.'' Upstairs he used the new padlock to lock the cellar door, putting the key into his pocket. ''Don't turn on any lights. At this point you are out of electricity.''

While Deedra refueled the fires, Aaron went out to the two-way emergency radio in his car to make the arrangements. Through the window Deedra saw Claude meander toward Aaron's car, and Harriet stood in front of her living room window watching.

Aaron talked with Claude a few minutes, gestured

toward the store. Claude strolled back to his house, but watched from a location near his front window.

During the time they waited for the helpers to arrive, Aaron sat in his car alerting the state police forensics unit and the M.E.

Within half an hour two trucks rolled up in front of the old store building. One was a utility company vehicle, the other a television repair service truck. Aaron stood among the men, instructing them, and then one man removed a ladder from the repair truck and climbed onto the roof. The others went inside with Aaron. When they returned from a hurried trip to the cellar, the men were pale and silent, the photographer had remained in the cellar taking photos of everything. Two men went outside and carried in an empty television set box, took it to the cellar and returned upstairs with the box containing the two bodies. After a few minutes when they went out several times for tools and various other implements, they carried the body-laden box to their truck. They motioned to the man on the roof, and when he climbed down, they drove away.

Meanwhile the utility men were going about the old store, testing wires, pretending to try to turn on the lights. No lights were turned on and only their flashlight beams shining through the windows. Presently the man carried in a box that seemed to contain wiring and a circuit breaker box. After the empty box was stored in the basement, they carried the box with the woman's remains upstairs. Aaron immediately re-locked the cellar door. Forensics would go over every inch of the cellar later. They tinkered around for several minutes then Aaron turned on the lights. The men seemed to cheer, gathered up their tools, and carried the body box out to their truck.

Aaron followed them out, went to his car and returned with a six-pack of beer that the men shared and conversed, though the smiles were forced and anyone up close would have seen how difficult that was for them.

Meanwhile Deedra kept the cabins under scrutiny though nothing seemed unusual. Harriet had watched through the window, as had Claude and Jocelyn. If the other residents were interested they showed no signs of it. At least Deedra didn't see them. The Black brothers were still away.

At last Aaron sent the men on their way, stamped into the store, took her in his arms and kissed her with a fervor he hadn't shown earlier. It set her heart beating a different rhythm than the earlier heavy heartbeat caused by terror.

"I'll be back around 9:00. Make sure that Lance walks you home!"

She bathed, spending an hour in the tub relaxing, then phoned Clete with the exclusive.

"My God, Deedra! You unearth the damnedest things! Is Aaron going to provide you protection?"

Deedra felt a spurt of surprise. Clete did not usually worry aloud about the danger she might find herself in. It was a pleasant change.

She told him that Aaron would return later and that she was having dinner with Lance Fenton.

"Do you think he might be the culprit?"

"No."

"Call for help if you need it!" Clete abruptly rang off...as usual. He would probably call Aaron to find out what precautions were being taken, and what procedure Aaron planned on implementing.

At 5:00, in the early evening darkness Lance arrived

to escort her to his home. He helped bank the fires and helped into her heavy jacket. After she locked the door, Lance then double-checked it.

"Aaron phoned and gave me strict instructions to make sure you arrived at my house safely, and that I was to walk you home," he said by way of explanation.

It seemed that everyone in Percifal witnessed Lance Fenton escorting her to his house for dinner. Claude watched, mouth open, from his wide front window, Jocelyn at his side. She gave Deedra a timid wave and smile. Neil and Marsha had merely glanced at them and returned to whatever occupied them.

Harriet, on the other hand, frowned as they walked by, seemed to call to Dwight who appeared briefly at the window then turned away. Ivan and Shelia gave them a friendly wave and pulled the drapes, eliminating part of the illumination along the roadway. The Blacks' cabin was dark, and the Randolph's had already pulled their drapes so Deedra wasn't sure they knew of her visit to Lance Fenton's house.

Lance had really gone all out, scented candles burned in the living room, and tall candles gracing the dining room table. Lance had prepared a pot roast with potatoes, carrots, and onions. The gravy was without flaw, and there was a dessert of freshly baked apple pie and vanilla ice cream.

"You are, indeed, a very good cook," Deedra murmured.

"You have something very weighty on your mind, my dear. You have scarcely heard a word I've said about my travels about the country."

"Oh, Lance, I'm sorry if I'm not very good company this evening!"

"I assume it's not my presence that causes this tremulous reaction?"

"No, of course not. I hadn't realized I was still shaking," Deedra murmured.

"Does it have something to do with Aaron's visit this afternoon, and the subsequent arrival of a utility truck and TV repair service truck? Then I received this unusual phone call from Aaron instructing me in a stern-don't-argue voice that I was not to let you out of my sight, that I was to walk you home just before 9:00."

"Ah, yes." Then realizing that Lance was bound to learn about her grisly discovery anyway, she described the ghastly experience, and the belief that the attack on her had stemmed from the killer's fear that she would discover the bodies in the cellar.

Lance had remained silent though obviously shaken, during her narration. When she had finished, Lance poured her a glass of very fine wine. "Drink that, my dear. It will help steady those nerves." He took a sip from his own glass. "No wonder I felt that…ah… crawly sensation there earlier. The old creative mind reaching out to perceive the sphere of that old store's ambience." A cloud seemed to pass over his features.

Deedra stared at him with sudden awe. Lance had not made that statement lightly, he had definitely been edgy while in the store, and she had at the time wondered about it. Did Lance, like some intuitive people she knew, have a certain psychic ability?

"Do you ever visit with Emma Randolph? Does she communicate in any way?"

Lance grimaced. "Now, that's a strange situation. I'm certain Emma can talk if she really wants to. I once heard her singing along with a tune on the radio she

was listening to on her front porch. She saw me, gave
me a stern challenging look, and clamped her lips shut.
It was a warning look, a pleading look. I pretended I
didn't hear her, just wished her a good day. I think it
suits her to let Melvyn think she can't talk, a sort of
my-lips-are-sealed. There was talk before that accident
that Melvyn was thinking about leaving her. We all suspected there was another woman though no woman ever
appeared and no proof there had been a woman."

"And now Melvyn is burdened with her incapacity?"
Deedra ventured.

"Now she is totally his. She can't get away from him.
People feel sorry for her, and admiration for him, for
his dedication and care of her."

"Does he know she owns all the buildings here in
Percifal?"

Lance gave a start. "You've learned that, have you?
No, I don't think he knows about that. My wife knew,
sworn to secrecy. She signed as witness to the transaction. Emma told her it was a security thing, that if
Melvyn ever walked out on her she would be okay financially. As far as Melvyn knows, the bank in Rufus
owns everything here."

Deedra, however, was not so certain. Surely there
was documentation and Melvyn could have learned
about it from business acquaintances. It had to be listed
in the public records at the courthouse.

"Do you think Emma knows anything about those
skeletons found in the swamp? Perhaps she saw someone lurking around there?"

Lance Fenton's eyes took on a silvery sheen, a sure
sign that his inner knowing, his intuition was suddenly
alerted. Had Lance recalled some incident or feared
Emma had witnessed something unusual there?

Deedra felt a shiver traipse down the length of her spine and settle in her lower back. A tenseness she hadn't detected in Lance's presence earlier. Lance had an unusual mystic aura that bespoke of dead-on intuition. It was time to change the subject.

Deedra nodded. "I told you I wanted to learn your writing secrets. Tell me how you happened on the plot for your latest best-seller?"

Deedra finished another glass of wine and now felt remarkably calm. It was a relief to hear Lance talk about his writing, listen to this creative man who probed the depths of human motives and heartbreaks for the grist of his popular novels. It was really too bad that he was older, in his mid-sixties, or Deedra would easily have fallen under his spell. Indeed, she felt herself wondering how it would feel if he kissed her. The wine had really mellowed her out.

It was nearly 9:00 when Lance took her back to her dismal abode, helped get the fires going again, and made certain the house was secure.

"Funny," he muttered, "I don't feel that...ah... spectral sensation, that augury of others here now. A relief. I didn't like the thought of you here in what I believed at the time to be a haunted place." He threw another chunk of wood on the fire. "I intend to stay until Aaron arrives. And I see that Claude has made his usual round of snooping."

Deedra glanced at the window in time to see Claude's reflection recede into the darkness.

"Lance, has it ever occurred to you that Claude might be the killer?"

"Of course. Then I abandoned that notion because it doesn't fit his personality. He has no obvious tendencies toward violence and no evident signs of repression.

Dwight is a much likelier culprit. And one with opportunity. After all, he and Harriet ran this store for many years, have probably stored things in the cellar ever since. I'm certain Aaron is seriously considering Dwight. I would were I in his official capacity. Aaron certainly is burdened down with the murky madness of this killer.''

The sound of Aaron's arrival prevented any reply Deedra might have made. She was very relieved when Aaron strode in, his strong presence filling the room. He glanced at Deedra, gave a slight nod, and thanked Lance for seeing her home safely.

''I guess Deedra filled you in, but I'd appreciate it if you wouldn't spread the word. We'd like to get all the forensics done before the public and media descend.''

''Right. Can you believe the nerve of that monster leaving those bodies right here in the cellar? Incredible!''

''I think the culprit hadn't figured out how to get them out and dispose of them elsewhere, and ended up just leaving them there. That also explains the change in M.O., disposing them along the highway. Much easier to accomplish and with a lot less danger.''

Lance nodded. ''How many does this make now? Three here, four along the highway, and two from the swamp. Nine recovered. How many more?

Aaron gave him an enigmatic look. ''We think there might have been fourteen, no way to tell unless their remains turn up.''

''Five to go,'' Deedra muttered. ''One is probably in the swamp, the companion of the first woman's skeleton. The killer just has to be completely mad, only I haven't seen anyone who could fit the role of serial killer here.''

"Might not be insane," Lance replied, "could just be an evil person, a human predator of women."

Aaron sighed. "I wish he had preyed in some other part of the country. It will take months to get these all sorted out. And Sandy Nevin's body is the only one we can release for proper burial very soon. Some of the autopsy tests take time."

"Do you think they were all killed with the same type baling twine?" Deedra asked.

"Yes, or something very similar. I have a list of everyone whose purchased that twine in Rufus over the past four years. Nothing I can use as a real clue." Aaron gave Deedra a look she interpreted to mean, keep quiet about the twine out at Clete's place.

"If Deedra feels uncomfortable staying here, she's welcome to stay in my spare bedroom. She'll be perfectly safe, I assure you," Lance told Aaron.

"Don't worry, Fenton, I'm staying the night. I have a duty to make certain the crime scene is undisturbed, and Deedra is now considered under the protection of this county."

Lance raised questioning eyebrows, but no words, and graciously took his leave.

Deedra was relieved to see him go, feeling exhausted, and a need to find out what Aaron had learned. She made a pot of tea and they settled in front of the fireplace.

"The young ones are the missing teenagers, the woman is a mystery, doesn't match any description we have and doesn't really fit the M.O. She wasn't young and wasn't from around here. Forensics is overwhelmed, so for now we're just sending out queries for missing persons who might match her description. Could take a while."

"Does the method of murder match?"

"Yes, strangled, but we don't know what was used to do that dastardly deed. Might not have been baling twine, and the amount of time since her death might eliminate her as our perp's victim." Aaron threw another chuck of wood on the fire. "Am I getting confused, or are these cases just getting really grotesque?"

"Ghastly, grisly, ghoulish, and grotesque!" she replied.

Aaron plunked down beside her again. He kissed her with sweet longing, then reluctantly released her. "I'm on duty, so we can't have a romantic interlude which would help us both, and I'm quite frustrated about that. However, rules are rules, and with Claude mincing around, I dare not break them. He would probably alert the governor."

This caused Deedra a giggle, and surprisingly, relief.

TEN

DEEDRA SETTLED IN BED fully aware of Aaron lounging on the sofa in the living room, aware that being together caused them both frustration due to a great deal of self-control.

Despite her longing, Deedra wasn't ready to commit herself to this man she had known less than a month. Their chemistry jibed, but what about the other necessities that made marriages work, what about the compromises that would have to be agreed upon? His career or hers? She was almost certain that her career would be the victim. Could she accept that? Aaron could always find work in law enforcement wherever he went, but in this part of the state there were no big city newspapers, no big salaries, no competition. She desperately wanted a home and family, but would need to make certain she loved the man enough to be content with whatever compromises that necessitated.

Occasionally she could hear Aaron putting wood on the fire, filling the stove with pellets. She wondered if he was thinking about her, or puzzling over the murders, going over and over what evidence existed. Was he planning on arresting Dwight Stratton for murder?

She awoke in the morning to the aroma of freshly perked coffee and thinking it was part of a dream. It wasn't. Aaron appeared with a cup of steaming coffee, the brew that most Americans used as eye-openers to start their day.

"Did you get any sleep?" She asked.

Aaron grimaced. "Enough. I must say I don't relish having to keep fires going all night. We are all spoiled with our central heating units."

"I have learned to appreciate modern conveniences in a way that never even occurred to me before." She sipped the coffee, giving Aaron a smile of thanks. "I'll take a bath and make breakfast. Then you can tell me what's on the agenda for today."

They lingered over breakfast, reluctant to get the mechanics of their duties into high gear and avoided personal remarks, though Aaron's glances spoke of controlled desires. The next few days were going to place severe stresses on Aaron.

"You'll have to go in to the district attorney's office and make a statement, including how you were tossed into the swamp. I believe that statement has been typed up, just needs your signature, but the D.A. may quiz you about it. He'll want to know every minute detail. He's a no nonsense guy, very direct, be very specific with your answers."

The forensics team arrived at 8:00 leaving no time to wonder at Aaron's advice, Deedra was shooed off to the district attorney's office.

Before entering Rufus, she pulled off to the side of the road and phoned Clete.

"Just to let you know I'm on my way to the D.A.'s office to make a statement, and am out of the way while the forensics team scours the cellar."

"Think they'll find anything?" Clete asked.

"In the cellar, no. In the boxes that contained the mummies, probably."

"Did Aaron say he was going to arrest Dwight?"

"No. I don't think he plans to do that until he has definite evidence. That old store building has been vacant for ten years. Dwight might not have been the only one with access to the cellar. And he doesn't own the building, Emma Randolph does."

"Um," Clete rang off.

The district attorney was a man in his early 40's, shrewd, all business and with a jaw-set that warned of his power. He could and would show no mercy to criminals, and most defense lawyers gritted their teeth when pitting their skills against his in trials he prosecuted personally.

Kurt Wagner was of German descent and had inherited strict militaristic characteristics from his father and grandfather who were soldiers under the Third Reich. Those who knew him well, said he seldom smiled and only when justice had been served against the criminal element. He had married a Hispanic girl who seemed to walk two steps behind him, and presented him with three sons and a daughter. The children were well-behaved, solemn, and seldom smiled to the consternation of their teachers. Kurt had earned the nickname of "the avenger," T.A. instead of D.A. Everything was done legally, however, just with fierce fervor.

Now, Deedra sat across from him and hadn't yet heard of Kurt Wagner's reputation. She was slightly taken aback by his direct questions. He made no attempt to put her at ease, didn't smile, and taped every word.

"Are you up here at the sheriff's suggestion?"

"No, at my editor's, Clete Bailey. He arranged for the rental of the store building."

"But you are assisting Aaron Blaine?" The gray-blue

eyes were like flint, a faint glitter that hinted at zealousness.

"Of course. He is the person I've contacted about finding the skeleton and the dead bodies. I also interviewed him about the other murder cases."

"And reported to your boss at the newspaper?"

"Yes, of course."

"I understand you're an investigative reporter?"

"Yes."

"Did you know that Clete Bailey and Aaron Blaine were friends?

"Not until after I arrived up here," Deedra replied, wondering what Kurt Wagner was trying to establish.

"Then the sheriff hasn't asked you to participate in an entrapment procedure?" The flinty eyes gleamed.

Deedra's mouth dropped open. "How could I do that when I don't have an inkling who the killer is and Aaron certainly hasn't confided that?"

"You do report to Aaron though?"

"I never withhold anything I think might assist in an investigation like this. Not only is it my duty, it's ethical and meets the journalistic standards of the newspaper that employs me!" Deedra felt angry resentment steal through her—he had stolen her cool. She returned Kurt Wagner's stare with one of her own, their eyes locked in a silent battle.

The district attorney was the first to look away. "All right then. What do you think about these murders? I, too, need your cooperation, and I want you to tell me your impressions of Lance Fenton."

Again Deedra experienced surprise. This man was a very thorough regimented person, and held no sympathy for vague and devious answers. He sounded as if he disapproved of Lance Fenton, and taking that as a clue

she carefully gave him an assessment of Fenton with no
personal overtones. She did not want the D.A. to think
she was intrigued by the famous author, that she didn't
think he could possibly be the killer.

Their session went on all morning, and when Deedra
left she felt as if her brains had been stirred about, her
thinking process altered a bit. Two ideas emerged, however. Kurt Wagner suspected that Emma Randolph and
Jocelyn Hoover were withholding important information, and that Dwight Stratton had not hidden the bodies
in the cellar, instead had secrets in his life, a woman
perhaps.

Deedra garnered these facts from the type of questions the D.A. had posed, and her reaction to them. He
had noted her surprise at questions about Dwight's involvement with a woman and whether she thought the
unidentified body could have been that woman?

After a few minutes she began to suspect that the
D.A. wanted her to start probing into the personal/hid-
den lives of the men in Percifal. Up to that point she
had been looking at opportunities, trying to fit in times
when the women could have been abducted. Kurt Wagner wanted her to look for concealed agendas, corrupt
desires. It was certainly true that Dwight had a strict
no-nonsense marriage, now at the age of mid-life crisis,
a time when men began to wish for the return of youth,
a restlessness when men thought their lives lacked
excitement and began seeking out sexual and even
dangerous entanglements. So, she mused, the D.A.'s
questions were logical, followed a pattern of long-
established motives. But was it true? So far no one she
talked to had hinted at such a thing about Dwight.

She left the interview with a different perspective
about Kurt Wagner…and of the murder cases…and

knew the prosecutor had learned a great deal more from her than she had from him.

At Sheriff's Headquarters she talked briefly with Aaron, learning that forensics had cut off the woman's right hand in order to soak the fingers thereby enabling them to obtain her fingerprints. Deedra experienced a moment of nausea, then reminded herself that the poor woman had obviously been subjected to far worse harm and indignities, and that she wouldn't feel a thing now. Necessary as it was, it seemed somewhat disrespectful.

The teenagers had been positively identified and the paper work was proceeding on them. As soon as forensics was through with them, they would be released to their parents for proper burial. The parents had been devastated, the mother of the boy taken to the hospital and now under doctor's care. The news of the discovery had been released to the media, and Aaron was dreading the consequences.

Deedra met reporters on her way out to her car. It was a frenzy for close-ups and word bites, which increased her headache to a throbbing beat, like the din of a distant drum. When at last she was able to drive away, she was damp with perspiration, stressed to the point of tears by having to appear "tough."

Tears dripped down her cheeks as she drove through the tree-lined highway to Percifal. It was a cold, overcast day, somber clouds hung overhead like a mantle about to drop over the landscape. The temperature had dropped a few degrees and though it didn't snow, the threat lingered all afternoon.

A crime scene notice was posted on the front door, and out of the corner of her eye, she saw Harriet and Jocelyn hurrying toward her with freshly baked offerings.

She gritted her teeth, hastily wiped the tears away, and allowed Harriet to cluck over her like a mother hen.

"You poor thing, finding bodies right here in the cellar! I can't imagine how terrifying that must have been! Does Aaron have any idea about who could have placed them there?" Harriet's eyes held a scared look, obviously aware that Dwight was now under suspicion.

"Do you need anything, dear?" Jocelyn asked. "If you are uncomfortable here at night, you're welcome to stay in our guest room. Claude said Aaron spent last night here, now of course, we know why."

Deedra sighed. How could all these things have happened around Percifal and Claude wasn't clued in? That was a suspicious fact in itself, and wondered if Jocelyn, too, realized that Claude was now under suspicion.

"Thanks, Jocelyn, but I'll be all right here. There's nothing here to hurt me, and if those mummies sent ghostly wraiths around, they are gone now. Sit down ladies. I'll make fresh coffee. I really need it after being quizzed by that district attorney!"

Deedra had to tell the women all the gruesome details, and to shock them, told how forensics had cut off the woman's hand to soak the fingers in an effort to get her fingerprints.

Jocelyn turned somewhat pale, but Harriet's eyes glistened behind her glasses as if a mist had formed over her eyes. Deedra was certain it wasn't tears, but some deep distress that Harriet dared not express.

"What kind of questions did Kurt Wagner ask?" Harriet inquired.

"Oh, just my observations of the men living here. They are trying to find the man who threw me into the swamp, asking me questions like did I smell cigarette smoke, after-shave lotion, that kind of thing. What can you smell in a heavy fog like that?''

Harriet and Jocelyn missed her attempt at humor, and exchanged glances that ended in silence.

"How is Emma Randolph? Is she terribly upset about all this?" Deedra had deliberately changed the subject, covertly watching their reaction.

"Why, I just don't know," Jocelyn sputtered as if she had forgotten something important. "We've been so upset and busy watching the officers over here, we haven't tried to talk to her."

Deedra nodded. "I just thought she might be upset, not knowing everything that was going on. Do you think since she sits near that window all the time that she has seen anything unusual?"

Harriet shook her head. "What could she see? These…ah…murders took place a long time ago, before her accident probably, and she worked at the bank then, was gone all day. She almost always drove home with Melvyn, and went to work with Lance Fenton's wife, Grace. The bank didn't open until 10:00, or course, and Melvyn's route began early. Emma and Grace Fenton were close friends. Grace died a few weeks before Emma's accident. I've always said that if Grace had been alive, she would have taught Emma how to talk again."

"Tell me about Emma's accident. I was in Rufus at the time it happened on that missing women's story. I drove out here to get a picture for the paper, but didn't follow through. Did that trooper recover?"

"The one who rescued Emma?" Harriet asked.

"Yes, but was unconscious for several weeks."

"His parents take care of him now, wife divorced him. He lives somewhere in Los Angeles County."

"The other trooper still around?" Deedra asked.

Harriet shook her head. "He moved up to Washington, somewhere around Seattle. I heard he wasn't in law enforcement anymore."

"He was reprimanded for the accident?" Deedra persisted.

"Well, nothing specific. He did resign right away, however," Harriet smoothed her dress.

After Clete phoned, the women went away, mainly because she took his call in the privacy of the bedroom, not wanting to be overheard. "Clete, can you locate the trooper who was in the patrol car that slid into Melvyn Randolph's truck two years ago? The accident that put Emma in that wheelchair."

"Yeah. You have suspicions of Melvyn?"

"More like I want to learn something about Emma. Harriet said Grace Fenton and Emma rode to work together in the mornings, but Emma usually went home with Melvyn. That's why she was in the truck. The doctor's say there's no reason for her inability to talk, that it's probably psychological. But someone said she did talk for a day or two after the accident. And anyway, you told me to try and find out what she knows...if anything."

"Yeah, good idea. I'll see what I can find out."

Brad phoned having learned the grisly news. "Sorry I didn't phone right away, but I've been swamped with media calls."

"Don't apologize, and please don't use the word 'swamped!' I'm just about scoped out on that word...and this place."

"Has anyone asked you out to dinner tonight?" Brad sounded sympathetic.

"No, but if you'd like to stop by with pizza and sodas, I'd really like that."

"Sounds great. I'll be there no later than 7:00. Might have trouble avoiding the reporters," he replied. "Are they still hanging around?"

"Yep. Big story. Some will stay hoping for an arrest. If nothing happens then most of them will go on to other events. You know what happens when the story hits the back pages."

"Solving this one isn't going to be easy. Even though the M.O. is different, I'm almost certain it's the same killer. After all, he couldn't stash all the bodies here in the cellar, and to escape Claude's scrutiny would be a feat in itself!"

"Unless it is Claude. Maybe that's why he watches all the time, afraid someone would go into the cellar," Brad suggested.

"You certainly could be right about that," Deedra reluctantly agreed.

Aaron arrived with a man from the state attorney general's office. Aaron was definitely perturbed, had to show the man where the bodies had been kept, went over Deedra's testimony about finding the bodies and the skeleton in the swamp. He seemed quite suspicious of her as if she was setting up a scenario to earn front-page stories. The attorney lost most of his pomposity when Deedra related the details of dragging the skeleton out of the swamp, and showing him the wound on her head.

Aaron led him away to meet the residents of Percifal. Deedra never learned how they received his visit, just knew that Aaron was perturbed about having to impose on them. Aaron waved as they drove away from Percifal, the frown on his face seemed set as if it might now be permanent.

Deedra wrote a feature on her discovery of the "mummies," faxed it to Clete, and another she sold to the national press. One thing about being involved in things, it was financially beneficial. She was definitely planning to shop around for a new car.

At 6:30 Brad arrived with a giant pizza and several kinds of sodas. They watched a movie-of-the-week and kissed a few times. Brad seemed to sense that she wasn't in a romantic mood and kept things warm and comfy rather than hot and steamy. They didn't talk about the murders though Deedra knew Brad was concerned about her staying there, again offering the use of his guest bedroom.

He left at 10:30 after glimpsing Claude prowling about. "I wouldn't want to start any rumors, and can't help wondering at Claude's peeping-tom addiction. He surely can't expect to witness any hot and heavy sex scenes when everyone in Percifal knows of his...ah... penchant for peeping."

Deedra laughed. "I'm sure if anyone has figured it out, it would be Jocelyn. She seems unconcerned about it, although Claude's first conversation to me included the statement that his wife was nervous, worried about strangers. Surely there were lots of strangers around here when the store and gas station were open. So what happened to make her nervous since then?"

"Yeah, strange. I don't recall anyone saying she was the nervous type when I was a kid and spent time around the lake. And my Dad never mentioned it. You don't suppose she suspects Claude of vile and murderous acts?" Brad frowned. "Be sure and lock the door after me."

Deedra watched Brad drive away, then prepared for bed, her eyes drooping with sleep. She did not dwell on the bodies that had been in the cellar and it was not thoughts of them that awoke her screaming in terror a few hours later.

ELEVEN

THE DREAM, a quite pleasant dream, was interrupted by a sensation of something crawling or creeping. She tried to push the irritant out of the dream, but it was insistent and smelly, an imp intending on spoiling the dream, intruding, pinching, then with a sharp piercing bite to her chin.

She groaned, sat up, turned on the light spilling the rat onto the sleeping bag. Her screams were the howlings of pure terror. Her nightmares suddenly real for the rat wasn't alone, there seemed to be several, a real army of avenging rats. Her bleeding chin interested them, and they clambered onto the bed to taste the fresh, dripping blood.

Deedra swatted at them, but they persisted until she stood up in bed. Her groans evidence of her terror, her flailing motions an attempt to fend off the wily rodents. One rat tried to climb up her leg. With savage force she hit at it, but its claws dug trenches into her leg, which began profusely bleeding. Smelling blood, the rats advanced.

Not coherent, she gibbered epithets and flailed about in helpless frenzy until the gun that Brad had given her slipped out from under the extra pillow. Her mind steadied. She grabbed the gun just as another long-tailed furry creature, its eyes gleaming even in the vague light, made an attempt to crawl up her leg. She kicked it away, aimed and fired the gun, splattering the rat all over her sleeping bag. The other rats paused in their pursuit, then gathered around the remains of the dead rodent, eagerly consuming it.

Deedra vomited, and the rats quickly scarfed up every smidgen of it causing her to gag with nausea, bile filling her throat.

Deedra fired again, killing another rat and sending the others skittering away. She aimed and shot again as they scuttled for safety.

She was still standing in the middle of the bed, shaking, moaning—the urge to vomit stalled when people began knocking on her door.

"Deedra! Deedra! Are you all right?" Claude's voice joined by others.

Deedra gulped down the bile that had risen in her throat. "Just a minute!" It was all she could do to avoid the gory mess, get out of the bed without stepping into the rat's remains, which already smelled of ancient vermin, a smell that lingered in the room.

Barefooted she went to the front door. Her hands shook so badly she had to struggle to release the deadlock bolt.

On the porch just out of the rain, were Claude, Dwight, and Lance, staring at her their expressions reflecting fear and dismay.

Only then did she realize she still carried the gun. "Rats! Ugly, vicious rats!" She squeaked hysterically. Blood was still oozing from her chin and running down her leg.

"Rats did that to you?" Lance sounded as if he found that incredible. "Where did they come from? There weren't any signs of them earlier, were there?"

"Deedra you've got to get those rat bites taken care of right away! Call 911," Dwight commanded.

Deedra found her cell phone, but her fingers didn't cooperate, and finally Lance took the phone and called the emergency number. He also phoned Aaron, who arrived almost as fast as the emergency response team.

Waiting for the medics, Lance and Dwight went in search of the rats while Claude stayed with Deedra trying to stem the bleeding on her leg with a washcloth. They found no signs of the rats except on and around the bed, and no way where they could get in until Dwight discovered a slit in the screen of a back porch window. The slit could scarcely be seen, cut next to the frame, and only six or seven inches long. The cut was recent, and deliberate. Someone had intentionally put rats into the old store building. The men stared at each other, fear and questioning glazing their eyes. When they returned to the living room they did not tell Deedra of their discovery.

The medics arrived with siren blazing, and on viewing her wounds, one of the men blanched though they began disinfecting and bandaging Deedra's wounds without question. When a very angry Aaron arrived, unable to disguise his true feelings for Deedra, he gathered her into his arms interrupting the medics. After a moment Aaron appeared to realize he was interfering, and with a muttered, "Sorry," went away to inspect the old store. When he saw the horrific mess on the sleeping bag, his curses made the other men cringe.

"Woe be unto the person who did this ugly, vicious thing," Lance muttered.

The men exchanged glances and their silent thoughts seemed to sizzle through the room like static electricity.

Deedra couldn't control the tremors that shook her

and after consulting with a doctor the medics injected a calming sedative which took affect almost immediately.

Aaron, obviously in a cold fury, ordered the medics to take Deedra to the hospital for the night so the "damn rodent mess could be cleaned up, and a new bed and sleeping bag installed here." He phoned the doctor and made certain he would be at the hospital so there would be no delay in admitting Deedra, she was under protective custody...again.

"I'll be there first thing in the morning to get a statement."

He turned to the men of Percifal who had been joined by Ivan and Melvyn. "This is obviously a mean and dangerous business. I'll want statements from everyone beginning now!"

Deedra heard Aaron's last statement through a mist closing her off from pain as the medics pushed the gurney she huddled on out to the waiting ambulance. She was in a deep sleep by the time they arrived at the hospital, and did not know that the doctor examined her injuries, ordered certain medications for her, a regimen of rest, and an order of no visitors with the exception of Aaron Blaine. Deedra had no idea that she was that close to a complete breakdown. If word of it got out, her tough image would have been ruined.

Aaron remained at the old store to oversee the investigation and clean up. At 4:30 a.m. he notified Clete and the two old friends talked for nearly an hour, Aaron alerting Clete that strands of the baling twine used in one of the murders had come from a spool in the barn at his place near Rufus. Aaron asked for, and got permission to go through Clete's house just in case anything there had been disturbed. He also requested that

Clete hold off on printing the story, preventing flocks of media people until they had time to do all the forensics.

Clete in turn, told him of Deedra's fear of rats and how that had happened—how Deedra had been trapped in the cellars of an abbey with a mutant boy who hated rats and squished them to death in his huge hands—and that it was rumored Deedra still had nightmares about rats, though never admits it.

At 9:00 a.m. Aaron appeared beside her bed at the hospital. He had brought her laptop and the novel she had been reading.

"Thought you might want something to do," he murmured.

"Yeah, need to fax a story to Clete." She smiled her thanks. "Did you find out how the rats got in there? I need to get it fixed."

"It's all taken care of," Aaron replied in a grim manner.

"What's going to happen next? Why is the killer still after me?"

"Probably wants to drive you out of that old store building though I can't see why now since we've already removed the bodies."

"Well, a few rats aren't going to do it! Though I really need a new sleeping bag!" Deedra's tone indicated deep anger, a thirst for revenge.

"Now, wait a minute! You really intend to go back there? There are other places to stay, you know."

"No s.o.b. is going to run me off by such ugly, disgusting, tactics! Being able to shoot a couple of those loathsome, vile creatures gave me the know-how to fend off other...intruders. I do plan to go back there, so please don't argue."

"Do I have to get Clete to rein you in?" Aaron's eyes gleamed with worry.

"Only if Clete thinks the story here isn't productive anymore, and I certainly don't want to be replaced by someone like Bryce Paxton!"

"And who is this Bryce person?"

"Never mind. You wouldn't like him." She rearranged the pillows. "What's new?"

Aaron sighed. "Nothing we didn't already know. Forensics hasn't discovered anything we can use from the skeletons or the mummies. Only that they were all strangled. Probably to prevent them from screaming and probably the method he used so he could take the victims unaware. We've discovered no connection between the youngsters and the woman." Obviously Aaron didn't want her to return to Percifal. Before he could put that pleading into words, his cell phone rang.

"I'll make an exception this time. But this visit is the only one. I don't want the media hounding the hospital staff," cutting the connection with a scowl.

He turned to Deedra. "It's Brad, he's downstairs. I've given permission for him to visit, and extracted a promise that he isn't going to print this right away. I don't want the hospital staff hounded by the media. I don't want anything out about this just yet. The people at Percifal are sworn to secrecy for the time being, and they certainly don't want to be the objects of speculation right now." Aaron moved closer to the bed, kissed her gently. "I couldn't stand it if this killer got to you!"

There was a gentle knock on the door that alerted them to Brad's presence.

"If I didn't see it with my own eyes, I wouldn't believe in a rat attack!" Brad muttered. "How the hell did they get in?"

Aaron, not pleased with his visit and definitely showing it said, "Slit a screen in that closed in back porch, and no, you can't print a word of it just yet. How the hell did you learn that Deedra was here?"

Brad, sensing Aaron's hostility, replied in a placating voice. "I drove out to see Deedra, wanted to take her to breakfast. When she didn't answer the door, I talked to Harriet who told me they had taken her off in an ambulance. A goddamn rat attack!" Brad muttered in a savage way as if he intended to do something drastic about it.

"Yeah," Aaron replied, eyeing Brad with suspicion, causing Deedra to wonder if Aaron suspected Brad had used a ploy to get her to move into his guest bedroom.

Aaron left with a promise to visit again that evening.

Brad spent ten minutes with her, and then a nurse appeared and sent him on his way. He promised to phone her that evening.

She phoned Clete. "You learn the whereabouts of those troopers?" Cutting off his questions about her rat encounter.

"Yeah. You can contact the driver in a town called Puyallup near Tacoma. He runs a security system business." Clete gave her his name and home phone. "Won't talk to anyone at his place of business."

That meant she would have to contact him at his home and that meant waiting until evening.

The nurse had given her another sedative and she slept through the lunch hour. She awoke too drowsy to write or read and watched something on TV, though she never remembered what.

Aaron arrived with news that the skeleton Deedra had snagged from the swamp was Marian Mossner, the woman who had disappeared after visiting her mother in Half Town.

"Have you identified the woman from the cellar?"

Aaron shook his head, his blue eyes slightly gray with fatigue. Four murders, three mummified bodies, and the attack on her was more than one sheriff's department could handle. Several troopers were on loan from the state police and an undercover detective with special authority sent up from the governor's office. The pressure from the state and media officials was like an ever-tightening vise. At this point, all Aaron could accomplish was the vast amounts of paperwork involved in locating, identifying, and collating all the information on the victims' last few hours of life.

"No, she isn't one of the missing women from this area. And we've received no response from other state agencies. Her fingerprints haven't made a match with the FBI's facility either. We just don't have a clue to her identity."

"Have they," Deedra pursued, "determined how long she had been dead?" Deedra had the uncanny notion that if they could just identity the woman they would have a direct clue to the killer.

"Just an approximate time. About three years, give or take a couple of months. It's going to take awhile. The teens were known to be alive on a certain date, so they can use that fact to base the determination on, with no knowledge about the woman, they have to rely on forensic techniques. And some of those take time." Aaron suddenly sat down in a chair beside her bed, a concession to fatigue.

He ran a hand across his forehead. "Clete gave me permission to go through his house. Didn't find anything out of the way. We did pick up a fingerprint matching that of Darlene Hernandez. So your hunch about her being held in that stall was correct. I'm certain she was killed there, too. A forensics team scoured the stall without finding anything else. There were old tire tracks around the place, but nothing we could ever use in court since the tracks overlap and rain had washed most of them away. I've notified Clete, but for the time being, that information is to stay in my department. However, it reinforces the theory that the perp is familiar with this area.''

''Are you concentrating on Dwight Stratton?''

''Yes and no. Neil Landen, owing a hardware store, could easily obtain keys to get in and out of the store. Dwight and Harriet both claim they did not padlock that cellar door. Harriet is quite vocal about it—said when would they even have had time to do such a thing? Dwight had been working in Brockton for several years by the time the woman was placed down there. And Harriet was insulted that I even questioned them. She looks on it as a betrayal of trust on my part. My status in Percifal has taken a hit.'' Aaron tried a grin that didn't work.

Deedra felt a stab of hurt for him. Aaron needed the respect and friendliness of the people he had known most of his life, and was distressed that they didn't understand his duty in this ghastly mess. Though he was a respected law officer, carrying out his duties in a fair and legal way, murder had never been on the agenda. Now, he was overwhelmed by multiple murders—all discovered in the past four months. Enough to put pressure on any large metropolitan police homicide's division let alone a small town's force.

''No new clues from the Nevin's girl's murder?''

''Nothing you don't already know about,'' Aaron

sighed. "I've assigned most of my deputies to work that case since the girl was local and the community is completely outraged. The rest of the deputies are assigned to the other three cases with a state trooper in charge of each case. So we have four on-going task forces that have to integrate their information from time to time since we're certain they were all killed by the same perp. The mummy cases are on hold for awhile, gives forensics plenty of time to deal with what they have to."

"Starting with the bodies in the cellar, how long were they down there…at least three years?"

Aaron nodded. "The woman's body, at least."

"The store had been vacant for six or seven years by that time then. The people who could have had access to the store are Dwight, Neil, Claude, Melvyn and Ivan?"

"Let's see. I'm not certain when Neil and Marsha moved out there," Aaron frowned. "And you forgot to add Lance Fenton to that list."

"Who lived in cabin 2 before Neil and Marsha?"

"Melvyn and Emma. They moved down to cabin 7 after Melvyn's truck went into the upper part of the lake. Number 7 had been used as a rental cabin until that time. Neil and Marsha moved into 2 after their house in Rufus burned down."

Deedra made a mental note to check on the dates of the teenagers' disappearance and when Neil and Marsha moved to Percifal.

"I assume news of the bodies in the basement has hit the media?" Deedra asked.

Aaron nodded in a glum way. "Yes, we had to inform the parents of the teenagers and the local people are up in arms. Percifal has earned a very dubious reputation now, and I'm afraid everyone living there is subject to open suspicion. The network news has really played the serial killer angle up to the proportions of another John Wayne Gayce. Only instead of young boys and men, these victims are women. Warnings to joggers have been posted all along the highway near Rufus, and special guards placed around the high school. My office is swamped with calls.'' Aaron ran a hand over his face again.

"Any calls offering information?"

"Several, and of course, we've followed up on those leads. Some are just the crank calls every law enforcement office receives from time to time. No deputy gets any time off until the caseload is reduced. Going to louse-up people's Christmas plans,'' Aaron muttered.

"Am I getting out of here tomorrow?" She challenged.

"Yes, Bradley is going to drive you to Percifal. That is, unless you are too uncomfortable about staying in that old building now?"

"No. I'll be all right." She tried to put the thought of the rats from her mind.

"I'd have a deputy take you home, but I can't spare it now."

It was too late to call the ex-trooper that evening, so she phoned Clete instead, giving him a scaled down version of the rat attack. Though she expected questions about it, he merely listened and when she finished asked, "Are you sure you want to go back to that old store?"

"No. I don't really want to, but that is where the story is, and that's why I'm up here in killer country, isn't it? Are you even entertaining thoughts of replacing me with Bryce or someone?"

"We did have a query from Deke Thomas," Clete replied in a non-committal tone.

"Well, where the hell is he?"

"Covering the trouble in the Middle East, of course."

"Well, tell him to stay there. I'm going back to that creepy old store in the morning. But it doesn't look like they'll catch this killer very soon. If this drags out for several months, I'll consider a replacement." Deedra cut the connection.

After taking the prescribed medication, Deedra slept the night through free of the specters that haunted her life.

Bradley arrived at 9:00 and drove her through a crushing rainstorm to the old store. Wind lashed tree limbs which in turn flung rain water whipping every which way, and sometimes across the windshield. The pavement was covered and the ditches rapidly filled accounting for their unusual depth. Deedra wondered if one rainstorm had ever filled them to over-flowing. Brad had all he could do to drive through the onslaught, so their conversation was restrained, the headlights making vague and sometimes confused illumination.

The houses of Percifal couldn't be seen from the highway, the heavy rain like a shower curtain preventing them from sight. The swamp nuzzled up to the roadside, it's gobs of greenish guck an unattractive, and to Deedra, a nauseating sight. The swamp was a place to avoid, a place of ghoulish events and grim secrets.

Smoke was rising from the chimneys of the old store causing Deedra a startled, "What?"

Bradley stared at the smoke for a minute. "Aaron probably started the fires earlier to make sure the house was warm when you arrived. Stay in the car until I check it out."

Taking her key, he slid out of the car and dashed to the door. After a few moments he reported everything was secure, there was plenty of firewood to last through the next few hours.

Bradley helped her get settled and rushed away. A newspaper, even a weekly, demanded time, energy, and a presence in the establishment. If he had ever entertained any romantic thoughts about her, he showed no signs of it now, she mused, as she listened to his car slosh away.

For a few minutes after he left, she felt strangely isolated, a feeling of having been deposited in the wrong time at the wrong place. Perhaps Clete was right, perhaps she should allow someone else to take her place here. Hadn't she gone through enough trauma? Was it so important that she show the world her "tough" image? Did it make one damn bit of difference? Only in her colleagues' eyes, no one else would care one way or another. After all, reporters were replaced all the time, when one was gone there was always someone there to take her place. Had she reached a plateau in her career? Had the rats sent her over the edge?

She huddled down next to the fire and listened to the rain lash away at the old store building. There was a strange feeling of emptiness there now, as if someone or something was missing. Had her presence alerted those murdered souls who lingered about just waiting, yearning to be found so their remains could be properly cared for, their loved ones notified of their fate?

She was still huddled there with these dismal thoughts when Harriet knocked on the door. This time she brought a jar of tomato soup and a toasted cheese sandwich protected from the rain by an old lunch box.

"Don't tell me you aren't hungry, dear. You're just

feeling sad and unhappy. This food will cheer you up."
Harriet set the food on the makeshift end table and sat
down on the sofa.

"Thanks, Harriet. I'm sure I needed a little TLC this
morning." She drank the soup from the jar, and nibbled
at the sandwich. The food was surprisingly helpful and
her mood cleared, her gloomy thoughts began fading
away.

Harriet smiled at her, satisfied that her neighborly
duty was appreciated and completed successfully. However, she leaned back as if she planned to stay for
awhile.

"Do they have any idea who put those rats in here?"
She nervously smoothed her dress.

"I don't think so. No one has told me if they have.
I just don't understand why that was necessary. It was
sort of anti-climatic after the discovery of those bodies
in the basement." Deedra was suddenly aware that Harriet was on a mission, that this visit had a motive, and
her mind clicked into alert.

"Probably done to scare you away," Harriet replied.
"Haven't you helped solve several murders? The killer
must be afraid of you." Harriet smoothed her dress
again.

"Well, he might have succeeded if it had been done
before I found the bodies, now it only strengthens my
resolve not to be scared away." Deedra replied.

Harriet pinched her lips in a tight line as if disagree-
ing on that decision. "Perhaps the person who put the
rats in here isn't the person who killed those people in
the cellar," Harriet suggested.

"Yes," Deedra answered thoughtfully, "that makes
a more logical explanation. Seems like the killer took

an awful chance by that rat thing. Seems like he would want to be very cautious, not call attention to himself.''

"You think the sheriff knows who put the rats in here?'' Harriet smoothed her dress again, not making eye contact.

Deedra's eyes narrowed. Harriet was hinting at something. The rat incident was definitely not in sync with the killer's M.O. though methods of killing could vary with situations. Especially if the killer feared detection or might be trying to divert everyone's attention.

"I have no idea. I haven't dwelled on it really. Aaron had the place cleaned up, and I don't know what happened to the rats. I've been concentrating more on who the woman down there could have been. Aaron said her fingerprints don't match any of the known missing persons from around here. And from the approximate time of her death it looks like she was the killer's first victim.''

"Really?'' Surprise showed in Harriet's pale eyes.

"Yes. They think she was killed three years ago, the others started disappearing about two years ago. Did anyone rent or use this old building after you closed the store?''

Harriet frowned. "I don't think so. For a few years it wasn't even locked, left open like the gas station. Then there were teenagers who began using the place as a rendezvous for drinking and such. Dwight called the bank and they had it locked up after that.''

"Was there any activity around here that struck you odd or seemed unusual?''

Harriet frowned again. "Only that Claude began traipsing about and spying through windows. At first he said Jocelyn had heard noises or saw movements. He laughed about it at first, but after a few weeks he didn't laugh, he took it quite seriously. He didn't say, but we all thought maybe Jocelyn had been frightened by something…or someone. Dwight thinks I'm imagining things because I've always said that the same thing that scared Jocelyn also frightened Emma into her speech problem.''

''You mean it all happened about the same time?''

Harriet frowned evidently on recall. ''Yes, I guess it all happened within a few weeks of each other.''

''Do you think Emma can really talk, that she's just pretending?'' Deedra felt her interest in the murders returning. Evidently soup and TLC did have its positive strategies.

Harriet gave her a direct look. ''Yes. I think she can talk if she wants to. I don't know why she chooses not to. She can't be that afraid of Melvyn!'' She sniffed.

''She is afraid of Melvyn?'' Deedra now wanted to know everything Harriet could tell her about Emma… and Melvyn.

''Well, not afraid exactly. There was a time when she said Melvyn might leave her, and Emma is a one-man woman. Her heart and home are with that man. Personally, neither Dwight not I have seen anything to indicate why Emma might be frightened of him. Melvyn treats her very well, doesn't go off at night leaving her alone. Not many men in the same situation would be that considerate.''

''Do they have many visitors?''

Harriet shook her head. ''Not since her accident. Before that they entertained occasionally and Emma visited her sister out of state a few times. Now the banker is about the only person from Rufus that visits besides Jocelyn and I.''

''How very sad. Has her sister been here lately?''

Deedra had a sudden flash of thought though it vanished before she captured it, leaving her with the notion she had misplaced a clue.

"Sisters. No, not recently. The older one keeps in touch, but no one seems to know where her younger sister is. If Emma has heard anything from her she hasn't indicated it. It must be just terrible to have so many things to say all bottled up inside and no way to release it. I compared it once as a possible cause of human combustion, and it made Dwight angry. He thinks I speculate about people and things way too much. But I can't stop my brain spinning even if I wanted to."

Deedra smothered a grin and asked, "Did you ever meet Emma's sister?"

"Yes. She's phoned me a time or two just to make sure Emma is being treated all right. I told her she shouldn't fret, and promised I'd get in touch if I was worried about anything. Said she often wondered if Emma was getting worse and Melvyn was not telling her, not wanting her to worry."

"It's kind of you and Jocelyn to visit her, she must lead a very lonely life," Deedra remarked.

"To some extent, but she has TV and is quite competent on the Internet. She keeps up a correspondence with several shut-ins that way. Some people find these modern technologies detrimental, but for people like Emma they are a real help. In the old days they didn't have those forms of communication. I often think the pioneer women of the prairies must have been the loneliest women on the planet." Harriet gave her dress another smoothing.

Again Deedra was struck with Harriet's homespun philosophy.

"I guess if you've never heard of modern technologies you can't miss them, but I'm certain you're right about the loneliness of those people. I'm having trouble adjusting to keeping these fires going, can't imagine how much work that took in those days."

Harriet nodded and fell silent.

Deedra realized that Harriet had information to share and was waiting for her to ask the right questions. She searched about in her thoughts, uneasy, with no real clue.

"Did you witness the accident that sent Melvyn's truck into the lake?"

Harriet's eyes darkened. "Yes. I heard the police siren. The state trooper's car turned onto the road leading into Percifal right behind Melvyn's truck as if he was following it. No one could understand it, Melvyn wasn't speeding, just returning home. Seemed like Melvyn stepped too hard on the brakes and the truck started sliding on the ice. There was no way I could see to stop it. The fear on Emma's face was something I won't soon forget."

"How did the trooper get hurt?"

"The patrol car skidded the other way and hit a tree. Knocked the driver out and the other trooper hurried over to help get Melvyn and Emma out of that icy water."

"So the patrol car never actually struck Melvyn's truck?"

"No. Melvyn just hit the brakes too hard. You know how that makes a car slide if the road is the least bit icy."

"If I recall that was in the early afternoon?"

"Yes, about 1:30 or 2:00. People were going home early because of the weather. I called 911 and hurried out to see what was happening. I was frantic worrying about Emma, seeing her go down with that truck. By that time the trooper had brought her to the surface, and I could hear the ambulance's sirens. There were two, one for Emma and one for the injured trooper.''

"Did Melvyn go to the hospital with Emma?" The hair at the base of Deedra's skull tingled as if she could feel the fear of the incident.

"Yes, he went along in the ambulance. Claude brought him home later. He was really upset, of course. Losing all that foodstuff and his truck. He had to notify all his customers that he wouldn't be delivering until his truck was replaced. They tried to raise the truck a day or so later, but it slipped off the chain and sank into a deep crevice no one knew was there. The insurance company couldn't get any divers to go down to chain it up again, it's just too unstable. So they wrote the whole thing off, bought Melvyn a truck and paid Emma's medical costs."

"Do you mean the crevice has moved or changed since the earthquake?"

Harriet nodded. "Actually it's moved twice that we know of, some of the lake water is seeping away down there somewhere. The way I understood the geologist to say, was that the bottom shifts slightly with the lessening volume of water. No amount of rain seems to deepen it anymore."

"How sad. I guess I've never heard of a dying lake before." Deedra added more fuel to the fires, then went to the window to stare out at the rainy scene. There didn't seem to be any sign that the rain would cease very soon. Ponderous clouds hovered over the pines just above Percifal, harbingers of a stormy, cold day.

"There's no sign of clearing," she muttered, resettling next to the fire.

"Give it an hour or so, and there'll be some clearing, perhaps for a few minutes or a few hours," Harriet said in a placating voice as if she suspected that the weather would cause Deedra depression.

"Did you get to talk to the trooper that saved Emma?"

"No. He was chilled to the bone, and needed to get out of those icy clothes. Dwight offered him a change of clothing, but another trooper wrapped a blanket around him and drove him away."

"I understand he isn't with the state police anymore. That he was reprimanded and he quit?"

Harriet nodded. "I never understood that. The patrol car never touched Melvyn's truck. Though why they followed Melvyn up that side road isn't clear."

Deedra had wondered about that earlier. It was why she wanted to talk to the ex-state trooper.

"Did the police search around these old buildings for those missing women? The first two that disappeared after having been shopping in Rufus?"

"Yes. They made a cursory examination of the empty cabin down there, the gas station, and here. Dust on the cellar steps assured them that no one had gone down those steps recently. The padlock must have been placed on the cellar door later."

"Do you know who installed it?" Deedra squinted, not wanting Harriet to realize the importance of that question.

Harriet shook her head. "No. We weren't aware of the padlock until Aaron questioned us about it. We had no reason to enter this old place, and no key to unlock the front door."

''It's obvious that someone knew how to get in and out of here. Placing those teenagers down there must have taken real effort,'' Deedra suggested.

''You mean you think the woman's body was already down there when they searched for those two missing women?''

''Yes. She had probably been there for several months by that time.''

Deedra saw shock then a flush of fear play across her features, emotion Harriet wasn't prepared to control. Her eyes grew round, the irises dark, glistening with an inner thought Deedra didn't think was fear, was perhaps secret suspicion. Harriet pushed the emotion away with a stern set of her lips. Her hand trembled as she smoothed her dress.

''Oh, my! Then Jocelyn's assertion that she had seen someone prowling about the old store at night was true!''

''This was before the women turned up missing?''

''Yes. About the time those teenagers ran away. Jocelyn had heard about that on the news, and saw movement outside. She made Claude go out and find out if the teens were hiding around here. No signs of anyone here or in and around the gas station. Do you think the killer placed those bodies down there at that time?'' Harriet's eyes were wide with shocking knowledge.

''Probably. Whoever placed those bodies there had to have easy access to this old building. Someone with a key.''

''That means,'' Harriet ventured, ''that the killer has been using this place for the disposal of his victims.'' Her voice almost faded to a whisper, the thought gruesome reality.

It had been Deedra's theory all along though she

didn't point that out, didn't want to interrupt Harriet's quite logical thinking processes.

Harriet took a deep breath.'' Then, it proved too difficult to put them in the cellar so he started leaving them in the swamp or along the highway. But where did he kill them? They said on the news that the Nevin's girl wasn't killed where her car was found. Raped and strangled. Must have driven off into the woods somewhere.''

''I believe that's what the police think. I'm sure they're scouring all the lanes and back roads in this area,'' Deedra said.

Harriet fell silent. Deedra was unable to fathom where her thoughts were taking her.

Finally, Deedra ventured a question she thought might offend Harriet.

''Of all the men living here in Percifal, which one would you choose as the killer?''

The effect was startling. ''I just knew you would get around to asking me that. I think Ivan Wallace fits that…ah…profile, isn't that what law officials call it? Not many people know Ivan's history and I haven't gone around telling it either. Ivan was born in Rufus, his true name, Donald Ivan Wallace. His mother died when he was six or seven years old. A year later his father hanged himself. Ivan was sent to live in Brockton with an uncle who had his name legally changed to Donald Davis. That's what he was known as all the time he lived in Brockton and went to school there. After high school he joined the military and returned here as Ivan Wallace. Emma knew this because of certain banking documents. Ivan inherited his uncle's estate.''

Harriet paused and smoothed her dress. ''All this doesn't create a killer, I'm sure, except that I understand that Donald, I mean Ivan, created problems in Brockton.

It was known that he hated his aunt. Dwight, working in the grocery, is the recipient of many gossipy items, and told me that Donald's aunt was very upset with Donald. I don't recall the details, it's been so many years ago, but I've heard law people say that angry teenagers sometimes vent their anger on other facsimile objects or people.''

Harriet had finally reached the motive of her visit, the information she hadn't wanted to volunteer outright as if she was pointing a finger, yet intended to lead us away from her husband and close friends. A smart and valuable move.

Jocelyn appeared at the front door and though talk about Ivan Wallace wasn't continued, Deedra had learned something important.

"Harriet was telling me about the day Melvyn's truck went into the lake. Did you see it happen, Jocelyn?"

Jocelyn nodded, her blue eyes alert. "Yes. I heard the siren and saw the police car turn onto the side road following Melvyn's truck. I knew Melvyn was bringing Emma home early because of the icy road conditions. I couldn't understand why the troopers were following Melvyn. Later, I heard one of the troopers say that they saw Emma in the truck with him and thought she matched the description of one of the missing women. They wanted to stop Melvyn and find out who his passenger was."

"You saw the truck slide into the lake then?"

"Yes. You could see Emma calling for help. It was chilling to watch that truck settle into the water. That trooper didn't waste any time going in after Emma though. Melvyn surfaced about that time."

Their talk continued on about the events of that day,

how Melvyn had changed into dry clothes and had gone off with the ambulance.

"I was standing near the injured trooper," Jocelyn told her, "and I heard the other one talking to him. Something about 'you were right about that.' Then they were both hustled away."

"And it was about a week later that Emma suddenly couldn't talk?"

They both nodded.

"Strange," Deedra muttered.

Again both woman nodded, and soon after left her there tending to the fires.

Deedra's phone rang. It was Bradley announcing that he was bringing lunch and would arrive in a few minutes. "I've got something to tell you," he said.

TWELVE

WHILE DEEDRA WAITED for Bradley she mulled over the information gleaned from the women's morning visit. Harriet had definitely wanted her attention turned from Dwight to Ivan. But Aaron's investigation of Ivan had proved that on days when many of the victims had been accosted, Ivan had a substantial alibi. Was Harriet working too hard to point the finger of suspicion away from her husband? Causing Deedra to mutter, "Methinks thou dost protest too much."

Bradley arrived with chicken dinners and a bottle of fine wine.

"You said you had something to tell me?" Deedra asked while setting out the usual paper plates and plastic cups.

"I looked into Ivan Wallace's past. The police know about it, of course, and don't seem to think he has anything to do with the killings. But he was the accountant for Priscilla Dawson's business, and was the mysterious married man in that missing waitress' disappearance a year or so ago. The one from Brockton. Her sister still lives in Half Town. She knew Ivan as Donald Davis, they all went to high school together. The sister didn't know that Ivan Wallace and Donald Davis were one and the same. No trace of the woman has ever been found, and the last thing the sister had heard from her was that she was going to meet someone named Donald. The sheriff over in Brockton County finally made the connection between Ivan and Donald. Early on they had traced Donald to the military and then lost track of him. So now Aaron has stepped up the investigation, going over all Ivan's alibis for the dates of the latest murders. The others are so old, can't really get a fix on them.'' Bradley downed his cup of wine in one gulp.

''Hm. That means Ivan has two sets of ongoing identification, uses it whenever he needed to cover up Ivan's activities.'' Deedra lapsed into a thoughtful silence. Ivan didn't seem to fit her recall of the man who tossed her into the swamp, and on reflection, didn't believe he was that man. Though strong enough with his broad shoulders, he smoked and there hadn't been even a hint of it on his clothing. It had been very foggy, however, and perhaps it had cloaked that telltale clue. Still, Deedra couldn't seem to fit Ivan in that role and knew she would be very surprised if Ivan turned out to be the killer.

''Do you think Sheila knows about Ivan's affair with the woman? What was her name?''

''No, I'm sure not. Her name was Belinda Ross. Her sister said she referred to the man as Donald. It's complicated with her disappearance from Brockton out of Aaron's jurisdiction, and her body hasn't turned up anywhere.''

''She could,'' Deedra mused, ''just be another case completely separate from the others. And she might not be dead.''

''That's what the Brockton people are saying. They don't want any more cases connected to these on Aaron's plate. It's enough with the jurisdiction of the teenagers. Aaron was wise to insist that the investigating team be headed up by a state police homicide detective."

"What do you think, Brad?"

"I don't know what to think. Aaron has gone over and over everyone's alibis for the last four murders. Everyone seems accounted for at the crucial times."

"Except we don't know exactly what those crucial times are," Deedra reminded.

"Only the day not the exact hour. That gives the killer enough leeway to resume his normal activities, especially if the killer had a place to hide his victims for a few hours."

"What do you think?" Bradley stared into her eyes in a challenging way.

"At the moment I'm inclined to think Dwight. After all, it was his place of business here, he could easily have stashed those bodies in the basement. Harriet can't keep track of him every minute. He knows people in Brockton, is on the road every day. He could get away from the grocery for an hour or two without the employees knowledge. He drives a pickup, could hide a body in the back, and dump it on the way home. Easy enough in those thick fogs."

Brad nodded. "I hope they aren't overlooking Claude whose schedule is never the same. He doesn't have to be anywhere at a specified time, and he does roam around here in the dark."

"Yeah. His roaming might be to keep an eye on whether the cellar was opened. Yet, it doesn't really fit into this killer's role. This killer is sly and secretive. Claude certainly isn't. He is strong enough to have thrown me into the swamp though."

"Who does that leave? Neil and Lance Fenton. Fenton isn't the physical type, not much taller than you,'' Brad reminded.

''I take it the Black brothers have been completely eliminated?''

Brad nodded. ''The state police have anyway. They've checked their routes in the East, and they couldn't have had anything to do with it.''

Brad left rather early and it was probably precipitated by Aaron's arrival.

''Wanted to make sure you were all right,'' he said by way of explanation. ''I'd like to make an excuse to spend the night, but can't add that to my overtime. These murders are costing the county millions.''

''That won't make the taxpayers happy,'' she remarked knowing full well Aaron had another motive for his visit.

''Have you gleaned anything new?''

She told him of Harriet's and Jocelyn's visit and of the news Bradley had imparted.

''What do you think?'' Aaron's eyes were bleary, his face reflecting the weariness of the responsibilities suddenly shoved upon him.

Her heart gave a strange tug, an urge to cradle his head, to kiss his stern lips.

He must have sensed her emotion, and shook his head. ''We can't now. Just needed to make sure you were okay. You have my emergency number, call if you need me.''

And suddenly he was gone leaving the room feeling very empty, and time for her to refuel the fires again. She sighed. That seemed to be her routine in life. Get interested in a man and he leaves for duties more important in their lives than she was. Nevertheless, her respect for Aaron grew, he would not overstep any boundaries. A man who could be trusted. She only wished she could help him solve these awful crimes, and had a nagging, persistent, notion that she was over-looking an important clue. The idea was so strong that she turned the laptop on and carefully reviewed her notes, looking for what wasn't there, listing the known clues in a notebook.

The identity of the woman in the cellar was now considered the killer's first victim. Who was she and why had she been in this part of the country? Did she have a personal relationship with the killer, the impetus that gave him a taste for murder?

Jocelyn had knowledge of a skeleton in the swamp, had obviously seen it to have it. Deedra was certain Jocelyn had glimpsed more than one, and her nervousness about the missing teenagers indicated that fear. Why would Jocelyn even suspect that the teenagers had been around Percifal?

Emma's strange loss of speech and why she'd kept knowledge of her owner-ship of the cabins from Melvyn?

The four recent murders seemed less secretive. Could there be more than one killer? The M.O. seemed changed by the disposal of the bodies. Of course, if it was the same killer, he obviously couldn't risk any more bodies in that cellar. The method of murders was the same, all strangled and raped, except for the teenage boy and the woman in the basement. Did that mean there were two different killers and a copycat killer?

She halted long enough to prepare a supper of tomato soup and a toasted cheese sandwich, and ate while studying the list. Tomorrow she would make another effort to communicate with Emma, try to find out why she didn't want to talk.

It was nearing 8:00 when she phoned the ex-trooper up in Washington. His voice was raspy when he answered.

She identified herself and her purpose in phoning.

"Yes, I know who you are, and have heard about your finding those bodies and that skeleton. I just don't know why you've contacted me." His voice indicated controlled patience.

"I wanted to ask about your rescue of Emma Randolph. Are you aware that she can't or won't speak now?"

The man sighed. "Yes, I heard. She talked right after I got her out of the water though."

"Do you remember what she said?"

There was a long pause. "Yes. She said 'Did you see the others?' When I asked her what she meant, she looked confused and shook her head."

"You contributed that to her trauma?"

Another pause. "At the time I didn't know what she meant. I was freezing and as long as she was all right, I went to get dry clothes and to see if my partner was going to live. I was at the hospital for the next few hours, and knew Emma had been brought in and was expected to live."

"Other officers had arrived to take charge there?"

"Yes, though their time investigating was limited because of the search for the missing women. We had chased Melvyn's truck because a witness saw a woman in the truck with Melvyn. It turned out to be Emma, but we didn't know that when we started following them."

"You were reprimanded for the accident?" Deedra held her breath hoping she wouldn't anger him.

"Yep. We had been ordered to another scene and didn't go there, instead we followed the truck and were involved in that accident. We hadn't called in the license plate number of Melvyn's truck either, which was a breach of procedure. My partner was injured so bad he can never be a police officer again, and I was ticked off by a certain unfairness in the discipline, so I resigned."

"You sound as if you've got bronchitis?"

"It's permanent. Caused by that icy water. I got thoroughly chilled and should have been hospitalized for a few hours myself." There was no bitterness in the man's voice.

"I'm very sorry to hear that. No other after affects?"

The man laughed. "Only to my ego. I was very proud to be in law enforcement. If we had it to do all over again, I'm sure we would follow Melvyn's truck. We were all on the lookout for those missing women at that time."

"Do you have anything to suggest about these murders?"

Again there was that pause. "I suppose the powers all think the killer resides in Percifal?"

"Yes."

"Do they think the latest victims disposed along the highway are an attempt to take the suspicion away from anyone living in Percifal?"

"Yes."

The trooper sighed. "Do you think it's someone living there?"

"Yes, but I haven't been able to get a read on them. Any of them could have had access to this old store building, and so far few clues to any real character deviations."

"Killer's don't always show deviations," he reminded, "their repressions are under strict control to the outside world. The first known murder if I understand the situation occurred about three years ago. Who at Percifal underwent any devastating problem at that time? It might be a place to start looking.''

There were sounds of people talking in the background, and the trooper quickly signed off.

She settled on the sofa with a cup of tea, and thought that the trooper was right. Until the woman's body was discovered in the cellar the investigation had been centered on a beginning time of two years ago when those women disappeared after shopping in Rufus. Most of the other people had disappeared since that time. Only the grocery clerk from Brockton had vanished five years earlier. The waitress had vanished four years ago after telling friends she was going to the movies with a man friend. There had been no trace of them since that time. They were still listed as missing. No connection to anyone at Percifal. Yet Deedra felt a tingle of dread. Yes, she mused, these were the killer's first victims. He had successfully gotten away with murder, she knew he took pride in outwitting the police. After each killing he felt another sense of pride, of self-vindication. He didn't plan the killings just let fate have them cross his path. He wouldn't, she reflected, be repressed in that sense of the word. He would carry on as usual, hugging his secret inside, allowing it to fill the empty spaces in his life.

But she also knew that somewhere along the way he had left a clue. She would have to find out what that clue was, and why it had been overlooked.

Planning to visit Emma the next day, she faxed a message to Clete, and after a hot bath climbed into her new sleeping bag.

The answer came to her in the night and she awoke

with the knowledge of who the killer was, and perhaps why he had turned into a monster.

After breakfast she watched the men leave for work, Marsha going in with Neil at the usual time. Only the women and Lance Fenton were left in Percifal.

The weather, though not raining had turned cold and frost glazed the vegetation along the shoreline and on the slope behind the cabins.

Aaron phoned and after assuring him she was okay, she told him of her plan to visit Emma and perhaps Lance that morning.

"Be careful," he grunted, obviously preoccupied with heavier thoughts.

She found it difficult to wait until 9:00 and after pacing the floor and checking her watch several times, she started out on the usual morning walk at 8:30. Her boots crunched on the icy gravel, the cold air squeezing her face with an unexpected caress. The scenery was magnificent with the trees covered in holiday frost. But when her gaze strayed to the swamp it looked dull, the surface like heavy, greenish-colored mud, thick and brooding. She couldn't prevent the shiver that swept through her, its chilling tentacles causing the sensation of having been touched by an evil hand.

Again her gaze swept the swamp, and she wouldn't have been surprised to see another skeleton. Only the stark limbs of some dead tree protruded like crippled arms above the swamp's ugly surface. A shudder shook her. The swamp was tainted with evil now, and she wondered if the residents would leave Percifal to its decaying fate. The dying lake had cast a pall over what had once been a scenic, lively place, causing her to wonder if it was a harbinger of what would happen to places affected by pollutants.

"What a scary thought!" she muttered.

"Did you say something?" Lance Fenton grinned from his front porch. "I've fresh coffee and conversation inside."

"Said the spider to the fly," Deedra whispered to herself. "Sounds great! It's really cold out here and that damn swamp has given me shivers and quivers."

Lance's house was warm, there was the aroma of vanilla-scented candles that had been placed in the center of a coffee table.

Lance gestured her to a seat on the sofa, poured her a cup of steaming coffee, and took a seat in an overstuffed chair. A reading lamp stood beside it and a stack of magazines and a new novel were on a table on the other side.

"I've been wanting to read that novel," Deedra remarked. "Interesting, exciting, thrilling, what?"

"A page turner. Excellent writing and the fellow really knows his subject. Beyond the comprehension of all of us but a rare few, I dare say."

Deedra nodded. "I'd heard it was a must read. Are you writing or reading these days?"

"Both. This morning I ran into a snag and decided to give myself a day off. Let's me stand back a bit, get a new perspective, see the flaws." Lance paused. "You seem more confident today. Something new turned up?"

"Not that I know of, Aaron only phoned to find out if I was all right. He sounded preoccupied."

"Not surprising, is it?" Lance added fresh coffee to her cup.

"No."

"I note that your interest in Aaron is more than friendship, and you're probably wondering if a relationship is going to blossom from it. Aaron is a man of honor and your choice would be a wise one. But you would have to give up your big city lifestyle, perhaps your career.''

Deedra nodded, not terribly surprised by Lance's insight. He was, after all, a talented and compassionate writer who would detect all the nuances in people's lives. It was part of his persona. And suddenly she wondered why he hadn't detected the monster among them.

''Lance, you're so perceptive, haven't you a clue to the killer?''

Lance's eyes changed as if she had shocked him. For a moment he stared into her eyes in a challenging way. ''I must admit I've had suspicions, but they never seem to last. No one here does anything unusual except Claude and he simply isn't the monster type. I've given it some heavy thought. I'm certain though that rat incident was committed by someone other than the killer. Someone else who wants you to leave.''

''Agreed. Do you think it could have been Harriet?'' Deedra suggested.

Lance's eyes gleamed. ''Yes, that occurred to me. But is her purpose to protect Dwight since she obviously isn't the killer?''

''I think she wanted the sheriff's attention diverted away from Dwight. After I found those bodies in the cellar she realized that Dwight would be the obvious suspect.''

Except that I don't think Dwight fits that profile.'' Lance said. ''Yes, I think it would be a stretch to believe Dwight guilty of these wicked deeds. He's too prim and proper.''

Deedra experienced a tweak of amusement. She wouldn't place Dwight in the prim and proper column.

Harriet had already done that, and Dwight had fidgeted. There was the suspicion that he had been seeing another woman. She did not tell Lance about that, instead finished her coffee and said she planned to visit Emma, then needed to get a story off to the newspaper. "And I'm keeping you from your skill with the printed word."

Lance laughed. "Yes. I'll be able to write now. Your visits are refreshing. My house needs the sound of voices again. Too bad you've given your heart to Aaron or I'd begin intentional pursuit which would probably end up with rejection, another dread common to writers."

Gearing herself to impose on Emma, she mounted the steps of her cabin. Emma opened the door before she had time to knock, a worried smile on her face, and hesitantly invited Deedra inside.

The room was warm and a television was turned on to a daytime soap causing Deedra to wonder if Emma was addicted to them. Lots of women lived vicariously through the characters on the soaps, filling some fanciful void in their own lives. A perfect foil for the housebound.

"Thought I'd stop by this morning. I'm aware that you don't speak, but I think you can." Deedra waited though saw no visible reaction.

After a moment Deedra continued. "They tell me you have two sisters. Do you hear from them often?"

Emma pointed to the computer.

"E-mail? Both sisters?"

Emma slowly shook her head. Then she gestured, rolled the wheel chair into another room and returned with a picture of three women. Emma was the one in the middle.

"Your sisters? Do they live in this part of the country?"

Emma shook her head and indicated that the youngest sister's whereabouts was unknown.

"When was the last time you heard from her?

The woman stared at Deedra, a sort of dread filling her eyes. She took a notepad from the basket of her wheel chair. "About 3 years ago. No one knows where she is."

Deedra nodded. "That's sad. Harriet and Jocelyn visit you every few days?"

Emma nodded, a gentle smile indicating her appreciation. Then she wrote, "Tell me about finding those bodies."

Deedra experienced a faint tingling at the base of her skull. Surely Emma had heard the gist of it on the various news stations, or did she suspect there was more information than had been released to the public? Deedra told her about the discovery, and then about the rat incident, which seemed to be news to Emma...and it shocked her.

She turned a wide inquiring gaze on Deedra, a questioning look, and slowly shook her head.

"Yeah, I don't think the killer put the rats there either. That was done to warn me away or change my idea that Dwight is a suspect."

Emma blinked, then slow realization filled her gray eyes. There was also a hint of pain in them. Emma, Deedra guessed, also suspected Harriet of that and didn't like it, possibly felt it an act of betrayal to a friend who was there when she needed her.

Emma rolled the chair toward the door and cut her little finger on the sharp edge of something. It began to bleed.

"Just a minute!" Deedra grabbed tissues from a box on the side table and held them against the cut until it stopped the bleeding. Emma produced a Band-Aid from a drawer in the table and Deedra placed it over the cut.

"That okay?" She asked.

Emma nodded with a slight smile.

Deedra gathered the tissues and looked around for a wastebasket.

Emma gestured to the bathroom.

In the bathroom Deedra carefully wrapped one of the soiled tissues in toilet paper and stuffed it into her jacket pocket, the rest went into the wastebasket. Deedra washed her hands and when she looked into the mirror above the sink met Emma's watchful gaze.

"I threw them into the waste basket," she gestured, "had to wash my hands."

Emma nodded and gestured a thanks, then swiftly rolled the wheel chair to the door and had it opened before Deedra reached it. Emma was not sorry to see her go.

When Deedra reached her abode, she placed the soiled tissue into a plastic bag, and hastily drove off to the sheriff's office.

Aaron was in his office trying to sort out various paperwork and fend off the media. At first he didn't seem inclined to shut the door and listen to her.

Finally she said, "Damn it, Aaron. I know who the killer is and I think we can prove it!"

He started, gave her a sharp look and quickly shut the door. "What?"

"First you need to get a DNA sample of this. I'm almost certain the woman in the basement is Emma Randolph's missing sister. You can get a reading on her from a sample of Emma's blood. I saw a picture of

Emma with her two sisters, looked like it might be a match.''

Without questioning, Aaron labeled the plastic bag and gave it to a deputy with instructions to get it to forensics immediately.

''Who?'' Aaron asked when he stepped back into his office.

''Melvyn Randolph. I talked to that ex-trooper last night. He didn't quite admit it, but they were chasing Melvyn because they thought he had the women in his truck...and he did.'' Deedra held up her hand. ''Let me finish before you ask questions. Emma's first words to the trooper when he pulled her out of the water was, 'Did you see the others?' I'm sure their bodies were in the back of his truck and when it went into the lake they floated or moved and she got a glimpse of them. Later, the shock of that knowledge caused her the psychological trauma. When her speech returned she kept up the charade so no one could really question her about it.''

''The missing women were in the truck, and one of them eventually floated into the swamp?'' Aaron's eyes were narrowed to gleaming slits.

Deedra nodded. ''I think Melvyn's killing spree started about the time Emma reported to friends that Melvyn might leave her, about the time she purchased the cabins at Percifal. Then Emma's sister made a surprise visit, and Melvyn didn't want her there. I think he probably met her at the train or bus station, and killed her in his truck. The old store wasn't locked up at that time, so he disposed of her body there, probably with the idea that he would dump her into the swamp later. By that time he had a taste for killing. After kidnapping and killing Darlene Hernandez he decided it would be easier and less dangerous to dump the bodies along the highway…and there would be no local searches which would have eventually found the bodies in the cellar.''

Aaron listened attentively. ''And you think we can prove all this by?''

''Identifying the woman's body. If it is Emma's sister, you have a direct link to Melvyn. Backtracking on Darlene Hernandez and the Nevin's girl should produce some kind of evidence.''

Aaron nodded, and gave orders for a deputy to begin checking on Emma's younger sister, to avoid questioning Emma herself, but to contact the out-of-state sister.

''Stay there,'' he said to Deedra, ''I'll be back in a minute.'' Aaron went out and she saw him talking to the state police homicide detective who was in charge of the Brockton murders.

Aaron returned with the detective, and Deedra was requested to repeat her theory. Suddenly there was feverish activity. Melvyn Randolph's files were pulled up on all the available computers, his route schedules were checked again, and within two hours there was definite information that placed him within two miles of every known victim except Sandy Nevin. It was believed that she had started walking toward Rufus after running out of gas, and that Melvyn had probably offered her a ride. After raping and killing her, he had probably gone back to her car and pushed it into the ravine.

Deedra was warned not to breathe a word of this to anyone, even to Clete, should Melvyn get wind of it he might disappear or resort to violence against Emma.

She drove back to the old store building with a thumping pulse. It was going to be very difficult not to call Clete. The store was cold and it took a few minutes to get the fires going again. She sat in front of the laptop and wrote the story…her front-page story.

There would be another bonus for this one, and she could start looking for a new car.

Just before dark she saw Melvyn drive in and park his truck behind their cabin. He didn't enter by the back door, but went around and entered through the front.

THIRTEEN

Lights went on in all the cabins.

She paced, impatient, wanting to really get this murderer, wanting this nightmare to end, afraid for Emma. What would Melvyn do if he found out or even suspected that Emma knew he had killed those women? Did she connect him with the other murders? She had probably been in denial, avoided even considering it. Had Melvyn ever threatened her? Somehow she doubted that. Emma had ample ways of communicating and Deedra doubted she would tolerate an outright threat.

How could they really prove anything against Melvyn though? Even if they could raise his old truck from the depths, the water would have destroyed any traces. Only if the other woman was still in the truck would they be able to bring charges, and that might be what they planned to do.

Still, there ought to be a simpler way. And then she recalled that Sandy Nevin's car had been pushed into the ravine. That meant that Melvyn had returned and sent it off the road to delay the identification of her body. Melvyn wouldn't have pushed it manually wouldn't chance leaving fingerprints or other forensic traces, instead he would shove it over using the truck.

Would there still be traces of blue paint on the bumper or fender of the truck?

She glanced toward the Randolph's cabin. They were probably eating dinner. A good time to get a look at Melvyn's truck.

She added fuel to the fires, put a flashlight in her jacket pocket, and almost as an after-thought placed the gun in the other jacket pocket.

Instead of walking along the graveled road, she went around the gas station to the path above the cabins. She knew the way and though sometimes stumbled, she scurried to the Randolph's cabin without incident. Melvyn's white truck was easily visible in the early evening darkness.

She halted above their cabin, waiting to catch a glimpse of movement inside. Then cautiously moved down the slope until she stood behind the truck. Again she halted, her heart thumping. A few leaden moments passed before she went around to the front of the truck. She waited a moment before switching on the flashlight, aiming its beam at the front bumper.

At first she didn't see the blue paint caught under the bumper. A moment of disappointment hit until she recalled that the Nevin's car was a small compact, knew the truck's bumper would push against it halfway up the back. And there it was, a long scrape of blue paint on the underside of the bumper.

A noise caused her to switch the light off, then a heavy hand grasped her shoulder.

"What the hell are you doing here, Miss?" A coarse, anger-laden voice demanded.

Deedra was too frightened to answer. She put her hand in her pocket and grasped the gun.

"Maybe," the raspy voice continued, "you want to

see the inside of my truck? You might like what I can do to you there.'' Before she could remove the gun he twisted both arms behind her back and marched her around to the rear of the truck where he threw open a door and lowered a step. "Up you go my pretty one. I have to finish my supper and placate my wife, then we'll have a party out here!" He emitted an evil giggle of anticipation.

Melvyn took the flashlight though didn't check her pockets and didn't find the gun. He forced her to sit on the floor, shackled her hands to one of the meat hangars, and with angry roughness covered her mouth with duct tape.

"I'll be back very soon, my love," he giggled again.

It was exceedingly dark inside the truck. She squirmed and tried to get her hands free. The more she tugged on the shackles, the tighter they held. The tape across her mouth seemed to smother her, so she stopped trying to get free to ease her breathing.

Dark fear began to settle within her. Was this to be her fate, for she knew when Melvyn was through with her he would toss her lifeless body into the swamp? Her only chance to live was if Aaron came looking for her…and if he found her missing would immediately look around and search Melvyn's truck.

She pressed her arms against her side, feeling the cold steel of the gun, knowing if she had a chance she would use it on Melvyn. The hunt was over and now it was her life or his.

The silence seemed to deepen, her heart thumped along so loudly she could hear the pulse beats in her ears. Fear heightened the senses, and it seemed she could feel the hair on her head growing.

A sound, not close by, but somewhere near, caused

her to tense with an additional effort to listen. Why was Melvyn taking such a long time? Then realized he had to wait until Emma was in bed, perhaps after he had given her a sleeping pill. That would make sense, otherwise Emma would be aware of his night activities. She shuddered at the thought of the other victims he had captured, shackled here in the truck just like she was, and after he had settled Emma for the night, had committed the rapes and murders in this very truck, in this vehicle parked in his own back yard.

Again she heard a sound, closer this time, followed by silence.

She twisted her wrist in an effort to get a glimpse of her watch with its illuminated dial, but her jacket sleeve prevented it.

Her arms began to ache, then to hurt, and then to excruciating pain. She almost hoped Melvyn would return and end this suffering. Pain, she thought, was a deterrent to a human's wish to live, then she began to wonder what death was like.

A noise brought her out of the stupor with the knowledge that Melvyn had returned and was opening the door. He stood outlined in moonlight, an evil grin besmirching his face. He giggled again and then he stepped up into the truck.

He did not see the dark shadow behind him.

"Now, my pretty one, we'll have a real party, won't we? No one to bother us. Has anyone ever told you how lovely you are? I'm going to unshackle you now because we can't conclude our…ah…rendezvous with you hanging there like a slab of meat."

He unshackled her hands and moved back.

It was then that he saw Claude looking inside the truck and with an angry grunt made a lunge for him.

The men hit the ground with a thud and rolled over, each clutching the other in desperate grips.

Deedra reached into her jacket pocket and fired the gun close enough to the men to startle them, and for a minute they ceased fighting. Claude took advantage of the moment and agilely moved out of Melvyn's reach.

With her free hand Deedra tore the tape from her mouth, and the pain of it caused her to silently vow she wouldn't ever allow that to happen to her again.

"Call 911, Claude!" She ordered. "Don't move, Melvyn, or I'll blow your head off!"

"You won't need to make another call, Claude," Aaron said as he stepped from the shadow of the truck. 'Thanks to you, Melvyn couldn't make Deedra his next victim."

A deputy stepped up when Aaron ordered, "Cuff the bastard!"

Deedra could scarcely take it all in. Suddenly there was a patrol car there with headlights silhouetting the scene, a scene forever imprinted on her mind.

"Deedra," Aaron said gently, "you can put the gun down now."

Shakily Deedra handed him the gun and stepped down from the truck. She looked around for Claude. He had gone home.

"Guess I owe Claude for saving my life!" Tears filled her eyes.

"Yep. But it was you who identified the killer." Aaron gave her a hug. "You're one damn fine detective!"

The sound of the back door opening caused them to look toward the house where Emma stood, not in her wheel chair but standing, leaning against the doorframe. "Melvyn is the killer?" Her voice quavered.

"Yes, Emma. Are you all right? Do you want to go into town to stay?"

"No, Aaron. I must stay here. I own Percifal, you know."

"Yes, I do know."

After giving instructions to the deputies to drive on ahead with their prisoner, Aaron led Deedra his patrol car. "Why don't you ride in to town with me? You have to make a statement about all this anyway. The old store will be awfully cold now." He gave her shoulder a gentle squeeze. "And you haven't seen my house yet!"

AN ELDERHOSTEL MYSTERY

PAINTED LADY

PETER ABRESCH

James P. Dandy and his ladylove, Dodee Swisher, embark on an Elderhostel adventure along the old Santa Fe Trail. But before the trip even gets under way, Jim sees a Native American woman plunge to her death from a Denver rooftop. He suspects that the woman was pushed.

Soon it's clear somebody thinks Jim knows the whereabouts of a priceless Mayan artifact—a misconception that is becoming dangerous to both Jim and Dodee.

Another grisly murder occurs on the historic trail through the Wild West, and mysteries old and new find Jim caught in a shoot-out with a killer determined to make this Dandy's Last Stand.

"...a suspect-rich plot with a revealing glimpse of small-town life... evocative descriptions of the desert and mountains of the Southwest."
—*Booklist*

Available April 2004 at your favorite retail outlet.

MYSTERY WORLDWIDE LIBRARY®

WPA488

MURDER IN A
HEAT WAVE

A MARTHA PATTERSON MYSTERY

A wilting summer heat wave is bringing out the worst in the tenants of septuagenarian Martha Patterson's Greenwich Village apartment building. She agrees to join the co-op board to help facilitate some badly needed change. It's a thankless job—and a deadly one when the president of the board, Arnold Stern, is murdered.

Martha soon discovers Stern was extremely unpopular. A trail of suspicion leads to several tenants, including her neighbor and good friend, an ailing archaeologist whose priceless Greek antiquity becomes a subtle but crucial clue. An innocent secret exposes the killer—and unravels a murder prompted by greed, jealousy...and undoubtedly, the heat.

"...the real prizes are the heroine's shrewd, unassuming intelligence and the authorial voice... consistently entertaining."
—*Kirkus Reviews*

*Available April 2004
at your favorite retail outlet.*

GRETCHEN
SPRAGUE

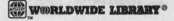
WORLDWIDE LIBRARY®

WGS489

DESPERATE JOURNEYS

Four trips you *won't* want to take…

DESERT DECEIT by Betty Webb
The murder of a media magnate turns a dude-ranch cattle drive into a trail full of unforeseen danger. Vacationing private eye Lena Jones attempts to unmask a killer in Arizona's most rugged and remote area.

THE FIRST PROOF by Terence Faherty
Ex-seminarian Owen Keane accompanies his former lover to Maine to bury her estranged husband. But dark mysteries surrounding the dead man's family converge as a murderer strikes at the heart of a tragic past filled with buried secrets, blackmail and vengeance.

DEATH ON THE SOUTHWEST CHIEF by Jonathan Harrington
Danny O'Flaherty escorts his eccentric aunt on a cross-country train trip, only to discover his uncle's corpse in the next seat. When the body is stolen and replaced with that of a freshly strangled man, Danny has seventy-two hours to find a killer.

STAR SEARCH by Nancy Baker Jacobs
Hollywood Star reporter Quinn Collins inherits a house from a writer she never knew. Looking into blacklisted writers of the 1950s proves dangerous as Quinn exposes a killer's desperate scheme—and the stunning truth about her own parents.

Available May 2004 at your favorite retail outlet.

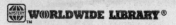
MYSTERY **WORLDWIDE LIBRARY** ®

WDJ491